"Sweet Jane," he said and gazed into her eyes for a moment before moving his hand to her cheek and caressing it lightly with the tips of his fingers.

Her breath caught and she almost swayed toward him as the need to feel his arm about her swept over her, but in an instant she had conquered the foolish desire. She did not know this man well enough to care for him—surely she could not be so inconstant. Only a few weeks ago she'd believed that she would never feel love or desire again. And now? Now she was not sure how she felt.

"You look beautiful, as always."

"You flatter," Jane said and laughed, but the look in his eyes was having a disturbing effect on her. She felt young and excited again, like a girl at her first ball. "But it is most pleasant...and the evening would not have been the same if you had not come."

Anne Herries

Claiming the Chaperon's Heart

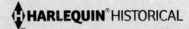 HARLEQUIN® HISTORICAL

Recycling programs
for this product may
not exist in your area.

ISBN-13: 978-0-373-30742-5

Claiming the Chaperon's Heart

Copyright © 2016 by Anne Herries

Printed in U.S.A.

www.Harlequin.com

Anne Herries lives in Cambridgeshire, England, where she is fond of watching wildlife and spoils the birds and squirrels that are frequent visitors to her garden. Anne loves to write about the beauty of nature, and sometimes puts a little into her books, although they are mostly about love and romance. She writes for her own enjoyment and to give pleasure to her readers. Anne is a winner of the Romantic Novelists' Association Romance Prize. She invites readers to contact her on her website, lindasole.co.uk.

Books by Anne Herries

Harlequin Historical

Regency Brides of Convenience

Rescued by the Viscount
Chosen by the Lieutenant
Reunited with the Major

Officers and Gentlemen

Courted by the Captain
Protected by the Major
Drawn to Lord Ravenscar

Melford Dynasty

Forbidden Lady
The Lord's Forced Bride
Her Dark and Dangerous Lord
Fugitive Countess
A Stranger's Touch
The Rebel Captain's Royalist Bride

Stand-Alone Novels

Make-Believe Wife
His Unusual Governess
Promised to the Crusader
Claiming the Chaperon's Heart

Visit the Author Profile page at Harlequin.com for more titles.

Prologue

'If you do this for me I shall be yours and all that I own will be at your disposal,' the woman said. Her pale olive-toned skin looked smooth and soft in the candle-light, her black velvet eyes as dark as night, but lit from within by a silver flame. She was a beautiful woman, sure of her power, and she sensed that he wanted her so badly that he could almost taste his need. The perfume she wore was heavy and had the exotic tang of musk and ambergris, and the jewels around her neck were worth a king's ransom. She was the daughter of an Indian prince and the granddaughter of an English earl, proud, haughty and vengeful—and the hatred of the man who had spurned her burned deep within her breast. 'He used me cruelly and deserted me—I want him dead. Only his death will assuage the wrong he has done me…'

She leaned closer to the man, allowing him to inhale the scent of her body, knowing that she had the power to drive men to near madness in their desire for her.

She could have had almost any man she wanted and yet one had eluded her and it was he alone she wanted. He had refused her offer to lie with her, to wed her and live in her palace, had told her that he did not love her—and she felt the bitter pain of his rejection like a snake's sting. He would learn that he could not walk away from her! In her anger she was lost to all sense of reason. She would make certain that he died a painful death for deserting her.

This poor fool who looked at her like a starving man was not the only one she had promised her favours, but the other was unlikely to do her bidding, though he loved her. This one had his own reasons for giving her the revenge she craved; she had picked him carefully and she knew that he would do whatever she asked for the promise of rich rewards. He was greedy, this one, and as desirous of vengeance as she was herself.

'He wronged you as he wronged me,' she hissed at him. 'Go to England. Follow him and do as I have asked you—and when you return you shall have all you desire and more…'

'Yes, I shall do your bidding, sweet lady, for I have business that takes me there. When it is complete and I have done as you ask, I shall return to claim my reward.'

A cruel smile touched her lips. He would have more than he desired for she would keep him only for as long as it pleased her…her heart was as cold as ice now, for *he* had broken it and she hated him.

The fool knelt before her and kissed the hem of her costly robes. 'I vow that I shall bring your enemy and mine to justice,' he said. 'Either he or I shall lie dead when this is over…but he is unsuspecting and I know him for the trusting fool he is. He will never know what is afoot until I take his life.'

She felt a trickle of fear slide down her spine and for a moment she wanted to take back all the hateful words. She loved the man who had refused her and his death could bring her no real satisfaction, and in that moment she knew that revenge could only bring her grief—and yet he had humbled her pride and he must pay. Anger and pride fought against softer emotions and won. She stared at the fool kneeling before her and knew he was not fit to kiss the feet of the man she loved, but her pain and grief was too deep and must be assuaged by blood.

After he had gone she was possessed by a wild restlessness that had her pacing until she realised that even revenge could not assuage the pain in her heart. Indeed, the thought of *his* death brought even more agony. Sinking to her knees, she wept until the storm of anger and despair had left her and then she knew that she had betrayed her own heart. She did not want the man she loved dead, but here with her, a smile of love on his face.

She must recall the fool who did her bidding so easily and tell him that she no longer wished him to kill for her.

Then, as she saw the sun had risen in the sky, she knew it was too late. His ship was already on its way and because he wanted the rewards she had promised he would do her bidding… *His* death would be her sin.

Giving a cry of terrible despair, she fell senseless to the ground.

Chapter One

'Ah, letters,' Viscount Salisbury said and looked at his elder sister Jane as she entered the room carrying a satisfying bundle. 'Any for me, Sis?'

'Yes, I think three,' Jane replied with a twitch of her lips. 'One of them smells of Miss Bellingham's perfume... Now, what would a young lady of sense be doing writing to you, I wonder?'

'None of your business, madam,' her brother said and snatched at the envelopes she held tantalisingly out of his reach. Lady Jane March laughed delightedly and withheld the letters for a second longer before releasing them to the younger brother she adored. She was an elegant lady, tall and slender, something about her making her instantly light up any room she entered, though her beauty could not disguise the sadness in those wonderful eyes.

Jane had chosen to make her home with the brother she'd always favoured, after her husband's untimely demise on the field at Wellington's side. Harry had been one of the Iron Duke's aides and so handsome it took her breath away, and his tragic death two years previously had broken her heart. The head of the family, John, Earl Sutherland, her half-brother, and his wife Gussie had offered Jane a home with them but she'd chosen to come here to William, her junior by just one year, because, as she said, *Will* was the only one who wouldn't either treat her with kid gloves or bully her.

'You will no doubt wish me the other side of the world within a month,' she'd told Will when he greeted her on her arrival at what had been their father's smaller country estate and was now his, John having inherited the main seat, of course. 'But Gussie would have driven me mad—and you know what John is…'

'I do indeed,' Will said ruefully. 'He's such an old stickler. Poor dear Mama used to go in fear of him until she married Porky…'

'God bless the Duke of Roshithe,' Jane said with a wry smile. Their mother had become a much loved and spoiled second wife, outliving her first husband by some years. Indeed, she had remarried after Jane's marriage because, she said, her dearest William did not need her help to find a wife. He had the fortune his maternal grandfather had left him, as well as the small estate from his father, consisting of a town house, a shooting box in Scotland and acres of land somewhere in Yorkshire. He was probably wealthier than his elder brother and never asked John to pay his debts, but that didn't stop the earl giving him advice on how to manage his fortune on every possible occasion.

'With your face and fortune, your problem will be in

fending off the ladies rather than finding a bride,' his mama had said before departing to the Continent with her doting second husband in tow for an extended wedding trip. Porky, as his friends and family persisted in calling him, despite his old and respected title, had been led by petticoat strings ever since Mama had taken him in hand and was blissfully happy to serve and adore her. He'd loved her all his life and been dismayed that her father had preferred the earl as a son-in-law; of course, Porky had never been expected to inherit the dukedom, and it was only after a string of unfortunate relatives met their deaths that he reluctantly came into it.

'I'm damned if I want that mouldering old house of Roshithe's,' he'd said on hearing the news. 'Of what use is the title and country seat to me? I never go near the place, never have and never will.'

'You will accept it to please me,' his lady said. 'I shall take precedence over John's wife—and that will not suit her consequence...'

To give him his due, Porky hadn't uttered another word of protest. If it suited his lady to become the Duchess of Roshithe it would suit him—and he understood perfectly the veiled hints and slights she had suffered at the hands of the earl's wife. Instead of complaining further, he'd given a grand ball, to which he'd invited anyone of consequence and it had afforded him a quiet amusement to see the countess having to curtsey to her mama-in-law, something she'd refused to do once her husband became the earl.

Jane and Will had watched their darling mama's success in society with barely held mirth, for she did so enjoy it. As a young bride, married for consequence and money, Helen had suffered at her pompous husband's hands as well as at the hands of his equally pompous eldest son, the child of his first wife—a lady of far greater family but less fortune. Helen had brought her husband a large dowry, but her father had been wise enough to tie most of it up so that it remained with her and her children after her husband died. Not that she needed it now for Porky was richer than any of them, perhaps one of the richest men in England—and he had little to do with his wealth but spend it on his bride and her children, Will and Jane. John, of course, was deemed to have enough of his own, though whether he would have agreed if asked was doubtful. He was far too polite to mention it, of course, though he frowned over the vast sums squandered on his stepmother's vanity—as he called it.

Immersed in her letters, Jane became aware that Will was hovering. She looked up and smiled, because she knew her dearest one so well.

'You want something,' she said. 'Come on, what is it?'

'Dearest Jane,' Will murmured, his blue eyes sparkling with mischief. 'You know me so well… It's Melia Bellingham. Her aunt has taken sick at the last minute and she won't be able to come to London next month… unless you will be her chaperon, Jane? Please say you will. She's been looking forward to this visit for so long…'

'Amelia Bellingham shouldn't have written to you,

Will. Her aunt must write to me if she wishes me to chaperon her niece.'

'I'm sure Mrs Bellingham's letter is in your pile,' he said. 'You had such a lot. Why do you always get piles and piles of letters? I never get more than two or three and most of them are just bills...'

'Perhaps because I write lots of letters,' Jane said, her mouth quirking at the corners. 'It is my chief occupation most of the time—unless we go up to London to visit Mama and then it's just non-stop balls and dinners and all the rest...'

'Mama loves to entertain, and she has so many friends.'

'Of course she does,' Jane said drily. 'They queue for the lavish dinners Porky puts on. It beats me how Mama can be exposed to all that rich food day in and day out and never put on so much as a pound.'

'Because she eats like a bird and always did,' Will said. 'You're just like her, Jane, and will never put on weight. You will invite Melia to stay with us, won't you?'

'Of course, if you wish it,' Jane agreed. 'It's your house, my dearest. I'm your guest and I dare say you may invite whomever you wish...'

'You know I couldn't invite Miss Bellingham,' Will said. 'She must have a chaperon—and you've known her all her life, practically grew up together.'

'Her elder sister was my friend,' Jane said and a sigh escaped, because her friendship with Beth Bellingham brought back memories of Harry. Beth had been in love with him, as had most of the young girls that season…but he'd only had eyes for Jane, and she missed him so much, so very much. Sometimes in the night the ache was like a sword thrust in her chest. 'I like Melia, Will—and I'll be glad to invite her.' She shuffled through her letters and opened the one from Melia's aunt, nodding as she rose to pen an immediate answer. That done, she rang the bell and gave her letter to the footman. 'Have that one sent immediately please, Flowers.'

'Yes, my lady,' the footman said, inclining his head correctly. Only the very observant might have seen the look of devotion in the man's eyes as he bowed and left the room. Will knew that all the servants adored Jane. It wouldn't make things easy for his wife when he married, because Jane was undoubtedly the mistress here—and he'd been glad of it until he began to realise that he was actually thinking of marriage.

'So?' Jane asked as she rose from her elegant chair and closed the writing desk she'd brought with her on her return from France. 'Am I to wish you happy quite soon?'

'Well, if Melia is of the same mind when she's had her season, yes,' Will said. 'You do wish me happy, Jane? I know it makes things awkward for you…'

'Nonsense,' she said. 'I've taken advantage of your good nature for too long. I have a perfectly good house of my own a few miles from John and Gussie and I shall probably take a house in Bath once I decide to settle. I should have done it a year ago, when I put off my blacks.'

'But how can you live alone?' her brother asked. 'I

know you don't want to live with John, but Gussie isn't too bad—or Mama…'

'I wouldn't dream of treading on her toes,' Jane said, laughing softly. 'And you know Gussie would drive me mad within a fortnight…'

'You could stay on here. Melia likes you so much…'

'And I like her and I want it to stay that way,' Jane said gently. 'No, my dearest brother, I shall not make your wife's life difficult. It's quite simple; I must find a companion…'

'Well, I suppose—but who is there that you could put up with? You're not the most patient of women, Jane.'

'I am not in the least patient,' she said. 'But—do you remember Cousin Sarah? You might not recall her because you were away at school when she came to stay. It was shortly before Papa died…'

'I seem to remember her at the funeral. She was tall and thin and plain…and her mother was always demanding things, making her life hell.'

'Yes, well, Aunt Seraphina died last month and Cousin Sarah wrote to me asking if I knew of a position that would suit her. I was thinking of asking her on a visit to see how we got on—and, if we can bear each other, I shall set up house with her in Bath.'

'But can you imagine what John would say to such a suggestion? Sarah Winters could never be a chaperon for you, Jane. She isn't old enough and she has no consequence.'

'And needs none in my house. I was married for a year before Harry died,' Jane said, her face pale. 'I am Lady March, a widow of independent means, and that is exactly how I intend to live…' She arched her fine dark brows as he stared at her. 'After the freedom of marriage and then living here with you—do you really think I could live with John and his wife?'

Will stared at her for a few minutes and then nodded. 'Of course you couldn't, Jane—but they will all be against it, even Mama.'

'Mama wants me to marry again, Will. If I went to stay with her she would present me to all the eligible men she knows, and keep on doing it until I gave in. I married for love and would never marry for any other reason—indeed, I value my independence.'

'You don't think it might be a better arrangement to marry someone you could admire if not love? You would have a large house and a husband to help you…'

'I couldn't even think of it yet,' Jane replied and her throat tightened. 'I know it's a year since I came out of blacks, but I still grieve; I still think of him all the time and wish…'

'Of course you do and I'm a brute to suggest anything that upsets you, love. Please forgive me.'

Will was sincere in his apology and his sister was pleased to tell him there was nothing to forgive. They parted on good terms, Jane to write to Cousin Sarah, and Will to ride his new young horse that he had great pleasure in schooling. It had taken him a while to tame the brute, but it could go like the wind and he'd a mind to race the young stallion, riding him himself, of course. He was whistling as he strolled down to the stables, content with his world, which looked like continuing in the same happy-go-lucky way it always had.

Will was lucky. Everyone said so and he saw no reason why his luck shouldn't continue. Melia would marry him and be content to live in the country, apart from a few visits to town, which was exactly the way he wished to live…

'Oh, look, dear Aunt—' Melia Bellingham opened her letter from Lady March and her deep blue eyes lit with excitement as she showed the very fine calligraphy to the lady, who had now recovered enough from her illness to sit in a chair but was still far too fragile to contemplate taking a lively young woman to London. 'You will not mind my leaving you here alone? Please say I may go—for I am sure I am of little use to you. You always say I make your head ache, Aunt Margaret.'

The older woman sighed and sniffed the lace kerchief soaked in lily of the valley perfume. 'You have so much energy, Amelia. It's no wonder I find your company tiring, especially when I feel a little fragile. However, I should not wish to disappoint you in this matter, and of course you may go to Lady March. I would have preferred you to be in your sister's care, but poor dear Beth is increasing and cannot entertain you. You must write a pretty letter to Lady March and thank her.'

'She says she will send her carriage to bring me to her at home in the country, and then we may travel to London together. I must write my reply at once because otherwise she will not get my letter in time…'

'Child, you are always in such a hurry,' her aunt said and waved the heavily scented kerchief at her. 'Please go away now and send Miss Beech to me. I need quiet companionship.'

Melia skipped away, only too happy to be set free of her duty to her aunt. Aunt Margaret had been good to her and Beth, though Beth had not needed much from their long-suffering aunt for she'd been eighteen when their parents were lost at sea on what was meant to be a pleasure trip to Papa's estates in Ireland. Such a storm had blown up that the yacht had been buffeted on to the rocks far off its course on the wild Cornish coast and both crew and passengers drowned in the terrible storm.

Grieving and not knowing what to do, the sisters had been taken in by their kindly aunt, for they had little choice but to leave their home. Papa's estates were naturally entailed and fell to a distant cousin they had never met and who presently resided in India. The girls both had small dowries, put aside by their father, and two thousand pounds each left to them by their maternal grandfather. Had it not been for the kindness of Aunt Margaret Bellingham, they would have been forced to live in a small house in a village somewhere—or so the very formal solicitor had informed them soon after the funeral.

However, six months later, when they had both removed from their home and Beth was already married, a letter had come to say that they might remain at the house for as long as they wished. It seemed that their father's cousin had no intention of returning from India at present and even when he did so would not wish to deprive the sisters of their home. He had written to an agent who would look after the estate and would let them know when the new owner was thinking of returning to England.

It had been too late for Beth and Amelia. Beth had married and was happily living at her husband's estate, and Melia was living rather less happily with her aunt. Aunt Margaret was not in the least unkind, nor did she make unreasonable demands of her niece, but she was too old to attend many parties and those she did were very dull. She'd promised Melia a season in London when she was eighteen, but a nasty bout of gastroenteritis had laid her low and then, just as she was recovering, she'd caught a chill. Her doctor said that London was out of the question, and Melia had almost resigned herself to giving up all idea of going to town until Beth was over the birth of her child and had finished nursing the babe.

'I shall be on the shelf by then,' Melia had told her friend Jacqui as they walked together through the grounds of Aunt Margaret's house. 'I shall die of boredom before I ever have a chance to fall in love and be married.'

'What about Viscount Salisbury?' her friend asked slyly. 'I thought you and he swore undying love when you stayed at Beth's house in the country?'

'Yes, we did,' Melia said, her eyes dancing with merriment. 'Shall I tell you a secret?' She laughed as Jacqui nodded eagerly. 'Well, he has been in the district visiting friends twice since then and we walked and rode together—and he has written to me and I to him...'

'You could not!' her friend cried, shocked. 'That is

so forward of you, Melia. Whatever would your aunt say if she knew?'

'Well, she does not know for Bess gets the letters from the receiving house and brings them to me without her seeing them.'

'She would be so angry if she knew you had deceived her.' Jacqui was in awe and yet a little censorious. 'Mama would shut me in my room for a month on bread and water if I did such a thing.'

'Well, you wouldn't,' Melia replied and hugged her arm. 'I dare say I should not had Mama lived. She would have invited young people to the house for me and I might have been engaged by now.'

'Has the viscount asked you?'

'No, but he will if I wish it.' Melia's eyes sparkled wickedly. 'I am not yet sure if I wish to marry him, but I do want to find out. If we were to go to London, I should have the chance to meet so many pleasant young men…'

'Well, you must get your aunt to write to Lady March and ask if she would be kind enough to have you as her guest when she goes up to town. I know for a fact that she has chaperoned other young girls since she was widowed, for one was my cousin. As you know her brother, Viscount Salisbury, I dare say he would prevail upon her to invite you.'

Melia had thought her friend's suggestion a good one, for the families had been close before Jane and Beth were married, but, to make certain of a favourable answer, she'd written of her aunt's illness to the viscount. The letter had clearly done its work and now she was to visit London, as she'd hoped—and, if she could achieve it, she would be engaged before the end of her visit, either to Viscount Salisbury or another...

Having finished her letter, Melia rang the bell for Bess. The maidservant had come to her aunt's house with her and was devoted to her. Bess would not mind walking down to the village to see the letter went as soon as the next post bag was sent off to London. However, when she answered the bell, Bess was carrying a silver salver on which resided a letter addressed to Melia.

'Thank you,' she said and smiled at the woman who had nursed her from a babe and now looked after her clothes and tended her hair. 'I want this letter to go off straight away. I'm going to visit Lady March and she is taking me to London—and you'll be coming with us, Bess. You will enjoy that, won't you?'

'Well, miss, I know you will and I don't mind anything if you're happy.'

'You are the best friend I ever had,' Melia said and pounced on the plump, kind woman, arms about her waist as she kissed her cheek. 'I do love you, Bess.'

'Get on with you, Miss Melia,' Bess said but her face was pink and smiling. 'I'll take your letter for you, no need for flattery...'

'I wonder who could be writing to me,' Melia said as she looked at the seal and then frowned, for it was a family crest. 'Good gracious! Can this possibly be from...?' She broke the wax seal and glanced at the letter.

Scanning the first few lines, Melia discovered that it was from someone calling himself her Cousin Paul.

Papa's cousin, not hers, Melia thought with a little frown. A look of annoyance settled over her pretty face as she continued to read the contents of her surprising letter.

I was concerned to learn that you had been asked to leave your home. It was against my wishes and I do most sincerely apologise for it. My hope is that you will forgive the mistake and return to your home. Clearly you cannot live there alone, though on my return from India in early June I shall be living at my house in London and will pay only brief visits to Willow House.

However, it is my intention that you shall be introduced into Society under the aegis of a friend of my mother's, Lady Moira Fairhaven. Lady Moira, widowed these eighteen months past, is preparing to take her place in Society again this year, and will live with you at Willow House until you come up to London. She will be with you by the end of May and you may become accustomed to each other before coming to the house I shall take for you in town.
Yours sincerely,
Paul Frant

Well, really! Melia could not see why he should write her such a letter—as if the fact that he had inherited Papa's estate made him her guardian. He was no such thing and she had no intention of doing as he asked. She would keep to her intention of being Lady March's guest, though, had she not already arranged things to her liking, she supposed she might have been grateful to her father's cousin for his offer.

Aunt Margaret must not know that she'd received this letter. If she read the contents she would say that Melia must remain here to meet her chaperon and do as her distant cousin asked. Putting her letter carefully away in the secret drawer of her writing slope, Melia wondered uncomfortably if perhaps her father's will had given this distant cousin power over her. Yet surely Papa would never do such a thing? Neither she nor Beth had ever met the gentleman. She knew nothing about him, and she did not wish to. It was most disobliging of him to return to England now, just when Melia had everything in hand. She knew that if she wished to marry a suitable gentleman, her aunt would be only too willing to oblige her—but this stranger might have other ideas...

Chapter Two

'This is being too kind, Adam,' Paul Frant said. 'I never expected you to accompany me to London, my dear fellow. Your help on the ship was invaluable, for I must confess that I have never felt quite as ill in my life as I did when that fever struck. However, I am on the mend now and you might have gone to your own estates after we docked at Portsmouth. I know you must have business to attend.'

'I've never before known you to have a day's illness,' Adam, once Captain of His Majesty's Own Guards, serving with the Indian troops, and now, newly, Viscount Hargreaves, said with a faint twist of his mouth. 'It was not like you, for you fought on the Peninsula in Spain and came through, despite being wounded twice. I was concerned, my dear fellow. You still look a trifle weary.'

'I feel less than my normal healthy self,' Paul replied truthfully. 'It pains me to say it, but for a while there I believed it was the end. I must have been carrying the fever with me, for some of my colleagues had it at the Company offices before I left. Poor Mainwaring died of it, leaving a widow and two young sons in England. His death was a part of the reason I decided to come home. Before he died, he asked me to make sure that his family received his pension and all that was due to him. I think he'd hoped to make his fortune out there, but unfortunately he was not good at business.'

'Unlike you,' Adam said with a wry twist of his lips. 'You must be as rich as Croesus, Frant.'

'I haven't done too badly out of the Company,' Paul said modestly. 'Enough to give that poor child of Bellingham's a decent dowry. I inherited the charge of her along with the title, for which I have not the slightest use, but I must accept it, I suppose, if I choose to live here. I'm not sure yet whether I shall do so. I may return to India when I've seen to things in England. I'm not certain I could settle to the life of an English gentleman.'

'Find it a trifle dull after fighting the wild tribesmen of the hills, eh?' Adam gave him an odd look. 'Or is it the lure of a beautiful woman that calls you back, my friend?'

'I had little time for ladies of any description; I left that to you and the rest of the Army,' Paul mocked him gently. 'Annamarie was beautiful; I give you that— but she was not to be trifled with. Only if I'd decided to marry her would I have thought of trying to capture her heart. If indeed she has one; I found her charming but with little real warmth.' Paul had thought there was something hard and cold about the woman so many men admired.

'She is a proud beauty,' Adam said. 'I admired her. It must be hard to be of mixed birth as she is, Paul. Her father was an Indian prince, her mother an English lady. Annamarie says that her father was married to her mother by a Christian priest; his other wives went into purdah after he died but Princess Helena was allowed to leave the palace and bring up her daughter as she pleased in a palace of her own. One might almost say that she'd been cast out by her royal relatives. Because of her marriage, which was not in the Indian way, some of her husband's people think her a concubine rather than a wife.'

'Yes, that is unfortunate. Princess Helena sent her daughter to the school for the daughters of English gentlemen,' Paul said. 'Annamarie was brought up to believe she was legitimate and, since her maternal grandfather still lives in Shropshire and is an earl, she has been accepted by some of the officer's ladies...but not all. If it had not been for Colonel Bollingsworth's wife, she might have found herself ostracised, but most followed her lead and accepted Annamarie into their company.'

'Out there, some of the ladies allow a little leeway.' Adam nodded to himself. 'You know as well as I do why her mother does not send Annamarie to school in England. She would not be accepted into the top echelons of Society here, I think.'

'Then Society is a fool,' Paul said angrily. 'She has every right to be accepted here, but it is the same in

India—her father's people treat her as an outcast. I believe she and her mother might do better to come home to England. I am sure such beauty as Annamarie's would find many admirers and, if she were taken up by the Regent's set, might do well enough.'

'Yes, perhaps...' Adam eased his long legs as the carriage drew to a halt. 'Ah, I believe we are here. This is your house, Paul?'

'It was my father's but now mine,' Paul replied with a twist of his lips. He was a good strong man, with fine legs and broad shoulders. Seen in company with Adam, he might not be thought handsome, but there was nothing coarse or ugly in his features. His chin was square and forthright, his eyes clear, his gaze sometimes piercing, but his mouth was softer than the rest of his features, a clue to the warmth of his heart. He had warm brown eyes and light brown hair, but not the pure blond of his companion's locks. Adam's profile was almost beautiful, his hair short but softly curled about perfect features, his eyes a blue some called cerulean and his mouth sensuous. His body had all the proportions of a Greek god and his skin the natural tan that came from being accustomed to a life outdoors in a warm climate.

'Ah yes, your father.' Adam frowned, uncertain now. 'As I recall, you did not exactly see eye to eye with Lord Frant?'

'No, and never could after the way he treated my mother and I...'

Paul's eyes narrowed in anger. The row with his father after his mother died had split them apart. Paul had left his home vowing never to return while his father lived, and he'd kept his word. He'd made his own way, rising first to the rank of Major with Wellington at Salamanca and then, after a wound to his leg from which he recovered well, gave up the Army that would have bound him to an administrative position and used his share of the prize money to go out to India and invest with the Company. Some shrewd business moves had made him richer than he'd expected, and a fortunate encounter with a rich Maharaja had resulted in him being made an honorary son and given lands and palaces. If he chose to return to India, he could live like a prince and marry almost anyone he chose.

Paul knew that Annamarie had hoped he would ask her to be his wife. Because he'd once saved the life of a prince, Paul had a unique position in the region. It would have suited the daughter of an English lady and an Indian prince to marry a man who had both English rank and Indian favour. Together they might have been second in importance to the present Maharaja in the district. She'd made it quite clear that she hoped for a proposal of marriage before he left for England, but Paul had not been sure what he wanted.

In England he had inherited his father's title and estates, but he knew that his younger brother—the son of his father's second wife, although still only in his teens, would have been delighted to step into his shoes. Paul had no need of his family estates in England—and in particular he had not needed the bother of the small estate that had come to him through a distant cousin. The young girls who were made his wards by Bellingham's will were a part of Paul's reason for returning. Although he'd been told the older girl had married well, that still left the younger one—at eighteen, she was ready for marriage if a husband could be found for her. To that end, Paul had written to an old friend of his mother who had recently been widowed, asking her if she would be kind enough to chaperon the young girl. She had graciously given her consent, though the exchange of letters had taken months to complete. It was imperative that the girl be chaperoned, for Paul was unmarried and could therefore not fulfil his task of guardian without female assistance.

Some years had passed since Paul had met Lady Moira. He'd been seventeen then and it had been just before his mother died of grief over her husband's infidelity, and the terrible quarrel that caused him to leave home and become an officer in the Guards. Fortunately, he'd had some small fortune left him by his maternal grandmother and when his own father cut him off without a penny was able to survive on his pay as an officer and his allowance from the inheritance. Later, he'd won prize money and honours and life had become much easier when an uncle left him a small fortune.

Paul knew that his father had bequeathed everything that was not entailed to his half-brother. He minded that not at all, and would have been glad to pass the rest of it over had he been sure he did not wish to live in England, but some small perverse part of him clung to what his father had been forced to leave him. How it must have gone against the grain with Lord Frant to know that the son of the wife he'd married for her dowry would have his title.

Paul would have freely admitted that the woman his father had taken in his mother's place was beautiful. Goodness knew, his own mother had been far from a beauty, but she had a beautiful nature, gentle and loving—and her heart had been broken by her husband's cold indifference.

Watching his mother fade, become frailer and sadder, had broken the young Paul's heart and after her death he'd railed at his father for his cruelty.

'I never loved her,' his father had told him bluntly. 'I needed her money to restore my estates—but it was not the fortune I'd been led to believe. A paltry twenty thousand…'

'Twenty thousand would have been a fortune to many,' Paul said. 'If you'd put it to good use instead of wasting it on gambling and women…'

'Your mother came from trade and it has not yet been bred out of you,' his father sneered. 'Had I known I should get no more when the old man died I'd never have taken the silly bitch.'

Paul had tried to knock him down then, but his father was a strong bull of a man and he'd sent the youth flying. Even so, Paul had tried again and again, until his face was cut and bleeding and he could not rise.

'Well, you can take yourself off where you came from,' his father said. 'Go back to the mills and dens of the North and stay where you belong…'

His taunt was a cheap one, for though his maternal grandfather's wealth had come from the mills of the North, they had been sold two generations back and the money invested in land. However, the Martins were better mill owners than farmers and much of their former wealth had been badly invested. Paul had received a bequest of ten thousand pounds on his grandfather's death, and was the owner of several hundred acres of farmland, but had the family still owned the mills they would have been worth more.

Lord Frant had inherited the ten thousand that would have come to his wife on her father's death, but thought nothing of the sum and promptly lost it in a week of frantic gambling at the tables.

Paul had known nothing of this or his own inheritance for some years, by which time he was well on the way to making his own fortune. Now, on the verge of entering the house that had been his father's, he felt chilled. Standing in the dark, unwelcoming hall, he thought of turning tail and finding accommodation in a hotel, but pride would not let him.

'Welcome home, my lord. It's good to see you back.'

Paul looked hard at the black-clothed footman who had opened the door to them and his brow wrinkled in concentration. 'Is it Matthews?' he asked at last and saw the smile on the man's face.

'Yes, my lord,' he said. 'I worked as a boot boy when you were a lad, sir, then as a man of all work. I was made up to footman six years back.'

'Were you now?' Paul nodded, looking him over. He glanced about him. 'I seem to remember this hall looked different when I last stayed here.'

The smile left Matthews's face. 'Yes, sir. I regret to say that his late lordship sold much of the furniture and the paintings last year.'

'In debt again, I suppose,' Paul said and sighed. 'Has he left me anything worth having?'

'Not much, my lord,' the footman replied. 'The bedrooms are mostly the same but the silver, pictures and some porcelain pieces have been sold. Your mother's rooms were stripped bare years ago...' Matthews looked awkward. 'Thought you should know, sir.'

'Well, what are a few bits and pieces?' Paul said and laughed ruefully as he turned to his companion. 'I'm sorry to bring you to such a place, Adam—but I dare say we've a bed to offer and, I hope, some food.'

'Oh, yes, sir. Your instructions have been followed. A new housekeeper and cook were hired and the rooms opened up and cleaned. Mrs Brooks says she's made one room look proper for you, sir; it used to be her ladyship's sitting room...that is to say your mother's room, my lord. I believe a fire has been lit there for you...'

'Thank goodness someone has some sense,' Paul said as he led the way through to a room he knew well. Matthews was directing two other footmen to carry his bags upstairs, and a woman had appeared from the room at the far end of the hall. She hurried forward, seeming flustered.

'We were not sure when to expect you, sir.'

'I think we should like some wine and a light meal in the green room, Mrs Brooks.'

'Yes, my lord. I understood it was the room you favoured as a lad—and the other room usable is what was known as the library, sir.'

'Don't tell me the books have been sold?'

'Some of them, sir. However, it is quite comfortable—until your lordship decides what to do about refurbishing the other rooms...'

Paul gave a wry laugh. The Frant library had contained some rare books and the loss of those meant more to him than any silver or paintings, but he could not do anything about that loss. His father had sold everything he could without actually breaking the entail, and he supposed he ought to have expected it. Had he come home with only a few guineas in his pocket he would have been in trouble, but as it was he could afford to smile at the pettiness of the man he'd called Father.

At least his mother's room was comfortable, though not as he'd remembered it. Nothing of hers remained, but everything decent in the house must have been placed here and the comfortable wing chairs by the fire were more than adequate, as was the mahogany desk and elbow chair, the large settee and the sideboard on which some fine glasses and decanters stood waiting.

'At least it seems I have some wine to offer you,' Paul said, casting an eye over the contents. 'Brandy, Madeira or Burgundy?'

'A glass of Madeira, please,' Adam said and stretched out in one of the chairs. 'Well, you'll be busy now, my friend, though I do not envy you the task. Buying furnishings is not my idea of amusement.'

'Nor mine,' Paul said and laughed. 'I imagine I can find someone to do it for me.'

'Know what you need?'

'No. What?' Paul asked with his lazy smile.

'What you need, my friend, is a wife,' Adam said, a faint challenge in his eyes. 'Just the thing for making a man's house look comfortable. I'm thinking of getting one myself now I've given up adventuring—and if I were you I should do the same...'

'It's odd that you should say it,' Paul said thoughtfully. 'I have been wondering if perhaps I ought not to offer her marriage—Bellingham's girl, you know. I'm damned if I wanted her father's estate, but perhaps I ought to offer her a home. I could only do that if I married her...'

'I should think about it for a while if I were you,' Adam advised. 'You haven't seen her yet—and she is a little young for you, is she not?'

'You are quite right, which is why my words were mere idle speculation. No, I shall not marry unless I find the right woman...'

'You at least do not need to look for a fortune,' Adam said and there was the faintest trace of envy in his voice. 'You have more than enough for any man.'

'Yes, I have been lucky,' Paul agreed, 'but it was honestly earned—and I have not yet decided where to settle...'

'You won't return to India?'

'I do not know.' Paul sighed. 'It has been my home for several years—I am not sure there is anything to keep me here. You came home to settle your affairs, Adam—shall you return after you have done so?'

'I am in two minds,' Adam said and his eyes stared at a point beyond Paul's shoulder. 'It depends on many things. Not least whether I have sufficient funds to live decently here...'

'Surely your father has not left anything away from you? You were his only son.'

'No, but the question is—has he actually left me anything but debts?' Adam asked wryly. 'I did not earn a fortune out there as you did, Paul—and, for all I know, I may be a pauper...'

Chapter Three

'This is so very kind of you,' Melia cried, looking round the pretty bedroom with delight. 'My aunt is very good to me, but, poor dear, she could hardly be expected to bring me to town. Such a delightful room…'

'My brother was concerned that you should have the best guest room, Miss Bellingham,' Jane said, smiling at the girl's pleasure. 'It is a lovely room. I have stayed here myself many times in the past.'

'Oh, you should not have given me your room,' Melia said. 'I do not wish to put you out, dear Lady March.'

'No, you have not,' Jane said, shaking her head. 'This was my room as a girl, but now I have a permanent suite of three rooms at the other side of the house. At least, it has been mine since…for a while now. Of course, when my brother marries I shall take a house of my own. I am thinking of making my home in Bath.'

'You will not desert the viscount?' Melia cried involuntarily. 'I know he is so fond of you, relies on you for advice in almost everything.'

'He will turn to the lady he marries once he becomes a devoted husband and I should not wish to interfere with her way of running the household.'

'Oh, but perhaps she would rather leave it to you.' Melia's face was an open book. Jane held back her smile because it was obvious that the young woman had no interest in the duties of a chatelaine, but thought only of the amusement of being a bride and being spoiled by a devoted husband. 'If his wife is young and knows little of household management. I hate dealing with servants; they are always so superior if they think you don't know—don't you find?'

Jane's merriment left her and she answered seriously. 'It is important that one does know what one wants. The first rule is to make your people respect you. It is good if they also like you—but a calm, firm manner when giving instructions is always best. You must have observed it in your aunt's house.'

'Oh, no,' Melia said ingenuously. 'Aunt is so lazy. Her butler rules the household and arranges everything as she likes it. He has been with her since she was a girl and treats her as if he were a benevolent uncle. She never seems to give orders. Benson just does everything without needing to be told.'

'How fortunate is Mrs Bellingham to have such a devoted man in her service.'

'She is always complaining about things, but never to Benson, of course. She might have everything as she likes if she stirred herself, but she can never be bothered and just leaves it all to him—and then she grumbles if the meals are not quite what she wanted.'

'Well, at least you know how not to conduct your household,' Jane said, amused by this description of the indolent Mrs Bellingham. 'Now, my dear, I want you to settle in first and come down when you are ready. I shall order some tea in half an hour in my sitting room downstairs, but you may have a tray brought up if you wish to rest.'

'I am not in the least tired,' Melia declared. 'I shall come down and join you… Do you mean that very pleasant sunny room at the back of the house?'

'Yes, it was Mama's until she remarried,' Jane said. 'Now, of course, she has a dozen pretty rooms she may choose from, and if she wants anything different she has only to ask Porky.'

'Is that what you call the duke?' Melia's eyes sparkled with mischief as Jane nodded and laughed. 'Oh, it does suit him—but it is a terrible thing to call such a lovely man. He was so kind to me when I attended the wedding as one of your mama's bridesmaids—and he gave me a beautiful gold bracelet as a gift.'

'Roshithe is a lovely man, and so kind to us all,' Jane said. 'I assure you, the name was given him years ago and stuck. He does not regard it, because he knows it is used with affection. His enemies are more likely to call him Roshithe in a supercilious manner, and that he does resent—though you should probably address him as sir, unless he gives you permission to use the name.'

'I would not dare. I shall probably address him as Your Grace…'

'He cannot abide that sort of toad-eating, as he calls

it, Miss Bellingham. Much better just to use the simple sir.'

'I'll try to remember,' Melia promised and gave Jane a small shy smile. 'Will you not call me Melia?'

'Yes, of course, if you wish it—and you must reciprocate. I am Jane to my family and friends.'

'Yes, I know. Viscount Salisbury always speaks of you that way. He is very fond of you, Jane.'

'We have always been close,' Jane said. 'I shall leave you to change if you wish.'

She left the bedchamber, which was indeed the prettiest in the house, its curtains pink and white striped silk, which matched the décor of pinks, cream and a deep crimson. Jane had ordered some pink roses to be placed on the dressing stand to complete the welcome offered to a lady who might, if she chose, become the next mistress here.

It would mean a big change in Jane's life, she thought as she made her way down to the sitting room she favoured. She would miss playing hostess for her brother and it would be an upheaval making the move to Bath, but she intended to make way for her brother's wife, despite Melia's hints that she would be welcome to stay on to run the house for her. No, that would eventually lead to resentment and perhaps unkind words between them; Melia might need help at first but once she found her own confidence she would not wish for another woman in her home.

Jane had already begun to make inquiries about a house in Bath. She was unsure whether she wished to rent a place while she looked about her or buy something immediately. If she bought she would need to furnish it, and she intended to look for suitable items while she was in town this time. Even if her brother Will was not successful in securing his bride immediately, it would happen, and Jane had no wish to live in the country house left to her by her husband.

'It's a bit dull and quite lonely,' Harry had told her the day he took her to see his small country house. 'I know we can make it nice, Jane—and with servants and children it will soon become a home. I dare say we'll make friends soon enough. There's plenty of time before we have to retire to a country life, because I want to rise in the Army. We can live in London when we're home on leave—and in time you will find a way to make this place into a home.'

Jane had assured him gaily that she would enjoy it, but that future had seemed so far away as not to be of much interest. Before they settled down to living off the land, they had so much fun to have—travelling overseas, putting up at the most frightful billets had all seemed amusing to the young couple in love. Her friends were Harry's friends, the ladies she met officers' wives, all living their nomad existence with a smile on their faces and secret fear in their hearts. Yet, even so, Jane had not thought it could all end so abruptly. She'd thought of her life as being married to Harry for years and years, but in fact she'd had only a year of happiness.

She would not think of that! Jane told herself severely that she must begin to look to the future. She had already written to her cousin. Sarah's reply had not arrived before they left for London, but Will's servants would send on any letters and, if Sarah wished, Jane would invite her to join them in town.

She would make a few inquiries about whom to consult on the matter of furnishing a house, but perhaps it might be better to hire a furnished house for a start, though Jane had some of her personal things at her brother's country house. She had intended to set up her own home long ago but living in Will's home had proved so pleasant for them both that she'd let her own plans drift.

'It is lovely to have you here again, ma'am,' Mrs Yates, Will's London housekeeper, came up to her as she reached the hall. 'There are quite a few letters waiting for you in the parlour, Lady March. I dare say your ladyship's friends knew of your intention and most of them look like invitations.'

'Yes, I dare say,' Jane replied with a faint twist of her lips. 'Mama knew we were coming, of course, and I imagine she has informed most of her friends—and that includes everyone who gives decent parties...'

Jane laughed softly as she saw an answering gleam in the housekeeper's eyes, because Mama was well known in this house. She picked up the large pile of letters and cards awaiting her and flicked through them. Three were in her mother's hand, each of them speaking of some party she really must attend or an exhibition she must see. Her mother intended to visit her the day after she arrived and she was to come to dinner that evening and bring the delightful young woman she'd invited as her guest.

Laying aside her mother's letters, Jane opened some

of the others. Most, as her housekeeper had guessed, were invitations to dances, masques, picnics, dinner and a grand ball. If she tried to attend them all, and this was the tip of the iceberg because as soon as it was known she was in town the invitations would pour in, she would need to attend three affairs in an evening so as not to offend the eager hostesses.

Picking up a neat cream-coloured envelope addressed to Lady March in a hand she did not recognise, Jane slit the seal and took out the piece of paper inside. She frowned as she read the few lines written on the single sheet.

Madam, Lady March,
Forgive me for writing when you do not know
me, but I have been informed that my ward, Miss
Amelia Bellingham, is to stay with you in town. I
would ask that you let me know when it is conve-
nient to call on you both.
Yours sincerely,
Paul Frant.

Brief and to the point, not particularly friendly, Jane thought as she scanned the lines again. She had not been aware that there was any other guardian than Mrs Bellingham. As Melia's father's widowed sister-in-law, she would surely be the proper person to have charge of the girl, Jane thought, but obviously Lord Frant—whoever he might be—thought differently.

It was slightly concerning, because the tone of the letter was distinctly cool. In fact, she would say that he'd been annoyed when he wrote the letter—only yesterday. She wondered if Melia knew of the gentleman and decided to ask when she came down for tea. Meanwhile, she continued to open her letters, discovering two more invitations for balls and one to the theatre from a close friend of her mother's.

Major Harte was some years older than Jane, but he had taken a fancy to her the last time she was in London and she'd received more than one proposal from him. As she knew he was a widower with two daughters under fifteen and needed a wife to keep them in order, Jane understood his persistence, but always gave him the same answer. She was not yet ready to remarry...

She had just finished sorting her letters into piles, those needing replies in one pile and the others in another, when the door opened to admit the housekeeper carrying a tray. Melia followed her in and tea was poured.

'I thought we would dine at home this evening,' Jane told her. 'It is the only night we shall be at home, because we are invited out almost every night for our entire stay, and will go from one to the other like bees gathering pollen from flowers.'

Melia laughed and looked delighted. 'Could we visit the duchess this afternoon? I do so like your mama, Jane.'

'She informed me that she would be out but would visit us tomorrow afternoon and expected us to dine at night. What we might do is visit my dressmaker and milliner, Melia. I think you might like some new clothes. Your own are pretty, but not quite as stylish as the fashions in town.'

'My aunt gave me fifty pounds, but I'm not sure how many clothes that will buy...' she said doubtfully and Jane smiled.

'Your aunt told me to have your dressmaking bills sent to her, my love. She would not expect you to spend your pin money on clothes. No, we shall have your measurements taken, and see if there is anything already made up that might fit you with some alteration.'

'Do you think there will be?' Melia looked anxious. 'At home it takes ages to have dresses made up.'

'Oh, I am sure Madame François will be able to accommodate us sooner than that,' Jane assured her. 'She has many girls working under her and takes no more than a day or so to complete a simple gown— and often there is a half-finished dress from a cancellation that we may have finished to your specification if you care for it.'

'Oh, good,' Melia said, excitement rising. 'How soon may we go?'

'We shall have our tea and some of these delightful sandwiches and biscuits Mrs Yates has brought us, and then we may fetch our bonnets. I shall have the carriage sent for in one hour...' She got up to ring the bell, then remembered the annoying letter.

'Do you know of a Paul Frant?' she asked. 'Is that the person who inherited your father's estate?'

'Lord Frant, yes...' Melia looked wary, her hand suspended as she was about to eat a tiny cucumber sandwich. 'He is in India I think...'

'According to the letter I received this morning, he must be in England as he has learned that you were coming to stay with me here—he has asked to meet us both at our earliest convenience. Did you know he was returning?'

'I didn't know when,' Melia said a little guiltily. 'He sent a letter but it was vague. I did not see why it should interfere with my plans…'

'No,' Jane replied, but she wasn't sure. Melia was underage and if her guardian had chosen to withhold permission for this visit he might have done so: Melia had clearly chosen to ignore his letter. 'What did he ask you to do?'

'Oh, he spoke of my returning to my father's estate and said that he would provide a chaperon for me,' Melia said with a shrug of her pretty shoulders. 'However, his meaning was vague, and I had already arranged this visit. If he wishes me to live at Willow House with a chaperon he must arrange it with my aunt—that is the proper way, do you not agree? After all, I know nothing of Lord Frant—or this lady he wishes to foist on me.'

'It would certainly be best for him to speak to both you and your aunt, to ascertain what your wishes are,' Jane agreed, but she felt slightly anxious on her young friend's behalf, for she surely did not wish to antagonise the man who might do something for her if he chose. Not that a dowry would signify if she took Will, because he could well afford to provide for his wife.

'Oh, well, I shall write this evening,' Jane said, dismissing the matter. 'Finish your meal, Melia, and then we'll change and visit my dressmaker. I wrote her that we might so she will be expecting us…'

'Oh, what a pretty little thing it is that you bring me to dress…' Madame Françoise cooed over Melia's trim figure. 'She ees perfection, no?'

'Yes, I believe Melia will take very well,' Jane said. 'Particularly, I think, if she is seen first in Society wearing one of your creations, *Madame*. Do you have anything at all that she could wear almost immediately?'

'Yes, I believe perhaps…there is the blue silk, Michelle—and the yellow net… Fetch them quickly!' Madame Françoise clapped her hands and the seamstress hurried to obey.

In all, four half-finished gowns were produced. They were orders that had been cancelled or changed after the work had begun and Madame was delighted to do the small amount of work needed to finish them to Miss Bellingham's liking. Melia was charmed with what she saw and easily pleased, agreeing to the four gowns and agonising over a wealth of materials, styles and trimmings until Jane declared it was enough for one day and assured Madame Françoise that she would receive more visits until an adequate wardrobe had been supplied.

Riding home in the carriage with Jane later that afternoon, Melia was excited and talked endlessly of the gowns they had ordered until at last she grew a little quiet, and then looked at her hostess anxiously.

'You do not think I have been too extravagant?' she asked in a small voice. 'I have very little money of my own and my aunt has already been generous…'

'Mrs Bellingham is not a poor woman,' Jane said. 'She assured me that she wanted you turned out in fine style, Melia. I should not worry if I were you. I shall pay for everything, and your aunt will reimburse me in good time.'

'You are both very good to me,' Melia said with the shy smile which Will's sister thought was probably what had drawn him to her. She had taken to the young girl and thought that if he did marry Melia he would most likely be very happy, for she had a sunny nature—even if she did bend the truth a little now and then.

It was as they approached Will's town house that they saw a man leaving it. He paused for a moment in the sunshine, looking about him in a manner that Jane could only describe as impatient, and then strode off in the opposite direction. She did not have long to wonder who it might have been for they encountered Will coming down the stairs as they entered and he exclaimed at once.

'Ah, there you both are! Lord Frant called in the hope of seeing you, Melia. At first he was quite put out at finding you both out—and seemed surprised that you should be staying here in my house. I had to explain that Jane lives with me and that you were her very good friend...'

'I do not see why he should be put out.' Jane frowned at him. 'I had his letter and intended writing to make an appointment for one morning this week. If he must call without one, he must not expect us to be sitting in waiting for him.'

Will looked a little surprised at her tone, for she did

not often speak so sharply. 'I wasn't aware that you knew him, Jane?'

'I do not,' she replied and laughed. 'His letter rubbed me up the wrong way. You had gone to your club, Will—and we decided to visit the dressmaker to have some new gowns made up for Melia. Had he said he would call this afternoon I would have put it off until to-morrow—though how Melia can be expected to appear in public without some decent clothes I do not know...'

'I dare say you've already taken care of all that,' Will said and grinned at her. 'Besides, Melia looks very pretty in what she's wearing.'

Since Melia was wearing a simple yellow gown of muslin over a thin petticoat with a charming bonnet of straw trimmed with matching ribbons, there was truth in his words, but only the silk shawl that Jane had lent her had given the ensemble a touch of town bronze. Since he saw his beloved through rose-tinted spectacles, he could not be expected to realise that—though, had his sister ever appeared in town in such a simple robe, he might have raised his eyebrows at her.

'Well, I shall write to Lord Frant and explain,' Jane said. 'Will, please ring for some tea for us all while I see to my letter—Melia will keep you company. Unless she has something more urgent pressing?'

Melia dimpled prettily and shook her head. She and Will walked into the front parlour, talking together animatedly. Jane thought the very ease of their manner together boded well for the future, but she was not certain that her young guest's mind was as firmly fixed on marriage as was her brother's.

She went into the smaller parlour that was her own when in town and sat down to pen a polite letter, explaining that she had taken Melia out to order some of the wardrobe she would need for the season. She apologised for wasting his time; had she known of his intention to call she would have waited in but, since they had arrived only that morning, Melia had been anxious to see a little of the town.

Feeling pleased with a letter that matched his in coolness, but was far politer, she sealed it with her own wax, mauve in colour, and pressed Harry's ring into it. Lord Frant should see that he was dealing with the widow of Lord March and not some little *nobody* he could order about as he pleased! She had informed him that she would be at home any morning that week from ten-thirty until twelve and he would be welcome to call in those hours, but at other times he might find them all out.

Paul frowned over the letter that had been brought to his house just as he was changing for the evening. He and Adam had been invited to dine at a gentleman's house and to play cards in the evening. Since the gentleman was an officer they'd known when serving with Wellington, both were delighted to accept.

Paul was not sure what to make of the letter. The paper smelled delightfully of a perfume that pleased the senses, but which he could not have named for it was subtler than the heavy perfumes he'd been used to in India. The writing was beautifully formed, but the message seemed glacial to him. What could he have done to deserve such excessive politeness? He'd seen middle-aged ladies giving the cold shoulder to some junior officers before this, but he himself had never been on the receiving end.

Lady March was probably some old trout with an acid tongue, he thought and grimaced. It was regrettable that he must call on her during the hours she'd set, for he normally steered well clear of those very haughty dames. However, since his ward had chosen to ignore his invitation to take up residence in her own home and await her chaperon and his ideas for her future, he had no choice. Had he been married, he would have had no hesitation in commanding Miss Bellingham to do as he bid her, but, as a single man of no more than one and thirty, he must be circumspect in his dealings with the young lady—and therefore he must try to get on to terms with the old biddy who had brought her to London. He had never met the Viscount Salisbury or any member of his family, but he'd been told by Mrs Bellingham that they were respectable people and rich. He'd thought Lady March a younger woman, but the tone of this letter made him think he'd been mistaken.

Well, he would forget it for this evening. Paul had already set things in motion regarding the furnishing of his house. Lady Moira had returned to town after discovering that her charge was not in residence at Paul's country house and, discovering that he was camping out in two rooms, promised to arrange for him to meet a very good man who would furnish his house in the latest style.

He'd thanked her, for although he had his own ideas

on what he wanted, he really had no idea where to start. Lady Moira knew all the best shops and the silk merchants—because, she said, when she called, all the drapes in the house needed refurbishment too.

Adam had told him he needed a wife, and a certain unease at the back of Paul's mind warned him that Lady Moira was thinking of herself as filling the position, which meant he would be reluctant to ask for her help furnishing his house. She was actually five years older, but because she dressed in the first style, was intelligent and up to date in her thinking, she seemed younger. Many men seemed to prefer a slightly older woman, and there was something very sensual about Lady Moira. Although Paul did not care for the perfume she wore; it was too heavy and reminded him of some that the ladies of easy virtue who pleasured the Army officers had a habit of wearing. Indeed, Lady Moira reminded him of a beautiful courtesan he'd been offered by the Indian Prince he'd saved from death.

'I owe you my life, *sahib*,' the young Prince told him. 'Selima is of royal blood and she is yours for the taking. She is trained to please men and she will show you tricks you never dreamed of, my dear lord and saviour.'

Paul had held his laughter inside for he knew the young man believed he was bestowing a great honour by giving him the services of the beautiful concubine, but he'd refused as politely as he could. A certain gleam in the woman's eyes had spoken of a sly nature and she'd held no appeal for him. However, to refuse point-blank would have been considered an insult, so Paul was forced to fabricate an excuse. He'd been preparing himself for marriage with his English bride, he'd said, and must forswear the pleasures of the flesh until his wedding so that he could do his bride justice.

This had found favour with the young Prince, who clapped his hands and said very seriously that he thought the *sahib* was wise not to waste his strength on a courtesan when he could have a sweet young bride. Selima would be waiting for him when he returned to India, his heir already born or on its way.

Everyone had felt certain that Paul would return. Why would he wish to live in a cold, wet climate when he could have a life of ease in the heat and splendour of palaces made cool by tinkling fountains and little pools, with lilies and beautiful courtesans to play in them and await the attentions of their master? A wife was necessary for sons, who could inherit his wealth, but after one had sons there was so much more to enjoy.

Paul did not truly know what he wished for. Since his return, almost two weeks since, he'd taken a trip into the country to look at various estates, hoping to find Miss Bellingham where he'd expected her to be. Failing that, he'd visited her aunt and finally returned to London in a less than contented mood. He was still not quite back to his full strength and felt the extra journey had been wasted. Finding that his ward was out when he'd called that afternoon had seemed the outside of enough, and now this letter… For two pins he would sell his estates here and return to India. There seemed little reason for him to stay and he had almost made up his mind to book a passage next month, leaving the winding up of his various estates to his agents and lawyers.

* * *

Jane had just come downstairs the next morning and was about to write some letters in her parlour when she heard the door knocker sound in a manner that was no less than imperious. She hesitated as the footman looked at her, inclined her head and said, 'I'll be in my parlour if it is for me, John.'

Going into her parlour, Jane sat at her desk and dipped her pen in the ink. She had just begun her first reply to an invitation when a tap at her door heralded the arrival of the impatient guest. She waited as the door opened and the man she was expecting was announced. Getting slowly to her feet, Jane looked at the man that entered, her heart suddenly beating faster. He was at least a head taller than she, and she was a tall woman. Harry had been slightly shorter but that had never mattered because they were so much in love, but this man could look down on her. Her first thought was that he had a harsh face, but was otherwise unremarkable, and then she looked at his eyes—fierce, and wild, she thought with a little shock, untamed.

'I have come to speak with Lady March and my ward, Miss Amelia Bellingham. Would you have the goodness to ask them to come down, ma'am?'

'I am Lady March, and I will certainly ask Melia to come down shortly, but perhaps it might be wise if we spoke first alone?'

'You—but you're far too young...' he said, looking astonished.

'What have you been told?' Jane felt a laugh escape her, try as she might to control it. 'Forgive me, sir, but

I believe you are Lord Frant—and I am certainly Lady March. My brother, the Viscount Salisbury, will verify that if you wish.'

'Of course not…forgive me,' he said and his eyes glinted, though she was not sure whether it was anger or something else she saw in them. 'I presumed from… but no matter. I hope I do not inconvenience you but you did say any morning at this hour?'

'So I did,' Jane replied. 'Melia is trying on some gowns that were delivered this morning, but I will send for her in a moment. When we have established why it is so very urgent that you see both of us.'

'I merely wished to make her acquaintance,' he said, looking as if the wind had been taken out of his sails. 'Without my consent or knowledge, her father made both Amelia and Elizabeth my wards. The elder girl is married but I thought…' He paused, as though he was not sure what he wanted to say. 'It was never my wish that they should be turned from their home and I wanted to make sure that they—Miss Amelia in particular— had all she needed for her comfort and happiness…'

'Ah, then we are in agreement,' Jane said and smiled at him. He stared at her as though he did not quite know what had hit him. 'Melia is my friend and—although it is not certain, she may one day be my sister. I believe my brother is fond of her and, if they find they suit, he intends to make her an offer of marriage….'

'Indeed…' Lord Frant went on staring at her. She thought he looked shocked and felt quite sorry for him. Jane suspected that he had come spoiling for a fight, and something—she had no idea what—had pricked the

bubble of anger, leaving him drained like an empty bal-
loon. 'I am glad to hear she has prospects. It was—and
still is—my intention to settle five thousand pounds on
her. I intend to do the same for her sister. Ten thousand
pounds is more or less the sum I shall receive once I
sell the Bellingham estate, and I have no wish to profit
from any of it.'

'It is your intention to sell then?' Jane appraised him
with her clear eyes. 'I had thought perhaps you had
come home to live?'

'Yes, perhaps I have,' he said, seeming to come back
to himself all at once. He smiled and she saw that his
mouth was soft and sensual, not at all hard or harsh as
she'd first thought. 'I have not decided; it will depend
on various things…'

'Well, I see we have reached a happy agreement,'
Jane said, realising she had quite misjudged him. 'I shall
send Melia down to you so that you may talk in private.'

'Oh, no,' he said quickly. 'Pray send your servant to
fetch her, ma'am. There is nothing I wish to say that
you may not hear…'

Chapter Four

'We have an engagement for the theatre tomorrow evening,' Paul told Adam when they met at the boxing club that afternoon. 'Please keep the evening free, dear fellow. I want you to escort my ward, while I entertain her chaperon.'

'Do you mean Lady Moira?' Adam asked, reluctant, for he had not liked the lady Paul had chosen for the task when she called at the house.

'Oh, no, that is all changed,' Paul informed him in a blithe tone that made him arch his brows. 'Lady March will be accompanying us. Melia is happy with her and there seems no point in taking her away from where she is settled. Besides, it was all arranged on the spur of the moment. I did ask Viscount Salisbury—Lady March's brother—to accompany us, but he was engaged to play cards that evening.'

'So you thought I would oblige?' Adam gave him a clear look. 'I suppose Miss Bellingham looks like a horse?'

Paul gave a shout of laughter. 'I think her quite pretty. Of course she cannot hold a candle to Lady March... . She is lovely, Adam. Truly lovely...'

'Good grief, if I did not know better I would think you smitten,' Adam said and his eyebrows rose higher as he saw the expression on Paul's face. 'Are you? Is she more beautiful than Annamarie?'

'Completely different and utterly wonderful...' Paul shook his head as he saw the astonishment in his friend's eyes. 'Yes, you may stare. Such a letter she wrote me! I thought she must be some old trout and went there prepared to put her down—but one look from those eyes and I was floored. I just stood there and couldn't speak for some minutes. I have never experienced anything like it, my dear fellow. She took my breath away when she smiled.'

'You have got it bad,' Adam said drily, still hardly believing that he was hearing those words from Paul's mouth. 'In India you could have had any woman you wanted...including the daughter of an earl, but you barely spared any of them a look.'

'Wait until you see her,' Paul said. He grinned at his friend. 'If you value your life, please do not fall in love with her. She's mine...'

'Prepared to fight to the death for her, are you?' Adam teased, thinking he was merely jesting, and then caught his breath as he saw the answer in Paul's face. 'What is so special about Lady March?'

Paul stared at him for a full minute in silence and then shook his head. 'I'm damned if I know, Adam. She is beautiful, but it isn't that...the laughter in her eyes, perhaps, and yet it isn't just that. To be honest, I have no idea why I feel this way; it just came out of the blue. I was angry, prepared to come the injured party and demand my rights, but then…it was just so sudden. One minute I wanted to strangle her, and the next it took me all my resolve not to take her in my arms and kiss her until she surrendered.'

'I should not advise that you do any such thing,' Adam warned. 'I met her brother this morning at my club and he told me that Jane is still grieving for her husband. He has only been dead just over two years.'

'Jane…her name is Jane? Sweet Jane, my love,' Paul said and sighed. 'Yes, I was told she was recently a widow but I didn't realise…I thought her older. She is the woman for me. If she will not have me then I shall never marry.'

'Nonsense,' Adam chided. 'You do not know her yet. Supposing she turns out to have a vicious temper and a sharp tongue?'

Paul looked rueful. 'She may have, for all I know. She certainly wrote me a cool letter but perhaps I deserved it, for mine to her was curt and I was angry when I left the viscount's house.'

'Be careful, my friend. You do not know this lady yet. Take your time, for if you plunge straight in one of two things will happen…' Paul looked enquiring and he smiled. 'Either she is on the catch for a husband and she will take you for your money—or she truly loved her husband and will break your heart by turning you down instantly.'

'I do not think there is a lack of money there,' Paul

said. 'Nor do I think she is on the catch for a husband—
but she would very likely turn me down flat. No, you
are right, Adam. I must play a long game—but I could
not help sharing my feelings with you. You are the only
other person I care for in the world. Had I had you for a
brother I should have counted myself fortunate.'

'Speaking of brothers, have you heard from that
lad—your stepbrother?'

'Mark? No, I have not and I do not expect to. He
must be at Harrow or Eton by now—and I heard that
his mother had remarried to a rich man. I believe she
thought my father wealthy and must have been disappointed when she discovered that he was far from it, and
a gambler to boot. He would have spent all she had, I
dare say, leaving her only with her widow's settlement.'

'You are not thinking of settling money on her, I
hope?'

'Certainly not,' Paul said and his expression hard-
ened. 'She and her brat may go to the devil for all I care.
She was already carrying her son when they married.
I believe the affair had gone on for a while before my
mother died of a broken heart.'

'Well, I am glad of your decision,' Adam said frankly.
'You have one weakness—a soft heart for those in trouble. Do not let your family take advantage of you—and
make certain this widow is what you think her before
you offer marriage.'

'I would go down on bended knee and beg her to
marry me today if I thought she would say yes,' Paul
told him and smiled wryly. 'Do not worry, my friend.

I shall exercise all the caution you advise in other matters—but where Jane is concerned…'

Adam shook his head and gave up, grinning from ear to ear. 'I never thought to hear those words from your lips, but if you feel that way, Paul, I can only wish you joy.'

'Save your good wishes until she takes me,' Paul said. 'You will come to the theatre?'

'Wild horses would not keep me away now,' Adam replied with a twist of his mouth. 'I am curious about Miss Bellingham—and even more interested in meeting Lady March…'

'I wish you had not agreed to go to the theatre with that fellow,' Will said to his sister that afternoon at tea. 'I would not have minded if I could accompany you—but we hardly know him, and I do not trust him near Melia…'

'I believe him to be a gentleman.' Jane smiled and placed a gentle hand on his arm. 'Do not concern yourself, dearest. Lord Frant has no interest in Melia other than as his ward. I think he found the whole business troublesome and was glad to leave her in my care once he understood that we were respectable. He is to settle five thousand on her, which is a decent sum. Not that you care one iota for a dowry, but others might.'

'It does not matter what others think,' Will said loftily. 'Melia is already sure of her future…should she wish it.'

Jane looked at him intently. 'Melia is very young, my love. I think her sweet and gentle and I am sure she would make you happy—but you must not be too certain of her yet. Bringing her to London may not prove to have the result you hoped for.'

'You think she might fall in love with someone else?'

Will looked so hurt that Jane felt terrible. Yet she had to make him aware of what she sensed. They had only been in company twice so far, but on both occasions Melia had been introduced to attractive, wealthy men, and she'd shown her pleasure in the attention paid her.

'I do not know, my love. I only felt that you should be a little wary. Melia has not given you her promise—has she?'

'No, but she knows how I feel. I spoke frankly the last time I visited near her home. She said that she needed to know me better and that's when the visit to London was first discussed…'

'Yes, I see.' Jane was thoughtful. If Melia had been a schemer she might have suspected her brother had been used, but she did not think it. Perhaps not always truthful, and sometimes careless of others' feelings, Melia might hurt Will but not intentionally. She liked him, considered him her friend and thought that she might like to marry him, but that did not mean she'd given her heart and, until she did, she might well bestow it on another. Jane hoped she would not, but Melia had to have her season; she had to have her chance, because otherwise she might do something regrettable after marriage. She was a girl who liked excitement and adventure, and Will preferred a quiet life in the country. Melia would have to be very certain that she loved him to settle for that life.

'Well, time will tell,' she said now and smiled lovingly at her brother. 'Things happen and people change…but I should not worry about us attending the theatre with Lord Frant. I do not believe you have anything to fear from him.'

In that much Jane was right, but if she wanted to safeguard her brother's interests she should have refused the invitation until Will could go with them, but perhaps even that would not have made much difference.

Melia was not sure how she felt about going to the theatre with Lord Frant. He had been kind to her, and she was grateful for the five thousand pounds he was settling on her through the family lawyer. Yet she thought him stern and was a little in awe of him, though her dear Jane seemed to like him and that must mean he was all right. However, the moment he introduced his friend, Captain, Viscount Hargreaves, Melia began to enjoy the evening.

His smile made her heart race and she thought him the most handsome man she had ever seen. Indeed, he resembled the pictures of Greek gods she'd once seen in an art book in her father's library, but was so much more impressive in the flesh. Not that she could see any flesh other than his hands and face—but after seeing that picture she could *imagine* what he might look like stripped to the waist.

How immodest she was! Her imagination did not go further than his waist, though his long legs looked powerful and strong in pale pantaloons and she thought would show to even more advantage in riding breeches.

She lamented that she had no horse in London, not realising that she had done so aloud until he at once insisted that he would hire her a good ladies' horse and take her riding in the park.

'Would you really?' Melia asked and fluttered her lashes at him. 'I have a darling mare at home. She has the softest mouth and has spirit, but is a gentle soul as a rule and would never dream of tipping me off.'

'I shall bring you a creature to rival your darling,' Adam ventured, vowing privately that he would buy such a horse if none suitable were to be hired. 'I promise you will not be disappointed. I am said to be a judge. Even Frant takes my advice on horses, though he is a marvellous judge and rider himself. We have been talking of setting up our racing stables together.'

'So Lord Frant intends to remain in England?'

'Yes, I think he does,' Adam said with a small smile and for a moment his eyes seemed to dwell on Lady March and his friend. 'Though we may keep our horses in Ireland and train them there…'

'Papa told me that the best horses came from Ireland…'

'Well, perhaps,' Adam agreed, 'but I like Spanish myself. Spanish bred and trained in Ireland—a winning combination…'

'How clever you are,' Melia said, gazing up at him. Her fingers fluttered on his arm and she felt almost faint when he smiled down at her. 'Do you intend to stay in England, Captain?'

'I dare say I shall divide my time between London and Ireland,' he told her. 'We shall race the horses here, you see—but I must visit them often. However, I prefer to live in London. It is the heart of things…but I do not mind travelling. I have had adventures enough for any man, and must find a good house where a sensible woman could be happy. I think my wife must love London, as I do, but be prepared to visit Ireland and other parts with me from time to time.'

'Oh, yes, she would surely wish to do that,' Melia said, quite carried away by such an enticing picture. 'To live in London for most of one's life must be heaven… though it is pleasant to walk in the country when the weather is good.'

'Yes, exactly,' Adam said and smiled again. 'I think we are to see a good play this evening. It is a comedy, I believe, and then we shall be entertained by a dancer. I am led to understand that she is wonderful to behold but I shall reserve judgement. I have seen a great deal of dancing in India.'

'Oh, yes, how exciting that must have been,' Melia said and her fingers curled about his arm. 'You must tell me all about it.'

'Not this evening for we must be quiet now the lights are going down,' he whispered, 'but perhaps I can take you driving in the park in the morning…'

She indicated that she would love that above all things and then was silent for the play had begun and Melia, like everyone else, was soon laughing at the scandalous romp Mr Sheridan had written for their amusement. Melia knew that it had first been acted upon the stage in 1777 and was much admired, but she had not expected to be so amused by the intrigues un-ravelling upon the stage.

When, after the performance, she and Lady March were taken for a light supper consisting mainly of ices, sweet trifles and jellies for the ladies, and bread, cold meat and cheese for the gentlemen, accompanied by wine or a cool, crisp sweet cider.

Later, after they had been escorted home in Lord Frant's very comfortable carriage, the gentlemen had said their goodbyes and they were about to depart to their own rooms, Melia asked Jane what she had thought to the play.

'Very amusing,' Jane said. 'I had seen it years ago when my mama took me, but I believe I appreciated it more this time.'

'Some of it went over my head, I must admit,' Melia said, 'but Viscount Hargreaves explained it all to me.'

'How very kind of him,' Jane said and hid her amuse-ment, for only a very innocent mind would need to have the play explained and she did not think Melia that innocent and she certainly was not stupid, and so it seemed she had enjoyed having it all explained to her. Perhaps for the purpose of inviting the viscount's whole attention? 'I am glad that you enjoyed your eve-ning, my dear.'

'Oh, yes, very much,' Melia replied, a small satisfied smile on her lips.

They parted, each to their own rooms—Melia to dream of a handsome face and a young god coming down from the heavens to bear her off with him to ce-lestial heights, and Jane to wonder if she'd served her brother a bad turn by accepting what she'd imagined a harmless invitation to the theatre.

For her it had been a pleasure. Paul Frant was an attentive host, making sure that the ladies were served with cooling drinks between the acts of the play, and taking them to a very pleasant supper in a private booth afterwards. Enjoying herself more than she had for some time, Jane had not become aware of the way Melia was flirting with Viscount Hargreaves until halfway through supper. She'd wondered then how long it had been going on—the little intimate smiles, the light touches on his arm and that ingenuous way of looking up as if in awe of his superior intelligence.

It was what every young lady on the catch for a husband learned to do, though some did it much better than others. Where some inexperienced young ladies might have seemed coy, Melia played the sweet innocent to perfection. Her aunt must have told her that gentlemen did not care for clever women or some such nonsense. Jane felt such behaviour to be deceitful, especially when the girl in question was perfectly capable of understanding and coping with most situations alone; to pretend misunderstanding or to act as if one were a weak and vulnerable female in need of a gentleman's strong arm was not something Jane would have resorted to. She believed in calling a spade a spade and taking one's life in one's own hands whenever possible, but perhaps some gentlemen did prefer the childish woman that Melia portrayed so well at times.

Knowing how firmly Melia spoke out for her own opinions in the matter of dress or other domestic matters, Jane thought her husband would soon be relieved of any such misapprehension once she was mistress of his home. Melia liked her own way and she'd heard her argue with Will over a horse he'd considered too strong for her to drive when he'd given her lessons in a light phaeton that his sister knew he'd had made especially for her. Will knew her as the wilful and sometimes headstrong girl she was and loved her, but in trying to trap the viscount with a sweet modesty that was not her own Melia was, in Jane's opinion, behaving badly.

She sighed as she unpinned her hair and her maid brushed it for her, the slightly waving length of it tumbling way past her shoulders. Jane had told Tilda not to sit up but she might as well have saved her breath, for her faithful servant had replied huffily, 'The day I can't sit up for you, my lady, you may give me my pension and send me off.'

'I couldn't possible manage without you,' Jane told her affectionately. 'You will have to go on for many years yet. I'm sorry, Tilda, but you must train a girl to care for me as you do before you think of retiring.'

Tilda had given her a dark look and muttered something that Jane could not hear and diplomatically ignored. The girl had come to her via her mother, a shy young thing of fifteen when she first worked for the family; employed in the nursery, she'd worked her way up to become Jane's maid, had gone with her to Spain and France when Harry was fighting under Wellington, and been a tower of strength when his death had almost killed Jane. Indeed, she did not know whether she could have borne it without Tilda and some other friends who had supported her in her grief.

After Tilda had wished her pleasant dreams and left her, Jane felt too restless for sleep. She looked at the portrait of her husband that she had kept by her bed since it was first given her as one of many presents from an adoring lover, for Harry had remained the ardent lover to the end. Sighing, she replaced the jewelled trinket in its place and walked to the window to look out at the night sky. Jane's heart had been broken when she lost the man she loved, and she would not wish such pain on her darling brother. If Melia's heart had been captured and her head turned by the dashing soldier, she would feel responsible—though, of course, they could have met at any time during the round of parties and dances that were about to begin.

Jane sat on the edge of the bed then lay back against a pile of soft pillows, another sigh escaping her. Was it only Will's disappointment that hung over her like a heavy cloud—or was there more?

She could not be certain. The evening had been pleasant, much of that deriving from the gentle smile and amusing conversation offered by Lord Frant. There was something about him that had made her very aware of him from their first meeting, but she could not put her feelings into words. He was direct, strong-willed and would make a bad enemy, of that she was sure—but to her he showed only courtesy, though she was certain he'd intended to quarrel with her that first morning.

What had made him change his mind? Jane puzzled over it, but could find no reason for the thunderstruck look on his face as he'd stared at her. A vainer woman might have hit upon the truth, but Jane had never thought herself either beautiful or desirable. She dressed in good clothes that suited her and were considered elegant by others, but, since she only glanced in the mirror when she dressed or changed her clothes, she was not aware that she was a striking woman with good strong features and fine eyes.

It would be vain indeed to imagine that a man like Paul Frant had fallen instantly in love with her and the thought never entered Jane's mind. He was a man of the world, obviously wealthy and experienced in business matters. She could only think that he'd been surprised—he had mentioned that he'd thought she would be older, so that must be it.

Her own feelings had shocked her, because she'd liked him despite her determination not to. His letter had been abrupt and she'd been ready to think him a villain for turning Melia and her sister from their home, but indeed that had been the lawyers, who had since been put in their place and were now doing all they could to make amends. Paul Frant was a long way from being the most handsome man she'd met; indeed, his friend Adam Hargreaves put him in the shade and was a viscount to boot rather than a mere lord. As a girl, Jane had been expected to look higher and her husband's title had not been considered one of importance. She'd married for love, with her mother's approval and her half-brother's grudging permission, and, until fate had taken everything away, she'd been very happy.

Jane did not feel it would be possible to love like

that again. Surely any other attachment she might form would pale into insignificance against the love she'd known—and, that being the case, she'd more or less made up her mind not to marry again. It was better to be a widow and independent rather than find oneself trapped into a less than perfect marriage.

Yet Jane could not deny that it was comfortable having a man to care for one's comfort, even if one was capable of arranging things for oneself. Will had never interfered in her arrangements, but she'd known he was there if she'd needed a male opinion on any matter of business. Living with her brother had suited her well, but she had her doubts about living in Bath with a female companion.

As yet there had been no reply to her letter to Cousin Sarah, which had surprised Jane a little. She'd thought the girl would be only too happy to accept the offer of becoming her companion. She'd made it clear that, though she would be accepted as family, she would be given an allowance that would make her independent and able to buy the small luxuries of life that made the difference between drudgery and content.

Perhaps the letter had been lost between Sarah's home and hers. She would wait another week or so and then write again.

Chapter Five

Having made what amends he could to the Bellingham sisters, Paul was giving some thought to disposing of their father's estate. He had paid a fleeting visit when he first came to England, expecting Melia to be living there under the guidance of Lady Moira. He had not stayed more than an hour to take some refreshment before pushing on, but he had naturally found his way to the library, and what he discovered there was pleasing. Bellingham had obviously been something of a collector and there were some books Paul would like to keep on the shelves. He'd decided he would have all the books transferred to his library in London for the time being, and gradually sort out those he ultimately wished to keep; the others could be sent elsewhere once he'd had the leisure to go through them and would in the meantime fill the large spaces in what had once been his great-grandfather's excellent collection.

Paul sighed as he looked up from the letters he was writing to his man of business. It had occurred to him that there might be some pieces of furniture at the Bellingham estate that he would like for his London home. As yet, he had purchased very little and in truth was not much inclined to it, though he knew he must furnish his town house in style before he could entertain properly—yet the prospect of searching various cabinet makers was daunting for a man who had never bothered with such things. He could leave it to an agent, of course, or— The thought that he might consult Lady March on the matter brought a smile to his lips. As his wife, she would have the freedom to purchase anything she chose, but he could not convince himself that he was making any impression on her inner calm. Perhaps if he were to beg for her help in choosing the furniture for his house it would bring them closer together—of course, she would quite likely refuse but nothing ventured, nothing gained...

He'd noted with some amusement the flirtation between Adam and the young girl who was by her father's will his ward, but as he believed the viscount to be trustworthy he had no qualms. Adam would not step beyond the line, and had already confided that he was on the lookout for a wife. Paul would have no objection, should his permission be sought, though he was not sure she was the wife he would have chosen for his friend. Paul did not intend to be critical, but her artless sighs, smiles and pouts seemed artificial to him and he wondered that Adam should be taken in by them—or perhaps he was making too much of the thing and the pair were merely enjoying a flirtation.

Had Paul thought much about his friend's state of

mind, he would have imagined that Adam had been more than a little in love with the beautiful Annamarie, though he had never said as much. The proud girl had shown her own preference for Paul, and Paul had seen her snub several of Adam's fellow officers. That would probably have been enough to prevent Adam from speaking, even if his heart were engaged, for his pride would not have taken kindly to such a snub.

Oh, well, there was no point in dwelling on something of which he had no real knowledge. Paul played with his pen for a few moments longer and then a smile touched his lips as he began to write. As yet he had not received a single invitation to an affair at which he could be sure of meeting the lady he wished to meet, but perhaps if he invited her to help him choose the new furnishings for his house, that would provide a reason for them to meet more often...

'More letters for you, Jane,' Will said and smiled as he handed them to her in her parlour that morning. 'How many more affairs are we to be invited to, I wonder?'

'Several, I imagine,' his sister said, looking at him in amusement. 'If I do not have at least four engagements each day I shall think myself abandoned. You must not grudge me my fun, Will. I come so seldom to London that my friends clamour to see me and have me attend their parties.'

'And the house is inundated with young smarts,' her brother said, a trifle put out. 'I think you were right, Jane. Melia hardly has time to pass the time of day with me of late. If she is not driving in the park with one of her admirers, she is riding, or attending an al fresco breakfast or a waltzing party in the afternoons.'

'You would not have her appear a country dowd?' Jane lifted her fine eyes to his. 'Naturally, she wishes to waltz well by the time she appears at Almack's, and Lady Sopworth's invitation to join her daughters at their waltzing lessons was a great favour that I was delighted for her to take up.'

'I do not mean to complain,' Will said with a wry smile for his sister. 'Melia is lovely and it is no wonder that she is in demand. I knew it would happen but I hope she will not forget me.'

'If she loves you this will be but a passing phase,' his sister said. 'If she does not—then I do not think you would wish to marry her?'

'Perhaps not,' Will admitted, a flash of pain in his eyes. 'But I do think the world of her, Jane—and I hoped she felt the same.'

'She is young, dearest, and must have a little time to flirt,' Jane said softly, feeling his hurt and wishing that she might help him, but there was little she could do.

'I do understand,' Will answered with a determined lift of his head. 'Take no notice of me. Have you arranged to see Mama today?'

'Mama is always engaged,' her loving daughter said. 'She did make time to call on us and we have all dined with her—but I am informed she means to give a large ball next week and we are all summoned to attend.'

Will's eyes lit with laughter. 'I should not dare to plead another engagement, and I know you would not think of it. Besides, everyone will be there. It will be the biggest crush of the season if I know anything of Mama.'

'Yes, I dare say it will…' Jane had been opening her letters. Most were invitations to various affairs, but the one she had just glanced down at made her sit up straighter. 'Cousin Sarah apologises for her tardiness in replying and asks if she may join me here on Thursday afternoon… Oh! That is the day after tomorrow. I must be at home to receive her, which means I cannot accompany Melia to Mrs Broom's for tea and a little music…' She turned beguiling eyes on her brother. 'I know it is the kind of affair you most despise, Will— but perhaps you could escort her?'

Will seemed to hesitate, then nodded. 'Of course, love. At least it will give me the chance to spend more than a few minutes in her company.'

'Yes…' Jane scanned the rest of her cousin's letter and frowned. Sarah seemed to be in a fret over something, hinting that she had a problem that she wished to discuss with her. Discarding the letter, she opened the next in her pile. 'I must make sure that one of the best guest rooms is prepared for Sarah…' A little cry of surprise left her lips as she read her next letter. 'How odd…'

'Something wrong, Sis?' Will asked.

'No, not wrong—just surprising. Lord Frant has asked if I can help him choose some suitable furnishings for his house. He says that he has been living in two rooms and that cannot continue if he wishes to entertain, which he does—and he has no idea where to start.'

'What can the fellow be thinking of?' Will frowned. 'You must say no, Jane. It is not your place to furnish the man's home.'

'No, but he does not expect that, merely some advice. He really has no idea how to start—and you know that kind of thing has always appealed to me. Mama says that if I ever lose my fortune I might make it again by advising others how to furnish their homes.'

Jane was very surprised that a man she hardly knew had suggested such a thing, but also flattered. She was aware that her good taste was often mentioned in polite circles and imagined he must have heard that she was famed for her style in all things. Mama was always extolling her virtues to others, particularly gentlemen.

'I suppose he has heard some sort of garbled tale about your flair for such things.' Will frowned. 'I still think you ought not to agree. There's something about him…and that friend of his. I cannot put my finger on it, but I don't like Hargreaves and if Frant insists on keeping him in his pocket it shows…'

'What does it show?' Jane enquired, believing she understood her brother's hostility. He was feeling a little jealous of the handsome gentleman for whom Melia had shown a particular liking. 'I find Lord Frant a very pleasant companion—as for Viscount Hargreaves, I hardly know him.'

'No more you know Frant,' her brother said harshly. 'I suppose he is well enough but I don't like his friend and that I tell you…' Will's face was a little red as he added, 'And it ain't just because Melia likes him either. I wouldn't trust that man further than I could throw him.'

Jane was a little surprised, for her brother was the most easy-going gentleman she knew. It was unusual for him to take such a dislike to anyone. Even allowing for Melia's attraction to the man, Jane had not expected this reaction.

'I wasn't aware that you knew much of him?'

'Well, I don't,' her brother said. 'When we first met I thought him a pleasant enough fellow, but I saw him fleece a young fool at the club one evening. I'm almost sure that he cheated, but I couldn't be certain. The youth in question was General Brent's grandson. He came into his estate when his father died last year and if he carries on at the card table in the way he did that evening, he will soon run through his fortune.'

'Oh, Will!' Jane exclaimed for she knew the general and the young man's mother quite well. 'I am shocked. Indeed, I am. Are you sure he was cheating? It is bad enough to go on playing when a young man like that is losing constantly, but to cheat him...'

'I saw him take a card from his sleeve. I almost intervened—but I could not prove anything. If he called me a liar and protested that it was only his kerchief, which he did take out to conceal the card...it would have ended in a duel. I did not wish to become embroiled in such an unbecoming brangle, Jane. He is Lord Frant's guest, his trusted friend—and it would seem as if I were trying to discredit him for my own purposes...'

'Yes, of course I do see,' Jane said, frowning. 'I am perfectly sure that Lord Frant is not aware of such behaviour. I do not believe he would count a cheat as his best friend...'

'No?' Will looked dubious but then he inclined his head. 'I dare say you are right, Jane. I know you to be a good judge of character. Please, keep your eyes and ears open as regards this man's character, as I shall. I promise you that it is not sour grapes. I trust I am man enough to accept Melia preferring another man, but I would not want to see her ruined or have her heart broken by a scoundrel.'

'Be careful you do not use such words to her—or anyone but me,' Jane warned. 'I am glad you've been frank with me, Will. I shall try to steer her away from his company gently, but to forbid her or cast a slight on his character would make her rebellious.'

'Yes, I know her temper and her heedless character,' Jane's brother said a little sadly. 'I love her for her faults as much as her good points. If she were a paragon, perhaps I should not love her half as well.'

'Oh, my dearest,' Jane said, but would not let words of sympathy tumble out. Will would resent it if she showed pity. He was a man and could fight his own battles. 'Well, we must do what we can to keep our dear friend from harm—but if I were sure of Hargreaves's unkind nature I should speak to Lord Frant of it.'

'I dare say he would not believe you,' Will said. 'However, be a little careful in your dealings with the pair of them. You've suffered enough, Jane. I would have no harm come to you either.'

'I do not think Lord Frant means me harm,' Jane said and gave him a loving smile. 'I am well able to control my life, dearest Will. You need have no fear for me— but we must certainly try to protect Melia, for she is a dear girl.' Jane might have added *despite her faults*, but refrained.

Will heard Melia in the hall and went out to join her, suggesting a walk in the park before nuncheon, something that found favour with her. Melia came in to tell her they were going out for an hour, leaving Jane to read her letters and write her answers.

Paul smiled as he read the answer to his letter, which had been sent round by hand. Lady March had suggested that they go to various merchants and emporiums that she had favoured in the past, but asked if she might be privileged to see the rooms she was advising on before they started. He immediately sat down and invited her to visit with his ward and, if he chose, her brother, any morning that week, suggesting the day after next if she had time.

Paul did not truly expect a reply to his second letter immediately because Lady March must have a score of appointments but, returning at four in the afternoon after a visit to the tailor he preferred, he discovered her letter waiting for him in the hall.

Lady March and Miss Bellingham would call at eleven on the preferred morning and be delighted to see the rooms in need of refurbishment.

Paul immediately penned a short note of thanks and assured her of his gratitude for her kindness. He was feeling more hopeful than before, because at least she did not dislike the idea of some hours spent in his company.

It was as he was drinking a small brandy and smoking a cigar in his library, his mood one of quiet reflection, that Adam walked in. He had clearly been riding and seemed in a mood as he flung down his whip on the sideboard and helped himself to a large drink.

'Something troubling you?' Paul asked, wondering at his friend's expression, of anger mixed with something more—was it fear or anxiety?

'Oh, nothing,' Adam said, but it was obvious that he was disturbed. 'I had thought to be out this evening—a card party with three friends, but it has been cancelled.'

'Is that all?' Paul asked, looking at him closely. 'I can offer you my company for I am dining at my club—but I sense something more. Can you not tell me?'

Adam hesitated, as if wondering whether to unburden himself, and then shook his head. 'I may have to leave you sooner than I'd thought,' he said. 'I'd hoped— but matters have gone too far and I may have no choice.'

'You visited your father's lawyers this morning,' Paul probed deeper. 'Are things not as you'd hoped in the matter of his estate?'

Adam snorted with disgust and threw himself down in the wing chair opposite. 'The damned fools have made a mess of things, if you ask me. They say I must sell…house, land, horses and carriages. Everything my father left me is owed to the bank and more. They tell me I am not responsible for more than his estate is worth, but they cannot tell me how I am to live— or who will loan me money for the scheme we had in mind. I do not have three thousand to put up, Paul, nor yet half as much…'

'I am sorry for it.' Paul frowned over the news. 'Are you certain everything must go?'

'It appears my father ran on the bank for years. Nothing is left after the bank is paid—so I must either marry an obliging heiress quickly or return to soldiering. Yet without the allowance my father made me I am not certain I could support myself in the manner expected of an officer.'

'I could put my lawyers on to it,' Paul offered. 'We might get a better offer than these fellows have told you. Why not let me see what I can do—if I can save enough for our venture, would that suffice?'

'Yes, for I should make my home in Ireland and visit London only occasionally.' Adam looked slightly odd. 'I am in funds for the moment because I won five hundred guineas the other night. I had hoped for similar luck this evening but…' He sighed and shrugged.

'Better to keep what you have for the moment,' Paul said. 'That sum would buy you a decent house in Ireland—and if I buy the land we need to train our horses, we shall be halfway there…'

'I do not care to hang upon your sleeve, Paul.'

'Nonsense. I intend to go ahead with the scheme and at the very least would offer you a partnership, even had you no money to contribute. I told you before, I think of you as my brother, Adam—and your friendship, horsemanship and sheer good sense would make me want you as my partner and manager. Whether or not we can salvage something from your estate is immaterial to me, though not of course to you.' He smiled warmly at the man who had nursed him through a debilitating fever on the ship from India. 'Come, Adam, do not refuse me.'

'You make it impossible for me,' Adam said and looked half angry, half rueful. 'You're too good, Paul. I don't deserve such consideration.'

'Nonsense,' Paul replied carelessly. 'You've been a good friend to me, Adam. Without your care and attention, I think I might have died on that ship—and I am grateful to be alive and recovering my health. I could not run my stable as I wish without your assistance, my friend, so let's have no more of this nonsense. You will remain my guest until my lawyers can sort out your affairs and then we shall go to Ireland and buy what we need.'

Adam shrugged his eloquent shoulders. 'Since you insist on being grateful for a mere kindness, what can I say?'

He tossed off his brandy and stood up. 'I must write some letters, and one to permit your lawyers to investigate my father's affairs.'

Paul watched him leave, puzzling over something he'd noticed for the first time…though it might have been there before but not as strongly. There was a slight resentment in Adam's manner of late, almost as if he disliked receiving favours from a friend. Yet why should he feel like that? They had been friends in India…or had Adam been a little resentful then, because of Annamarie?

Paul would have dismissed the idea as mere fantasy had he not seen that smouldering look in Adam's eyes when he'd told him he would give him a partnership even had he no money to put into the scheme. On the ship Paul had been totally reliant on his friend and nothing could have exceeded Adam's care for him. The ship's doctor had been busy, for more than twenty others had taken the virulent fever and nine of them had died. Paul believed that he owed his existence to Adam and would willingly have settled the sum of ten thousand pounds on him had he thought it would be accepted, but he believed that to flaunt his wealth in such a way must spoil what he had thought a perfect friendship.

It was difficult when one had rather too much good fortune and the other had none, Paul reflected. He could not give such a sum to Adam without giving offence but perhaps…yes, perhaps there was a way that it might seem to be a stroke of luck and not charity…

Jane was pleased when she saw the two gentlemen enter the ballroom that evening. She had not seen either of them at a fashionable affair like this one and had decided that Lord Frant must dislike social events of this kind. However, both he and Viscount Hargreaves looked very elegant this evening, immaculately dressed in their black evening clothes with frilled white shirts. One slightly taller and heavier, the other an Adonis. Jane was amused to see almost every feminine eye follow their progress through the room. Two newcomers were always of interest, but these men were both striking—and one at least was reputed to be wealthy. Of the other's estate she had no knowledge and would not have given it another thought had she not seen Melia's immediate reaction.

Her face lit up and Jane sensed the suppressed excitement in her. She was clearly waiting for the man she admired to come to her. He did not do so immediately, but joined a group of gentlemen who were laughing and talking excitedly, possibly about a horse race. Several of the gentlemen had been talking about a particular race that evening. Not one of the usual meetings at Newmarket or another of the racecourses but a private affair between two gentlemen, who had placed a large bet on the outcome at White's. Lord Bedford and Captain Marchant had been a trifle the worse for wear when the bet was placed, it seemed, but now everyone was placing odds, mostly for Captain Marchant's grey, which was held to be the better horse, but, since the race would take place on a private estate, only those invited would be privileged to see the outcome. Everyone else would have to wait until the news reached town.

'Lady March, I trust I am in time to secure a dance with you?' Lord Frant's voice behind her made Jane turn in surprise. 'I should like a waltz—and the dance before supper so that I may claim the privilege of taking you in.'

'Why, yes, I see no reason to refuse you since my card is still untouched.'

'I cannot believe that,' Paul said and took her card from her to write his name in two spaces. Two dances were the permitted number allowed before one was thought to show an attachment. 'There, I did not expect to have my choice and can only think that Someone Above thinks kindly of me.'

Jane smiled, looking up at him with a mixture of amusement and an odd shyness. She had come to the ball prepared to act as Melia's chaperon, but there was really no reason why she should not dance—although it was the first time since she'd become a widow that she had even thought of it. For a moment grief and regret smote her. Was it right that she should dance and be happy when her dearest Harry no longer shared such pleasures?

'Perhaps He does,' she replied, but the sparkle had gone from her eyes. 'However, I must admit to curiosity about your request, sir. Have you no other lady to oblige you?'

'None I cared to ask,' Paul replied with an innocent air. 'I have noted your perfect taste, in all you do and wear—and your mama told me that you have a flair for knowing what will look well.'

'You have met Mama?'

'Yes. I happened to meet Roshithe at my club and he was very interested in the situation in India. He asked me to dine and I accepted. Your mama was a kind hostess and talked to me about you later that evening...'

'Oh, dear,' Jane said and sighed. It was as she'd half expected: Mama had been meddling again. 'I fear my darling mother may have exceeded what is necessary or proper in extolling my virtues—you see, she wants to find me a second husband. I have disappointed her in refusing all her suggestions.'

'You wrong her sadly,' Paul said, mouth twitching. 'I found your mama delightful company and enjoyed my evening. Since I believe I have made a friend in her husband, I look forward to many more such affairs—when perhaps I may also have the pleasure of your company.'

'Did Mama tell you I should be here this evening?' Jane asked, half annoyed that her mother should try to throw her in the gentleman's way. She toyed with the idea of refusing his request for help but decided that would be churlish after she had first accepted.

'Everyone is here this evening, are they not?' Paul remarked, waving his hand to indicate the rapidly filling reception rooms. 'Shall we make our way to the floor? I believe our dance is starting now…'

Jane placed her hand lightly on his arm, marvelling that he seemed to have the knack of making his way easily through the crowd—a word, a look, a smile and the thing was done. When he placed one hand at the small of her back and then took hers in the other, Jane felt a small tremor run through her. She looked up at him a little uncertainly but he merely smiled and swept her out into the throng of dancers.

He was so light on his feet for a large man. Jane was immediately aware that she need have no care for her feet; she had only to follow his lead and let herself flow with the music. Dancing with this man was sheer delight and a pleasure Jane had seldom known. As a young girl she'd been popular enough, but too often gentlemen had either trodden on her toes or been stiff and awkward when dancing. Harry, of course, had danced well, but then, he did everything well. However, he preferred hunting to dancing and once they were married he had avoided attending a ball unless it was a regimental one and he was ordered to attend.

She had learned that Wellington expected all his young officers to dance well and enjoyed entertaining the ladies who accompanied the Army; wives and daughters were made much of and always treated with respect. Indeed, the worst thing any officer could do was to flirt with or compromise a brother officer's wife or daughter. It was an unwritten law and Jane had been treated scrupulously by Harry's friends.

'May I share them?' Paul said, making her aware that she had not spoken for a while. 'Your thoughts—or are they too personal?'

'I was thinking that I had not enjoyed a dance so much for a long time,' Jane said. 'I have not danced since my husband was killed…but before that I did not have much opportunity. It is rare to find anyone so perfectly in tune with oneself on the dance floor, sir.'

'I have never danced with anyone who gave me so much pleasure,' Paul said. 'But I learned when I was with Wellington, of course—as all his officers do. If they have no skills before they become staff officers they are obliged to learn quickly, and well.'

'Yes, indeed. When I was with Harry in France all his friends danced well…' Jane caught her breath but discovered she could continue without tears. 'However, I could not say that any of them were quite your equal, sir.'

'Now you have put me to the blush, for you will think me a vain creature seeking compliments,' Paul said, but his eyes smiled at her. They lapsed into a pleasant silence, each enjoying the sensation of the dance and the magic of the music as they swept about the floor.

It was some time before Jane noticed that many of the dancers had drawn back to the edge of the dance floor, seemingly to watch them as they moved fluently across the floor and back again. She laughed, caught with sudden excitement and reckless as she twirled round and round, never thinking for a moment beyond the moment the dance must end. Yet end it did at last and there was a little buzz of spontaneous applause, which only then Jane realised was for them. It brought a flush to her cheeks and she felt warm with embarrassment. Had she been able, she might have escaped to the veranda to take a little air, but immediately Paul escorted her from the floor, Jane was surrounded by young gentlemen clamouring for a dance with her.

'I was not sure you would dance.' A man she recognised as one of Harry's closest friends asked for her card and wrote his name in two spaces, each of them waltzes. 'Had I known you were in town I should have called.'

'Captain Forlan,' Jane said. 'How nice to see you this evening—the last I heard was that you were wounded in Bonaparte's last battle.'

'Yes, but it was merely a scratch,' he replied with a smile.

Jane nodded, knowing that every young officer spoke of the most appalling wounds as just a scratch. As he walked away from her, she noticed a slight limp and understood that he did not wish to speak of his wounds, especially at a ball. He was a charming young man; Jane remembered him from those dreadful days after Harry was killed, when his friends had been so kind. She'd been in such grief, dazed and shocked, unbelieving that the man she'd adored could have been taken from her so cruelly. His friends had seen her on to a ship; some of their wives had been dispatched to stay with her until she was home with her family. She re-called Captain Forlan begging her to send for him if she were ever in need of a friend, which of course had not been the case. Mama had fussed over her, and then Will had carried her off to his home and simply been there, neither fussing nor ignoring her, but ready to do whatever she required.

However, this was not the time to be thinking of such things. Now that Jane had been seen willing to dance, she was not permitted to sit out. At supper she was once again surrounded by young officers, though Paul had secured their table and had the waiters bring a selection of all manner of trifles to tempt a lady's small appetite. However, this did not stop the gentlemen from wandering over to offer a glass of champagne or anything else Lady March desired. Jane might have preferred a little time to engage her companion in private conversation, but she was not granted the time, and consoled herself that she would certainly have time the next day since she was to visit his house.

'We shall talk tomorrow,' she said in a low voice when it became apparent that they were not to be granted a moment of peace. 'I had not expected to have so many friends around us at supper...'

'I shall look forward to it and give you to your admirers with a good grace, ma'am.'

The smile in his eyes brought an answering one to hers. He could not know it, but she had little interest in all the flattery that was bestowed on her that evening. She almost wished she had not danced, for that seemed to have opened the floodgates, but she could not wish away the two wonderful dances with Paul, one that magical waltz and the other a more sedate two-step before supper.

She had only time to go upstairs to make herself comfortable before being claimed once more. A few times Jane had felt the prick of conscience and looked for Melia, but every time she was seen to be dancing with various young gentlemen, clearly enjoying herself. However, she did not sit in Viscount Hargreaves's pocket and so Jane felt there was nothing to concern her in the young girl's behaviour.

It had been a very pleasant evening, and quite unexpected. Jane had many female friends but until this evening she'd had few admirers other than those her mama placed before her, who were inevitably rich, older and too often boring for Jane's liking.

Mama had not been present this evening, because Porky was feeling a bit under the weather, but she was bound to hear of Jane's success, and it was sure to bring a visit.

It was not until she was alone in bed that Jane examined her feelings. For a while that evening she had been swept away by the excitement of an evening spent in good company—but now she was alone and the familiar ache and longing for Harry returned.

It seemed almost a betrayal of her love to have been so happy. Jane liked Lord Frant because he was charming and good company—but it could never be more than liking, of course. Jane's heart had been given to Harry and she could never love again.

Chapter Six

Leaving her brother's house at a quarter to eleven the next morning, Jane was driven in her carriage with Melia the short distance to Lord Frant's home. They were admitted by a footman in what looked to be a smart new uniform; he was smiling and seemed very interested in his master's guests, telling them they were most welcome and must ask him for anything they desired. He had been instructed to take them to a pretty parlour, where they found Lord Frant standing by the window looking out at the gardens through an open French window. He turned instantly, his eyes lighting up as he saw Jane.

'Lady March, Miss Bellingham,' he said, coming forward to take Jane's hand. 'I am delighted you have come, though ashamed of my poor house. It has been treated ill and I must make changes quickly. However, my people are loyal and I have secured the services of an excellent chef. May I offer you some refreshment, ladies?'

'Could we have a small tour of the rooms you wish refurbished first?' Jane asked, looking about her with interest. She had almost sent to say that she had changed her mind, but now she was glad that she had not been so foolish. All that was required of her was a little advice and surely that was little enough. The room had nice proportions and was furnished properly, but might have been better, in her opinion, since some of the furniture was of too large proportions. 'This has a pleasant aspect, sir—and those windows let in plenty of light.'

'This and my library house the only decent pieces left to me. My father was forced to pass on the title and the entail, but he left nothing that he believed was his own to dispose of, I think.' And some things that ought to have been passed to him had been sold, but Paul did not mention this circumstance.

'Yes, I thought something of the sort must have happened. This room should have fine delicate pieces that do not overcrowd it, perhaps—and some of these things might be transferred to another room. Unless you prefer what you have here?'

'Oh, no, my housekeeper did what she could with an almost empty house. You may have remarked that we have no pictures or silver, nor yet any important porcelain.'

'Yes, I have noticed,' Jane said, believing that frankness was best. 'Do you wish to make this your principle home, sir?'

'When I am in London, yes. The structure is sound and of course I do have my own estate in the country—not my father's, which I believe he somehow contrived to leave to his younger son, but one left me by my mother's father.'

'Yes, I see.' Jane looked about her again. 'But you do intend to spend much of your time here?'

'As much as any gentleman of fortune,' Paul replied. 'I was left a certain amount through my mother's family and an uncle…but I was able to make my personal fortune in India. As yet, I have not disposed of much of my land and property out there, for I was not certain of remaining here when I left—but the Company will sell it for me. I do not have many calls on my purse for I am single and I suppose I might support a wife in luxury—if I were to find a lady who could love me for myself.'

'You are very frank, sir, for which I am glad. I shall not scruple to advise you to purchase only the best. Cheap furnishings are always a false economy.'

'Oh, you need not bother to count the pennies; Frant has more than enough to purchase a houseful of furniture,' Adam said from the doorway. 'Miss Bellingham, might I show you the garden? There is little to see in the house at the moment.'

Melia dimpled at him and after a nod to her guardian took Adam's arm and went out to look at the pretty gardens to the rear. Jane frowned over it for a moment, but decided that there could be little harm in a stroll round the garden on a pleasant morning; they would be in sight of the house at all times, for the gardens were not extensive.

'You may trust Adam, you know,' Paul said, obviously picking up her doubts. 'Have you any reason to doubt his behaviour towards my ward?'

'No, none—other than the foolish girl may give her heart where it is not truly wanted.'

'Yes, that is possible,' Paul agreed and cast a glance after them. 'I know that Melia's fortune would not recommend her to him.'

'Perhaps he requires a larger portion,' Jane said, her gaze very direct. 'I have not tried to forbid her because it would be useless—but I shall hint her away from him, and you might do the same.'

'I am very sure he would do nothing to disoblige me,' Paul replied but was thoughtful as he led Jane through the various rooms that contained only the occasional piece of furniture: a very large cabinet that was a fixture and could not easily be moved, and some built-in shelves in an alcove that were rather attractive and had swags of ribbons carved into the wood beneath. Occasional tables, chairs, all small objects that made a house a home, had been removed and there were faded patches on the walls where a mirror or a picture had hung. 'As you can see, we are in a sad case—but I have found someone to repaper the worst of the rooms. I am told it may be done while I am away at the Newmarket races.'

'That would be excellent,' Jane agreed. 'Nothing is more disagreeable than having workmen in when one is in residence. If we ordered the furniture you require and some mirrors, some candlesticks of silver and a few pieces of porcelain, you may buy your pictures at your leisure. I think they should be chosen when one finds something that appeals—furnishing pictures are not to be admired.'

'Yes, I agree. I hear there is an exhibition of new young artists due to start in three weeks. I might find one or two there, though anything of real merit must come through an auction, I think.'

'Yes, I believe that would be best,' Jane said. 'If one hears of a country house to be auctioned with all its contents, some fine things may be purchased that way.' She stopped to admire an exquisite ceiling and a run of long windows. 'I am glad to see that you do not cover those with drapes, sir. It is a lovely view out to the garden and must be pleasant in here during the summer.'

'Yes, and damned draughty in the winter,' Paul said and laughed softly. 'We only ever used this room to entertain; it soon warms up if there are enough guests— but I always preferred my mother's parlour and the library for comfortable evenings…'

'The rooms we saw first,' Jane said and nodded. 'I should certainly prefer your mother's parlour if it were furnished well—either in the French fashion or that set by Mr Adam, I think. That large Chippendale cabinet would do much better in here, I believe—against that far wall. You should have two settees here, facing each other, and an occasional table to the side. Behind this one you might have an elegant sofa table—indeed, why not order a pair with some important candelabra to set them off? Over there by the window I think a desk of good proportions, a chair to match the sofas at the desk—and at that end of the room a pier table with a shaped mirror above. We might have two areas, one at either end, of a small table and comfortable chairs set conversationally: a pair of fine cabinets against the long wall, flanked by a set of good single chairs, and some display tables between the windows at the back…'

'You make a fine start,' Paul said and scribbled some notes on the pad he'd brought with him for the purpose.

'You will need things like candle stands, torchieres and a reading frame, but perhaps not too many in here. The cabinet makers I have used in the past will send things we like and if we do not find a place for them, they will take them back.'

'I am enthused by your ideas,' Paul told her. 'When may we begin?'

'Tomorrow I must wait at home because a young cousin is coming to stay with me and I must be there to greet her,' Jane said. 'However, we might make an appointment for Friday morning. Some of what you require will need to be made up for you, and therefore the sooner we start the better…'

'You must not let me take up too much of your time…'

'Oh, I do not often bother with morning engagements,' Jane said. 'Melia may be charmed by an alfresco breakfast but I prefer to rise later, do a little shopping, perhaps visit a few friends in the afternoon and then prepare for the evening, for then, you know, we might have three engagements—dinner, a soirée and perhaps a supper and dancing elsewhere…'

'I wish I knew which events you favour,' Paul said without thinking. 'I cannot always rely on your mama to tell me.'

Jane stared at him, a little surprised and wary too. She was prepared for friendship, but was Lord Frant flirting with her?

'I am very sure that some of the events I attend would

not amuse you. I dare say you are invited to more than you can attend?'

'I have my fair share of invitations, but some of them hold little interest… Last evening was the first I have managed to meet you in company.'

Jane's spine tingled, a little unease creeping into her mind at the exquisite compliment. He was flirting and because of that she made her tone cool as she replied, 'I cannot think your evening wasted if you do not see me, sir.'

'No, perhaps not,' he said, recovering his mistake. 'It was just so pleasant to dance with you. I should not wish to miss a chance to repeat it.'

'Then you must accept all the invitations to balls and dances you receive,' Jane said and smiled because she could not quite resist.

'Yes, I shall of course be certain of meeting you sometimes then,' Paul said. 'In the meantime, perhaps your brother, Melia and yourself would join me for an evening of pleasure at Vauxhall Gardens—unless you have already been invited to such an event?'

'Will has promised to take us one evening,' Jane replied, 'but I am sure he would be happy to make up a party with you, sir. You must speak to him. However, I must warn you…' Jane stopped, her cheeks warm. She had been about to tell him of her brother's feelings of distrust regarding his friend, but realised that she could not confide such a thing to him. At times she felt he was a friend and to be relied on, but she hardly knew him and must exercise caution for the moment.

'No matter…I am sure my brother would be happy to see *you* at any time, sir.'

His eyes narrowed and she wondered if she had stressed the word *you* too much, for she did not wish to give offence and Paul Frant was an intelligent man who would not need things spelled out to him. They had returned to the parlour they began with just as Melia and her escort returned from taking the air and therefore no further conversation of an intimate nature took place. She suspected that he might have questioned her on her meaning had they still been alone, but was unable to in the presence of the others.

Refreshments were brought and they talked of the ball they had all attended and of future engagements, many of which Melia had mentioned to Viscount Hargreaves and which he seemed eager to attend. Jane had noticed that her young friend had seemed a little flushed when they first returned to the parlour, but she gave no sign of distress and seemed in high spirits when they left in Jane's carriage.

'Adam told me that Lord Frant's father behaved shamefully to him,' Melia said, chattering, her eyes very bright. 'That is why he has to refurbish the house completely—but of course he is very wealthy and can afford to do so.'

'I had understood something of the kind,' Jane said in a repressive tone. She did not think it seemly of Paul's friend to have discussed his personal circumstances with a young girl, but felt it unwise to speak against the gentleman to a girl who was clearly enamoured. 'It is hardly our business to speculate, Melia. I hope you will not speak of this to anyone else. To discuss another person's wealth is unseemly.'

'Of course I would not.' Melia flushed and looked uncomfortable. 'Adam was explaining that he is to go into business with Lord Frant, though he is not wealthy himself for his own estate is but small.'

'Ah, I see.' Jane gave her a direct look. 'You speak of the viscount as Adam. Do I take it that he asked you to do so?'

'Yes, of course.' Melia smiled saucily at her. 'Oh, I know better than to do so in Society, but privately we are Adam and Melia.'

'I do not wish to criticise your behaviour,' Jane said. 'Yet I am your chaperon and I would not wish you to be hurt...or to be thought fast. It might be prudent to be a little careful, Melia. Viscount Hargreaves is charming, but we know so little of him or his affairs.'

Melia's face flushed stubbornly and for a moment she looked as if she would argue, but then she inclined her head. 'I would never do anything you felt shameful, Lady March. Surely you cannot think it? I am grateful to you for bringing me to London for I am sure you did not want the bother of a young girl.'

'You could never be a bother to me,' Jane said. 'Indeed, if you think me harsh I am sorry for I did not mean to scold—I think only of your future, my dear. Both Will and I are very fond of you.'

'Yes, I know.' Melia looked a little ashamed. 'Pray forgive me, Jane. I did not mean to sound petulant but... the viscount is so flattering and it is nice to have a gentleman say pretty things...'

'Yes, of course,' Jane said. 'However, some gentlemen say more than they mean. I do not think it of Viscount Hargreaves necessarily, but a little care in one's dealings with a gentleman one hardly knows...'

'Do you not like him?' Melia asked, looking bewildered.

'I have formed no opinion,' Jane said truthfully. 'However, I do like Lord Frant and I would suppose any friend of his to be a gentleman—but for your own sake, Melia, take your time.'

'Yes, I shall.' Melia sparkled at her suddenly. 'He is not the only gentleman to pay me exquisite compliments. I might have had my head turned a dozen times at the ball if I were a foolish child.'

Jane smiled, the look in the girl's eyes making her wonder if perhaps Melia was not well able to take care of herself. Perhaps she too was merely flirting and would not lose her heart to a rogue...

Now why had she thought of Viscount Hargreaves as a rogue? It was not because of her brother's hints about his card playing... No, more a certain note in his voice when he'd spoken of Paul Frant as having plenty of money to buy a houseful of furniture. Something in his tone and his face had made Jane suspect that underneath the smiles and the assumption of friendship for his host there lay a simmering jealousy.

Melia felt a flicker of guilt as she went upstairs to put off her bonnet before nuncheon. She had lied to Jane about her feelings and her intentions, allowing her to think that she was interested in a score of admirers who had paid her such pretty compliments at the ball, when in truth the only one that made her heart flutter was Adam.

He had pressed her hand to his lips in the garden, gazing ardently into her eyes as he told her that she was the loveliest girl he'd seen in England and he was rapidly falling under her spell.

'I am so unworthy of you, my dear Miss Bellingham…'

'No, no, do not say so,' Melia had begged him. 'You must call me Melia; everyone I like does…'

'In private, perhaps,' he'd said in a voice husky with passion. 'I am Adam to you, and you are Melia in my heart—but I can never presume to hope for more than friendship, sweet lady. I have little to offer and, though Frant and I are to go into partnership in the matter of our racing stable, my estate is unable to support the wife I would wish for. In time, perhaps, I shall have my own houses in Ireland, London and perhaps Leicestershire for the hunting—but that may be some years away, and I could not ask any lady to wait for me…'

Melia's heart had swelled with a mixture of love and grief. How noble he was in renouncing her because he could not afford to give her the things she deserved. The portion Lord Frant had given her no longer seemed enough, for though it increased her fortune to seven thousand pounds in all, it was not enough to buy her a husband who needed the means to support a wife and live in comfort in the way he described.

How could Papa have left his whole estate away from his daughters? Melia supposed it must have been worth some twenty thousand pounds or more—which meant she ought to have had ten thousand pounds, not the measly five that Lord Frant had granted her.

She stared at herself in the dressing mirror, her mouth pulled down in discontent. It was not Adam's fault that his own father had wasted his inheritance to almost nothing. He'd told her that Lord Frant's father had done much the same to him.

'It is all right for Paul,' he'd said and she'd seen his rueful look of regret. 'He has the luck of the devil. In India we rescued a young prince from a pack of vengeful tribesmen from the hills—but it was he that received the gratitude and rewards from the Prince's father. I received almost nothing…'

Melia had been given the impression that Adam had been the principle rescuer and Lord Frant had taken the credit, which had resulted in him becoming the owner of palaces and lands out there in India.

'You should have spoken out,' Melia had said, outraged on his behalf. 'Lord Frant should share the rewards with you.'

'He was the one who snatched the Prince from a burning building,' Adam had said. 'My men and I made it possible by fighting off the tribesmen, but of course the Prince called Frant his saviour. I did not wish to push myself forward—and the Maharaja sent wine, food and one hundred gold coins, which I shared out amongst my men.'

'Yes, I do see it would be impossible for you to push your claim,' Melia had said, her heart won by his selflessness in sharing the small reward he'd received with his men. 'Yet I still think Lord Frant should have given you half of the rewards he received.'

'I should not wish you to think ill of him,' Adam had told her. 'You must not speak of this to anyone, Melia—it was merely that I wished you to understand why I cannot offer marriage to any lady, even if it breaks my heart. I must earn my fortune by hard work and skill.'

Melia changed into an afternoon gown, for she was going out with Viscount Salisbury after luncheon. She was aware that she had once given a careless promise to him, but she'd never said that she loved him or that she would marry him, merely that she would wish to get to know him better before answering his question.

Melia did like both Jane and Will very much; they were her friends and she would not shame them or hurt them for the world—but she'd discovered a new and exciting world here in London and meant to make the most of her chances while she was here.

Her heart was given to Adam, but he was set against marriage until he could earn enough to keep his wife in style. Only if Melia could persuade her guardian to give her a larger portion might she be able to persuade him to think better of his noble sacrifice. A man who would not speak out when he was cheated of a fortune would not marry just for money—and yet she believed that he'd been telling her he loved her. If she had ten thousand, perhaps he would marry her...

Jane was about to change for the evening when she heard the rattle of carriage wheels outside the house; the sounds of postilions shouting and a loud rapping at the door made her throw on a silk wrap and hurry to the top of the stairs. Hearing a commotion in the hall and then the sound of a young woman's voice, she gave a glad cry and looked down. Cousin Sarah had arrived some hours early and her arrival had thrown the servants into disarray.

'Come up to me, Sarah,' she called down. 'I am changing and may not come down, but please do come up to me. You were expected tomorrow but your room is prepared and we shall have some tea in my sitting room while they carry up your bags.'

'Jane…' A tall girl with dark eyes and a pale complexion started up the stairs towards her. 'I am sorry to throw your arrangements out, but I had the offer of a carriage part way and it brought me here some hours earlier than I'd expected.'

'It doesn't matter in the least,' Jane said, meeting her with outstretched hands. They kissed cheeks warmly, Jane looking intently into her face. 'You look pale, Sarah. I was so sorry when your dear mama passed away.'

'It has been a terrible time,' Sarah confessed, her voice catching. 'My father left us with little to live on and poor Mama was living in fear of being turned from the house. I do believe it was that…' She shook her head and forced a smile. 'I am determined not to cry all over you, Jane. It was so good of you to offer me a home and saved me from…but that will keep for later. You are dressing for the evening, I think?'

'Yes. Melia and I are engaged for an evening of music and supper, also perhaps a little dancing later. I do not wish to disappoint Melia, but I should not like to leave you alone, Sarah.'

'You must not concern yourself,' Sarah said and sighed. 'To own the truth, a little light supper in my room and I shall be very well for this evening. Please, Jane, I should feel so awkward if I kept you here when all I wish for is to rest.'

'Very well, I shall instruct my housekeeper to bring you your supper on a tray—and I will take you to your rooms, my dear cousin. Tomorrow we shall have a long talk and you may tell me all your news.'

'Thank you for your kindness,' Sarah said, and again there was a break in her voice. 'I was near desperate when I wrote to you and for a while I did not think I could escape my fate…'

Jane looked at her enquiringly, but she shook her head. Realising that Sarah was indeed exhausted, Jane led the way to the large and pleasant chamber she'd had prepared for her.

'Oh, what a lovely room—two rooms,' Sarah said, realising that she had both bedchamber and sitting room of her own. 'This is sheer luxury, Jane. I cannot thank you enough.'

'We shall discuss my plans and yours tomorrow,' Jane promised her, kissed her cheek and left her to the maids who had come up to attend to her unpacking.

After giving the housekeeper instructions for her cousin's comfort, Jane left her and returned to her bedroom to finish changing. Had she not been entertaining Melia she might have cancelled her engagements for the evening, but she did not wish to disappoint the girl—and Sarah's story would wait for the morning.

Chapter Seven

Paul picked up the invitation from Lady Featherstone and read it once more. He thought it most likely that it would be an insipid affair and would normally have rejected it in favour of an evening playing cards with some friends at his club. However, Melia had told Adam that she and Jane would be guests of Lady Featherstone this evening, and that meant it would not be a complete waste of time—and yet was it too soon? He did not wish Jane to feel that she was being pursued, for he sensed that although she was intrigued and interested in the project he had invited her to oversee, her feelings towards him were, as yet, merely those of a casual acquaintance. She was quite clearly still grieving for her husband, even though she'd put off her blacks. Had he not been Melia's guardian, he doubted that she would have obliged him in the matter of furnishing his house.

Paul looked at himself ruefully in the mirror. His natural impatience made him long to make her an offer of his heart, his name and his fortune, in that order, but he believed that she would become embarrassed and turn him down. Had he seen any sign of anything warmer than what he thought was the beginning of liking, he would have shown his feelings for it was not in his nature to be secretive.

Paul remembered the day he had snatched the young Prince Kumal from the building in which his captors had imprisoned him. When the preparations for an assault on their camp was noticed, one of them had set fire to the wooden hut and the youth's terrified screams had caused Paul to rush straight to his rescue. The tribesmen had been caught by surprise but that did not prevent them from shooting at him as he rode up to the small building and dismounted, attacking the door with an axe until it gave. Rushing into the fire against the shouted orders to wait from the captain in charge of the soldiers that day, Paul had carried the now almost unconscious lad from the building, sustaining burns to his back and one of his legs. He'd covered the Prince and his own head with a blanket, thus preventing much of the harm that might have been done; his scars were hidden and he never spoke of them.

Prince Kumal had suffered only minor burns to his hands, incurred in trying to pull away burning wood from across the door before Paul's arrival. He and his father had been overwhelmingly grateful, for his quick actions had undoubtedly saved the Prince's life.

'You must also thank the soldiers who helped drive off the tribesmen,' Paul told the grateful father. 'I could not have done it alone.'

'I have been told it was your quick thinking that

saved my son. Your soldiers and their captain were interested only in subduing the tribesmen. It was you who insisted they go in at once—and indeed they could only follow once you led the way. Kumal told me that he thought he would die until you started hacking down the door. He heard no shots until after you plunged in to rescue him.'

There had been none for Adam had been waiting to assess how many rebels there were before committing to the attack. He and his men had been sent to subdue the tribesmen, who had been causing a deal of trouble in the area, but Paul's reason for being one of the party was the suspicion that it was these particular renegades who had kidnapped the young Prince.

He knew that Adam and his men had received two thousand gold pieces as the Maharaja's reward for helping to save his son. His reward had been more personal: a pink-walled palace, lands—and the offer of a half-royal bride who would come with a rich dowry, besides many other gifts. His son had offered one of his own concubines for Paul's pleasure, but the Maharaja had offered him a prestigious wedding that would have brought both power and wealth.

'The Princess Helena's daughter is beautiful and carries the blood of my uncle,' the Maharaja said, smiling on him. 'It would honour her to become your wife—and it would honour us if you would make your home amongst us and share our lands.'

He had been tempted for a moment or two because Annamarie was very lovely, and any man might be happy to live like a prince. Paul's fortune had come through his own endeavours, but the lands and palace he'd been given were worth what many would think a small fortune in themselves—and Annamarie had a rich dowry settled on her by her father before he died. Adam had thought Paul a fool to turn down the offer and he'd had to be very careful for he did not wish to give offence, either to the Maharaja or Annamarie herself.

Perhaps if that letter from his distant cousin's lawyers had not arrived when it did he might have stayed and taken Annamarie as his wife—and what a terrible mistake that would have been. The proud beauty would soon have guessed that he did not love her, and she would not have been happy at being part of a bargain made by her uncle. She no longer lived in the palace and thought herself a free agent, bound to do only her mother's bidding.

Pushing all thought of India and the past from his mind, Paul finished his preparations for the evening. He was fortunate that his face had not been scarred as his back was, and one of his legs. He'd never been as handsome as Adam, but sometimes he wondered if any woman would put up with the scarring on his back... yet a nightshirt would cover it and the old scars never pained him now.

It was strange but he'd never thought he would ever fall in love—so deeply in love that nothing else mattered—but one look at Jane, one smile from those lovely eyes, and he could think of nothing else. He had for one fleeting moment considered wedding his ward, but that thought had been forgotten the moment he'd looked into Jane's eyes.

Deciding that he was ready, Paul picked up his hat, cloak and cane. Adam had decided that he would prefer an evening of cards amongst his friends and excused himself.

'You do not need me,' he'd told Paul, an odd look in his eyes. 'I shall visit a club I've been told of with some new acquaintances.'

Paul had wanted to warn him about trusting new friends and new gambling establishments, but the advice might have caused offence and would not have been heeded.

In India they had been friends, though not often in each other's company since Adam was a part of the Army that protected the Company and the district from various warring tribes. On the ship coming over, Paul's illness had formed a bond between them and he had sincerely wished that Adam was his brother—but, since then, Adam's behaviour had planted a small seed of doubt in his mind.

Paul was not a gambler. He was willing to play a hand or two with friends at his club for reasonable stakes and usually rose with either a small loss or an equally small gain. However, he believed that Adam was playing for high stakes and hoping to win enough to repair his fortunes. Adam's father had been a reckless gambler, which was why he'd lost most of his estate, and it seemed that it was in the blood. Paul feared for his friend because of it, but he could not interfere.

His lawyers were looking into Adam's affairs and the outcome of that might be the only way that this madness could be brought to a close. If Adam discovered that after all there was a reasonable sum left from his father's estate, perhaps he would be happy to go off to Ireland as they'd planned and put aside this reckless gambling.

Sighing, Paul put his friend's problems from his mind. The fever he'd suffered on the ship had dragged him down but he was at last feeling more like himself again. He would have to visit the country to sort out his various estates soon—and he wanted to visit Newmarket for the races. If he saw any young horses he liked the look of he would purchase them at Tattersalls. Perhaps if he could carry Adam off with him to Ireland, he might settle down and forget his foolish dreams of winning back all that his father had lost…

Jane was conscious of a feeling of pleasure when she saw that Lord Frant had come that evening. It was to be a simple evening of a little music and some cards for those who wished for it. Many of the gentlemen had accompanied wives, daughters and young cousins, and would disappear into the card room as soon as the music began. However, when she found a seat for herself and Melia where they might sit and listen but not be too close, it was not long before Lord Frant came to stand near them.

'Good evening, Melia, Lady March,' Paul said. 'I believe Madame Meloria is a fine soloist and we are in for a treat this evening.'

'Yes, so I have heard,' Jane said and smiled at him. 'Are you comfortable there? I believe there is a chair just behind that you might fetch to sit beside us if you wished.'

'Yes, I see it,' Paul said and moved away to pick up the single chair and place it next to Jane as she sat on the small sofa beside Melia. 'That will be more comfortable if the music continues for a while.'

Melia leaned forward in her seat. 'Is Viscount Hargreaves not with you this evening, sir?'

'No. I believe he had another appointment,' Paul said and frowned.

'Is something wrong?' Jane asked but he shook his head and assured her that all was well.

They spent a very pleasant evening listening to the music, taking supper together and talking. Melia had seen some friends and was carried off by one young lady to join her and her brother and his friends in a light-hearted and very noisy and amusing card game. No money was wagered by the young people but there was a great deal of rivalry and Melia's laughter was heard on several occasions.

'Your brother did not accompany you this evening?' Paul asked towards the end. 'I had thought he might have done so.'

'It was his intention, I believe, but Mama summoned him to attend her to the theatre. It seems the duke was indisposed and suggested that Will took her instead, which of course he was delighted to do. We are both very fond of her.'

'Yes, I dare say you are,' Paul said and laughed softly. 'I imagine not many can resist the duchess's charm?'

'Oh, it has not always been so,' Jane assured him.

'Mama was very young when her father arranged the marriage to my father and it was not a happy one. Papa was too critical for poor Mama, but Porky adores her. I do believe he has remained faithful all his life.'

Paul looked thoughtful. 'Marriage should always be for love or at the very least where liking and respect are sufficient. For myself, nothing but love would content me. If I were to ask a lady to be my wife she would know that I should never look elsewhere and make it my purpose in life to see that she was happy.'

'Yes, I believe that you would,' Jane said, her interest caught. 'For myself, I could never marry unless I loved. I was very much in love when I married Harry March.'

'Yes, I believe your husband was a brilliant soldier. You were unlucky to have lost him so soon, ma'am.' His eyes dwelled on her with a warm sympathy that made Jane's heart catch, for in that moment she felt that she could find comfort against his broad shoulder.

'Yes, it was ill luck—but Harry was never one to sit at the rear and send his men forward. He led the charge and was shot down…' Jane's throat caught and for a moment she felt close to tears, but held them back. 'I was devastated when they told me. I have begun to accept and move forward—but it is the only source of discord between myself and Mama. She cannot see why I say I shall not marry again…'

'You think it would not be possible to find such happiness again?'

'I do not think I could settle for second best,' Jane admitted candidly. 'Only if I felt another person necessary to my very life would I think of taking another husband.'

'I can only say that the man you chose would be fortunate—and since I think it a shame you should live alone I must hope you find him one day.' Something in his words touched her in a way that other expressions of sympathy had not and she almost wished that he would put his arms about her and hold her safe.

'I shall not be alone,' Jane said with her sweet smile that, unknown to her, clutched at his heart. 'My cousin Sarah has come up to town to bear me company. When Melia's visit is done I may think of taking a house in Bath. If my brother were to marry I could not continue as his hostess because it would be unfair to his wife— whoever she might be.'

'Yes, I see…' His expression did not change, but Jane knew that he was thinking about what she'd told him. 'Would I be wrong in thinking that your brother still has hopes of her?'

Jane glanced towards the group of young people and sighed. 'I believe he thought she returned his feelings, but now he is not sure. She is young and pretty and it is only right that she should have her chance to shine in Society—and to make her choice. I do not wish for Will to be unhappy, but I would not have Melia feel constrained to marry where her heart did not follow.'

'You think her head has been turned by gentlemen paying her compliments—or by one gentleman in particular?'

'It is not easy to be certain,' Jane admitted. 'Melia likes flattery and attention—who does not? She seems happy this evening, and yet I believe she was disappointed that Viscount Hargreaves did not come.'

'Adam is not truly in a position to take a wife—unless she has a fortune and is willing to bestow it on him. Melia's portion would not be enough for him, Jane. I think he would marry only if he were to find an heiress—or a rich widow, you see. You might hint at his lack of real fortune if you think it would save her pain. He is not penniless; I would not have you think that—but not rich enough to support the lifestyle he enjoys and a wife and family.'

'Yes, I had supposed something of the sort,' Jane said. 'However, I think it unwise to try and influence her. Melia must decide for herself what she wants of life.'

'You are very wise,' he said and once again that thoughtful look was in his eyes. 'It is seldom wise to meddle in the lives of our friends, unless they ask us—and even then too often they will not thank us for it…'

'I fear you are right,' Jane said. She rose to her feet and offered her hand. 'It has been a most pleasant evening and I am reluctant to leave, but I think I ought. I have neglected Sarah long enough and must go home and enquire how she is.'

'Ah yes.' He glanced at Melia. 'My ward will not take kindly to being asked to leave, I think. She is still intent on her game—and winning, by the sound of it.'

'Even so, I must take her away.'

'Unless you thought I might bring her home safely in—say another hour?'

'Oh…' Jane was about to say she did not think it a

good idea, but then remembered that he was Melia's guardian and might, if he'd wished, have insisted that she live with him and a chaperon. 'Yes, I think that might suit—if she likes the idea.'

Melia hesitated and then agreed. She said she hoped that Jane found her cousin well and she would not disturb her when she came in but go straight to her room.

'I prefer that you say goodnight. I shall not be asleep by then and indeed I could not unless I knew you were safely home.'

'Oh, if you wish it.' Melia gave a shrug of her pretty shoulders. 'But Lord Frant is my guardian—and far too old to be of any consequence...'

Jane gave her a puzzled look, wondering how she could speak of a man who had done so much for her. Five thousand pounds was a considerable gift and, properly invested, would bring in enough to keep the girl in comfort until she married. Living with her aunt, as she did, she would have no need to spend the interest on anything but trifles she fancied.

Having taken her leave of her charge, Jane had her carriage brought round and was driven home. A sigh escaped her as she settled back against the squabs, for she half wished that she had stayed another hour. She had seldom passed a more pleasant evening and could only thank Lord Frant for that since he had been attentive and an interesting conversationalist, telling her some tales of life in India that she found fascinating.

She spoke to her housekeeper, who told her that Miss Sarah had settled for the night and had drunk a tisane she'd given her.

'She had a headache, my lady, and I gave her the special mixture I used to make for your dear mama. It will make her sleep through to the morning, never fear.'

'Then I shall not disturb her,' Jane said. 'I should like some hot milk and sweet biscuits, if you please—and I will sit up in my dressing room until Lord Frant brings his ward home. Please let me know the moment she is in the house.'

'Of course, my lady.'

Jane went up to her own apartments and allowed her maid to undress her and brush her hair. It seemed that she'd left the company early for no good reason, but she had not liked to think of Sarah sitting alone in her room, despite her declaration that she was perfectly content to go to bed and rest.

After she had dismissed her maid, Jane tried to read a book in the comfort of a large wing chair, but her mind kept returning to Lord Frant and his smile. His years in India had caused him to have lines at his eyes, caused perhaps by the relentless sun and the need to screw up the eyes against it at times. She did not find it unattractive that his face should have a slightly craggy look, for it showed that he had lived—and, if she were not mistaken, suffered in some manner.

Something about him had caught her interest. Jane could not have said what, but at each meeting she discovered more about the man and his character, and she liked what she'd learned. Paul Frant was a man to be trusted and relied upon, Jane thought, and there was something honest and straightforward in his manner of address that appealed to her.

* * *

'I am glad to have this time alone with you,' Melia said when she was sitting in Paul's carriage on the opposite seat facing him. 'I wanted to talk to you about Viscount Hargreaves…of the predicament he finds himself in, which makes it impossible for him to marry where he will…'

'Indeed?' Paul's eyes narrowed but Melia ignored the warning sign. 'Do you think it quite proper for you to speak this of a man you hardly know?'

'Not when it affects my whole happiness, for you must know that I am in love with him and if he cannot wed me for lack of fortune I shall break my heart.'

Paul was silent for a moment, then, 'Has Hargreaves spoken to you of marriage? He should properly have asked my permission for you are under the age of consent and, even had you reached that age, mere politeness makes it imperative that he do so.'

'Oh, pooh, as if I should care for such things if I were of age and had a suitable fortune. Had Papa only lived I am certain he would have given me at least ten thousand pounds on my marriage.'

'I very much doubt your father could have found such a sum,' Paul told her. 'To do so he must have sold the estate, which, as you know, was entailed.'

Melia stared at him, a rebellious look on her pretty face. For a moment she was silenced, but then began the second prong of her attack. 'Do you not think you owe the viscount something for what he did when that young prince was rescued? You received a large reward while he had nothing but a few gold pieces, which he shared with his men.'

'Did Hargreaves tell you that?'

Melia hesitated, as though realising that she'd been not only rude but unguarded. 'Can you deny it is true?'

'The truth of the matter is my affair and no other's,' Paul replied in a measured tone that hid the anger he felt inside.

Her accusations were unfair and he could not be sure how much of it was due to her resentment against him and how much Adam had said to her. Did the man he'd thought of as a true friend feel resentment because Paul had received so many gifts from the Maharaja? His part in driving the tribesmen off had indeed been heroic and vital, but it would all have been too late had Paul not done what he had—and the Prince's father felt that the soldiers had merely done their duty to protect the province, for which service he'd already paid handsomely. His generous gift of two thousand gold coins was not something to be dismissed as paltry, even when shared with Adam's men.

'I do not think two thousand gold coins an unfair reward for a man doing his job. The Army is paid to keep the tribesmen in control and two thousand was a generous gift.'

'It was nowhere near as much! Surely…'

'I assure you that was the sum given to Hargreaves and his men, together with wine and food.'

'Even so—why should you have so much more?' Melia asked, looking sulky, but she stared in disbelief and he realised Adam must have mentioned a different sum.

Paul might have told her why he'd been so favoured, but he held his tongue. 'You speak of things you do not understand,' he said in a mild tone. 'I think you should reflect a little longer before you speak to me on this subject again. If you knew the truth…' He sighed. 'No matter—you are in love and young. You believe that only your wishes are important. Until you grow up a little and learn to think of others, I should not give my permission for your marriage even if Hargreaves had asked and had the fortune to keep you as you expect.'

'I hate you and I wish my father had not named you in his will.'

'I dare say he meant my father to be your guardian,' Paul said. 'They were friends, I believe—but my father died and yours just before him. It is unfortunate. I dare say my father's wife might have brought you out, but I can assure you he would not have given you five thousand pounds. You should try to be content with your lot, Melia. Sulking does not become you.'

Melia glared at him but did not reply, and, since they had arrived at Viscount Salisbury's house, Paul got out, giving her his hand to help her down from the carriage and see her to the door.

'Will you not wish me goodnight, Melia? It will be better for us to remain on good terms, I think.'

'Oh, goodnight then,' she said ungraciously. 'But I think you might help Viscount Hargreaves, so that we can marry.'

'I know you do,' he said with a faint smile. 'Try to

be patient, Melia; things often have a way of working themselves out. One day you may be glad I did not do as you asked.'

The door opened and she was admitted. Paul returned to his carriage. He was thoughtful as he was driven home. Melia had no doubt been spun a tale that led her to believe Adam had played the leading part in the Prince's rescue; it was the only possible reason for her attitude. He did not care for her character and could only be pleased that he had not been too hasty in the matter of offering her marriage; they would not suit, even had she agreed.

Was Adam as resentful of him as Melia's unguarded words seemed to indicate? If she believed that he'd taken all the honours and rewards for himself—rewards that rightfully belonged to Adam—it was possible that he thought much the same.

Paul felt a slight unease. He'd been so grateful for Adam's attentions on the ship that he'd fallen into the habit of thinking him a great friend—but in India they had not been close. He recalled that he'd once thought the young Army officer was in love with Annamarie. Now that he was remembering, Annamarie had only begun to show her preference for Paul when he'd recovered from his injuries. Her mother had visited him several times when he was suffering from the burns to his back and leg, and she'd invited him to visit them when he was able to resume his normal life. It was then that the beautiful young girl had made it clear she thought him worthy to be her husband.

A wry smile touched Paul's mouth; he'd become a

hero overnight in the small community, and Annamarie was not the only girl to throw him encouraging smiles. Glad to be well again and wishing only that people would forget his actions and not make so much fuss over what had, after all, been instinctive, Paul had taken little notice. He'd been aware of Annamarie's marked interest because she'd been offered to him as a wife— but before that…before the night that was only a blur in his mind and the weeks of pain, had Adam believed she might favour him?

Paul sought in his mind for a scene he only partially recalled. It was at a regimental ball. He'd been invited as an ex-officer and an influential businessman—but Adam had been there, dressed in his uniform, new to the post and looking very handsome. Was he imagining it, or had he seen the pair go out to the veranda, returning some thirty minutes later looking flushed and excited?

It was an image Paul had long forgotten. Of no importance to anyone but the girl and her mother who she chose to spend her time with…but now it made him wonder.

Was it possible that Adam held a grudge against him because Annamarie had transferred her attention to Paul after the dramatic rescue? Had he been hoping that she would marry him? Annamarie had quite a large dowry and a man with no fortune and, in peacetime, little hope of earning prize money, would never have been considered a suitable husband?

Paul would have supposed she might be married off to an Indian prince, unless her mother intended to bring her to England and find a husband amongst her own people for the girl. It was not his concern. He shrugged his shoulders as he entered the house. As he intended to make his home in England and would never marry the beautiful girl who had been offered to him by a grateful father, he had no interest in the matter—but it did affect his relationship with Adam.

He'd looked forward to running the racing stables with his friend, but if Adam was harbouring resentment perhaps it was not such a good idea... Paul put it from his mind. Melia clearly resented her father's will and perhaps she'd misunderstood what Adam said to her. Paul could only hope that had been the case...but he would keep an open mind.

Chapter Eight

'Mama was left almost penniless,' Sarah confessed over the coffee she and Jane were drinking in Jane's parlour that morning. 'When she discovered that Papa had been getting further and further in debt for years, it was a terrible blow to her.'

'Yes, I imagine it would be,' Jane said. 'Why did you not come to me at once? I should have done what I could to help. You might both have lived in my house. I would gladly have given you a home.'

'We did not want to ask for charity from anyone. Mama's brother sold what was left of Papa's estate and loaned us a cottage on his estate, which is where we've been living. We had enough to live respectably, but when Mama died my uncle told me he did not think it right for me to live alone there—and his wife does not like me...' Sarah hesitated. 'He suggested that I should marry and brought two gentlemen to my attention—Sir Jonathan, a pleasant gentleman of some sixty years, and Colonel Brush. He is a widower and needs a mother for his six children. Since his wife died because she was simply worn out with childbearing I did not care to take her place. Sir Jonathan was kind and told me that he needed only a gentle companion but…'

'Oh, my dear,' Jane cried and sat forward to catch her hand. 'Your uncle was most unfair to impose such conditions. Of course you should not marry either of those gentlemen.'

'Well, I considered taking Sir Jonathan's offer just to satisfy my uncle—but then I thought of you, Jane, and wrote my letter more in desperation than in hope.'

'I'm so pleased you did,' Jane said, giving her a frank look. 'If Will marries I must set up my own house. I think I shall take up residence in Bath—though I may spend some time in the country. Naturally, I must have a female companion, and your letter made me think of you. We might be very happy living in Bath together, Sarah. Visits to London and the country, and my brother occasionally, of course, but mostly in a pleasant location in Bath—what do you think of that?'

'It sounds like heaven,' Sarah said and sighed. 'Do you not think of remarrying?'

'No, I do not think so…' Jane hesitated. 'I had made up my mind to remain Harry's widow, but now I must admit that it might happen one day. However, you too may meet someone you wish to wed, and if that happened I should wish you well, dear Sarah. If I did marry before you, you would always have a home with me.'

'You are so kind,' Sarah said. 'I do not wish to be a burden…'

'Nor will you,' Jane said at once. 'I should have to

employ someone to bear me company, and I would so much rather you were my guest for as long as we both wish it. Melia is staying with me now, but she—she is a young lady of strong opinions and this was only intended to be a visit for the duration of our stay in London. Will had hopes of her, but I think her head may have been turned. I hope it is her head and not her heart, for I cannot like the man she favours...'

'Surely she cannot prefer another man when she has the offer of...' Sarah's cheeks flushed as she halted. 'The viscount is so very kind and thoughtful, Jane. When I came down this morning...nothing could have been more pleasant in the way he welcomed me to his home.'

'Yes, I am fond of Will and I shall be upset if Melia hurts him—but I hope that he will find his own way. Either she is the girl he loves or she is not...but I speak out of turn. Melia has not told me what she feels and I must not presume to know her mind or Will's.'

'As a sister you think of him first,' Sarah said. 'I longed for a brother or sister when I was a child, but now that I know of Papa's behaviour... I am glad there was no one else to be hurt by it.'

'I know how you feel. My father was a stern man, though he did not waste his fortune. Instead, he dictated to his family and made all our lives difficult—most of all for poor Mama.'

'But she is happy now? She sent me a most delightful letter and told me she would help me to buy some pretty clothes when I came to you—and...' Sarah blushed delicately. 'She suggested that she could find me a husband from her many acquaintances...'

'Poor Sarah,' Jane said with a wry laugh. 'Mama has almost given up trying to find me a husband so now she will turn her attention to you. I shall tell her to leave you in peace.'

'Oh, no, for she means well, I am sure. She promised not to bully me but to introduce me to lovely gentlemen who would make me happy if I let them...'

'Mama has paraded so many handsome and rich men for me to see,' Jane said, smiling at the memory. 'But for some reason she seems to have given me up this time. I dare say it will amuse her to introduce you to her friends—and if it does not upset you, there is no harm done.'

'It will not upset me,' Sarah told her. 'The duchess is to call for me at ten this morning and she insists on taking me to her dressmaker.'

'In that I shall not interfere,' Jane said. 'Mama has perfect taste and will know just what suits you. I had intended to offer you a dress allowance and I shall, but you must let Mama spoil you a little—Porky gives her far more than she can spend on herself and she enjoys spending it on those she cares for. She will inundate Will's wife and children with gifts once he is married, I have no doubt.'

'Why should she not?' Sarah said and laughed softly. 'It is surely what money is for—to spend on those one cares for.'

'Yes, indeed, which is why you must let us spoil you, Sarah. This trip to London was meant to be enjoyed and, like Mama, I enjoy giving presents.' Jane touched her hand once more. 'I have an errand to run this morning—unless you would like my support?'

'No, not at all; I adore the duchess,' Sarah said. 'You must not let me interfere in any way with your plans, Jane.'

'I had none for this morning, other than to make you welcome. This afternoon I shall take you visiting and this evening there is a small dance, to which we are all invited. Will intends to accompany us so it will be all the family together. Tomorrow I shall be visiting some furniture warehouses and emporiums with Lord Frant. I am sure you could come if you wish.'

'I shall be quite content here. Perhaps there is something I could do for you, Jane—flower arranging or keeping your correspondence in order. I did those things for Mama.'

'Oh, the flowers perhaps, if you choose,' Jane said, 'but you are here to enjoy yourself, Sarah. You will soon make friends, and of course your name will be included on all my invitations once it is known you are in town.'

'I must go up and fetch my shawl,' Sarah said. 'The duchess will be here at any moment and I must not keep her waiting.'

Jane nodded and let her go. She wandered over to her desk but she had hardly settled to her letters when a small commotion in the hall told her that her mother had arrived. The next moment the door was flung wide and the duchess walked in; she was a delicate, pretty woman with good bone structure and hair that was still the colour of spun natural silk or white blonde as some called it. Dressed in the height of fashion, she contrived to look half her age and she had often been taken for Jane's sister by strangers.

'My darling Jane.' Mama embraced her lovingly in a cloud of expensive perfume. 'How is poor little Sarah? Such a terrible time she has had...'

'Sarah is very well, I think,' Jane said. 'A little sad still, I believe, but ready to come out of mourning and be dressed by you, dearest. I think she would not wish to wear bright colours yet, but I know you will do the thing perfectly.'

'Of course I shall,' the duchess said. 'No one has ever doubted my taste in such matters, Jane. She shall wear what suits her, but nothing loud or distasteful in a girl so recently bereaved—it is only a month since dear Seraphina died, is it not?'

'Yes, it is,' Jane agreed. 'Sarah is just such a person as I can set up my own home with, Mama. We shall agree very well and I think our tastes are not dissimilar.'

'Well, that's as maybe,' Mama said, a little smile playing about her lips. 'Yet who knows? I may find husbands for you both long before then...'

'Mama, no!' Jane warned her but with a smile. 'Please no schemes for me—and do not put pressure on poor Sarah. She has had enough of that from her uncle.'

'Yes, indeed, I know it,' Mama agreed. 'I would not press her for the world—but if she should meet someone, perhaps who loves her but of little fortune, my dearest Porky will see her right. He would do anything to oblige me, you know.'

'I know, dearest one,' Jane said and laughed. 'You have him wrapped about your little finger, do you not?'

'Jane, it is no such thing,' the duchess said, her eyes alight with mischief. 'Porky likes to be generous. How could he spend a tenth of his fortune if I did not show him how? He has never been happier than now and tells me so every night and first thing in the morning.'

'Yes, I know that to be true,' Jane agreed. 'And you are truly happy, Mama?'

'Of course. Porky adores me, and that is rather lovely, Jane. I am very fond of him and I like to look after him. He needs me, you see; he was so lost and lonely before we married.'

Jane smiled inwardly for the duke had a vast crowd of friends and legions of faithful servants to care for his every need—but perhaps, in adoring his pretty and mischievous wife, he'd found his happiness.

Sarah came back downstairs and Jane went to the door to see them off in Mama's smart carriage, with its cream leather cushions and shiny black paint. She returned to her parlour just as Melia came downstairs, dressed for walking.

'Are you going out, Melia?'

'Yes, with Miss Anne Smythe and her brother Captain Smythe,' Melia said. 'It was arranged at the party last evening. Do you not recall my telling you last night when I returned?'

Jane was certain the girl had merely poked her head in to ask if she was well and then gone off to her own room. Looking at her closely, Jane thought she looked a trifle pale and heavy-eyed, not as fresh and lovely as when they had come to London.

'Is something upsetting you?' she asked, thinking that Melia looked as if she'd been crying.

'No, I am perfectly all right,' Melia said but did not look comfortable. 'I must go. My maid is waiting and I am to meet the others at half past eleven. I shall not be home for nuncheon, but I am not hungry.'

Jane let her go. Melia was her guest but she was not her guardian and it was not for her to speak of propriety—at least not yet. Providing the girl took a maid with her, there was no reason why she should not meet her friends in the park.

Sighing, Jane continued to look through the invitations that had arrived that morning. Most evenings they had their choice of at least three and quite often made an appearance at all three, though on the evening of an important ball or a private visit to the theatre she wrote apologies for her absence at some affair or other.

Jane had been standing at the window lost in thought for a while when she heard a sound behind her and turned to see her brother enter. He looked so handsome and so dear that her heart caught; if Melia broke his heart she did not think she could forgive the girl.

'All alone, Jane?' he asked, seeming concerned.

'Yes, for the moment. Mama has taken Sarah shopping and Melia has gone walking with Captain Smythe and his sister.'

'Not out with Viscount Hargreaves today then?'

'No, I think she was a little annoyed because she

particularly told him where we would be last night and he chose to go elsewhere.'

'Oh, I see… Yes, that would not please her.' Will smiled at her. 'It will be just the two of us for luncheon then.'

'Yes, just like at home,' Jane said and moved towards him. 'Are you enjoying your visit, my dearest?'

'Yes, I always enjoy the chance to visit friends, entertain them and purchase a few clothes. I have ordered three pairs of boots and two new coats—the last from Weston. I believe his style will suit me in the country.'

'If you marry, your wife may wish to be in London more often, Will. Melia seems to love it in town.'

'Yes, she does quite clearly,' Will said, seeming thoughtful. 'Well, we shall cross that bridge when we come to it. I hope you've given up this nonsense of living alone?'

'Oh, I never intended to be alone,' she said mildly. 'Sarah will make an ideal companion—do you not agree?'

'She seems a pleasant girl to me,' he replied and laughed. 'It is wrong to call her that, for she is the same age as you, Jane—and very much a woman.'

'Yes. I imagine she has had to be. It seems she and her mother have had a hard time of it since her father died—and Sarah has had a worse one since then. Did she tell you her story?'

'Yes, a little, but it was easy enough to read between the lines. I admit to feeling sympathy for her, Jane. You must make sure that she knows she is welcome to live with us for as long as she wishes—though she is too attractive to be unmarried for long.'

'She has no portion, Will.' Jane smiled inwardly for her brother had changed his tune concerning her cousin, whom he'd thought plain at the start.

'Yet her good nature will attract suitors—and I would be glad to settle a dowry on her, if she would accept it.'

'As would I,' Jane agreed. 'Mama would adore to have Sarah live with her, for she is much taken with her—but, as you say, I do not think it need be long before our cousin weds.'

'A second cousin only,' Will reminded her. 'Sarah is Mama's cousin, though we have been used to call her such…'

'Yes, of course…our second cousin,' Jane said and wondered why her brother had stressed the more distant relationship.

'You have perfect taste,' Paul said when they had completed their tour of the furnishing emporium and made several choices. He led her out to his waiting carriage, helping her inside and then climbing in after. 'I liked everything you picked and shall be happy with them, I know.'

'We have accomplished but a third of your needs,' Jane said and laughed as she saw his look. 'Yes, I know. Gentlemen often consider such purchases as slow work, but it must be done if you are to be comfortable again.'

'Yes, I know it,' Paul said and laughed wryly. 'I am

forever in your debt, Lady March. I should not have
known where to begin had you not lent me your aid.'

'You are most welcome, my lord,' she replied de-
murely but with a wicked twinkle in her eyes. 'I have
enjoyed myself a great deal this morning and shall look
forward to visiting your house once the furnishings are
installed.'

'Naturally, I shall offer you the chance before anyone else,' he said. 'However, I must tell you that I am
about to leave town for a few days. We attend the races
at Newmarket and in my absence I hope that most of
the redecorating will be done…'

'Ah, yes, that is best,' Jane agreed. 'A house is not
your own when invaded by builders.'

'Very true,' he said ruefully. 'I confess it is the first
time I've attempted it. I've never owned a house in England before—and in my palace in India all was done
before I saw it…'

'Your palace?' Jane stared in surprise. 'Do you own
such a thing, my lord?'

'It was given to me by the father of the Prince I rescued—a small palace by his estimation, but a palace
all the same, with pleasant gardens, cool tinkling pools
and trees to shade you from the heat of too hot a sun…'

'India sounds fascinating,' Jane said. 'I have sometimes thought I should like to travel again…'

'You travelled to France or Spain with your husband, I dare say?'

'Yes. Harry warned me it would be hard at times, and
it was—but I would not have changed it for the world.
I loved my husband and that time was precious; it mat-

tered not to me that we sometimes lived in cramped and draughty quarters.'

'I think I envy Lord March,' Paul said softly, but Jane hardly caught the words and blushed at what she thought she heard.

'So when do you hope to return?' she asked. 'Would it be of use to you, sir, if I visited some other warehouses alone and asked them to send certain items on approval? You may view them at your leisure and reject anything you dislike.'

'If you choose as you have today, items of quality and taste, then I am certain I shall not need to return them,' Paul said. He hesitated and then went on, 'I am always in your debt. You must tell me if I can do anything to please you, my lady.'

'Then I shall use the time to good purpose,' she promised. 'I enjoy shopping and will perhaps find some items I shall need when I set up my house in Bath. My cousin has arrived in town and she seems happy to make her home with us—until she marries, of course.'

'I shall look forward to making her acquaintance.' Paul took her hand and kissed it as his carriage halted before her door. 'And now I must thank you again and leave you, for I have things to attend before I leave.'

'I enjoyed your company,' Jane said. 'Have a pleasant visit and enjoy the races, Lord Frant.'

Paul smiled and helped her down, escorting her to her door, which was opened as she reached it. Returning to his carriage, he was thoughtful. Jane's taste matched his own perfectly, and his feeling that she was the only woman he would ever wish to marry had grown steadily throughout the morning they had spent together.

He had fortune enough to please any woman, and his birth was good—though her father had been of higher rank. Yet there was nothing to stand in the way of a match between them in that regard—but could he turn her heart towards him? Jane was pleasant, friendly and he believed that she enjoyed his company—but would she ever trust her heart to him?

He was a man who faced reality and he had to admit that not once had she shown any warmer feelings towards him than that of a pleasant acquaintance. Perhaps it was hardly surprising. She had loved once and lost tragically. Could she let go of the past and give herself in marriage again…had she even thought of it, or of him, in such terms?

Paul was rueful as he reviewed her manner and words in his mind, but nothing she had said or done could convince him that he was more to her than an acquaintance.

How could he make her fall in love with him? He was not sure it was possible. He'd tried compliments and that had seemed to cause her to draw back. She was not a vain woman and flattery would be useless. He sighed as he realised that love either happened or it did not…

Sighing, Paul turned his thoughts. He had an appointment with his man of business. Spencer had investigated the affairs of the late Viscount Hargreaves, and would tell him if anything could be salvaged— and if not they must discover a way of making it seem to be so…

* * *

Jane found Melia and Sarah sitting in the front parlour together when she had taken off her pelisse and
bonnet. Sarah was reading and Melia was sitting at a
table with a pack of cards, playing patience, but without much evidence of being in that mood, for she threw
them down with a sound of disgust.

'I cannot make them come out,' she cried. 'It is a useless game. I am glad you are back, Jane, for Sarah said
we should not ring for tea until you came.'

'It is a little past our time,' Jane said. 'Forgive me.
We were longer than I'd imagined—but it was so pleasant that I quite forgot the time…'

'I do not know how you can find choosing furniture
for that man pleasant,' Melia said with a sulky look. 'He
but uses you, Jane. You should not allow it.'

'Oh, I do not think myself used,' Jane replied, determined not to lose her patience with the girl, even
though she found herself resenting Melia's tone concerning Lord Frant. How could the girl be so ungrate-
ful after what he'd done for her? 'Like many gentlemen
he does not care to spend his time choosing furnishings
and I am happy to do it for him—besides, I have seen
a few pieces that I should like for my own house when
my brother marries.'

Jane saw a guilty flush in Melia's cheeks and suspected that she no longer wished to be Will's wife.

'Is the viscount to marry?' Sarah looked up from
her book.

'Oh, in time,' Jane said and glanced at Melia. 'I do

not think it is imminent, though I had thought it might be…'

Melia's cheeks grew red. She got up and went over to the window, looking out at the street below. 'Did you know that Lord Frant and Viscount Hargreaves go to Newmarket?'

'Yes, Lord Frant has just this minute told me. You had it from Viscount Hargreaves, I dare say?'

'Yes…' Melia avoided her eyes. 'He mentioned that he might be leaving town soon.'

'They leave tomorrow for Newmarket…for the races, I think. Afterwards, they will buy young horses for the stables they intend to set up.'

'Yes, so I believe,' Melia said and sighed. 'I understand they will buy land together in Ireland…'

'Ah, I did not know that,' Jane said. 'It appears you have been privy to more information than I…' She rang the bell and when a maid appeared asked for tea to be served. 'We must prepare for this evening…just music and cards. We do not dance until Mama's ball next week…'

Of its own volition, a sigh left Jane's lips. She had hoped that Lord Frant would attend the duchess's ball, but if he were in Newmarket—or even Ireland—he would miss it…and that meant the prospect of dancing, of being held close to a man's chest, held little appeal for Jane.

Chapter Nine

'It seems that I have the means to pay for my share of the stables,' Adam announced from the doorway of the inn chamber. 'The letter arrived this morning. I shall have five thousand clear when everything is settled—enough for the three thousand needed and a decent house in Ireland, should I wish it.'

'With your winnings these past two days you have enough to live on for a while,' Paul said and smiled. 'It seems your fortunes have changed, my friend.'

'Yes, thank God!' Adam looked elated. 'When I placed that bet of a hundred guineas it was my last, leaving me barely enough to settle my score here had I lost it.'

'You are braver than I.' Paul chuckled. 'I do not think I could have placed such a bet.'

'You are not a gambler,' Adam said wryly. 'You have courage, Frant—but you would not gamble your life on the fate of a horse. If it had lost, I fear there would have been nothing left but to put a ball through my head.'

'Then I thank the fates for making your horse win,' Paul said, his brows rising. 'I should not want to lose a friend on such an account…'

'Well, it seems that for the moment I am saved.' Adam grinned at him. 'We should take a look in at Tattersalls today, Frant. We may be able to purchase some decent stock.'

'Young horses with good bloodlines that we can rear ourselves,' Paul said. 'But we need also a good mare to breed from—and one or two horses that show promise of good form in the near future.'

'Will you race that beautiful horse of yours? The one the Prince gave you and you brought with you on the ship.'

'I fear my poor Suleima fared worse than I did on the journey,' Paul replied. 'One day I hope to race him, but it may be that I shall simply keep him for stud purposes.'

'None other could match him in the race you rode in India…'

'No, that is true,' Paul said. 'I was offered riches to sell him, but I wanted to bring him home to England…'

'You intend to settle here then?'

'Yes, I have made up my mind to it,' Paul said. 'I shall keep some of my horses here at my estate in the country, but the young ones can go to Ireland with you.'

'We have but one more day at the races,' Adam reminded him. 'Do you wish to take ship for Ireland immediately?'

'No, for I am engaged to the Duchess of Roshithe for her ball in two days hence,' Paul said. 'I shall return this evening, after the meeting—and we will talk of a trip to Ireland, perhaps next week.'

'Yes, of course, you would not wish to miss the duchess's ball,' Adam murmured softly. 'Shall we to the races then and see if we can find another winner?'

'Win or lose, I bet modestly,' Paul said. 'You would do well to do the same, Adam.'

'Of course,' Adam said but the gleam in his eyes sent a shiver of apprehension down Paul's spine. If Adam bet recklessly, he could easily lose all he had won and more besides...

'You look lovely,' Jane said to her friends as they came down to the parlour where she and Will were waiting for them. 'Melia, that gown suits you so well—and Sarah, I think I have not seen you look as beautiful before.'

'Oh, I am not beautiful,' Sarah denied with a blush and a shake of her head. 'You look wonderful yourself—is that a new gown, cousin?'

'No, one I have worn once before,' Jane said. She did not add that she had forgone her new gown in order to see both Melia and Sarah supplied with the beautiful creations they were wearing. Madame Françoise had been inundated with requests for new gowns for one of the most important balls of the season, but Jane had waited patiently. She did not expect Lord Frant to attend, therefore it hardly mattered that she was wearing a gown she'd worn before, though Mama had scolded her for it.

'Jane, you are too unselfish,' she said. 'You should

have put yourself before Melia. She has already had two new ball gowns.'

'But she is young and this is her first season. It is more important that both she and Sarah should look well.'

'And why is that, Jane?' Mama demanded. 'I would have my daughter look well—and perhaps find herself another husband…'

'Mama, please do not…' Jane sighed. 'I have told you before that I do not wish to marry the Marquis Vermont—or Lord Hamilton's nephew or…'

'No, of course not. Why should you when a much better match presents itself? He is not a marquis, but fortune and good nature are more important and Lord Frant has these qualities in abundance.'

'Mama!' Jane's cheeks burned. 'Please do not suggest such a thing…'

'I merely point out that the man is there…and is already halfway in love with you, Jane. If you were to give him a hint, I dare say he would propose to you in an instant…'

Jane felt hot and uncomfortable. Yet her mother was only suggesting what she had suspected once or twice, but immediately dismissed. Sometimes there was a look in Paul Frant's eyes that seemed to suggest that his feelings for her were more than mere liking.

'Oh, no, I couldn't…' Jane looked away from her mother's too bright gaze. She tried to dismiss the idea, as she had others—but this time she could not quite manage it. Was it possible that Lord Frant's regard was something deeper than friendship? And what would she feel about it if that were true, fantastic as it seemed? No, no, it was ridiculous because they had known each other such a short time…

Jane found that the idea was not as distasteful to her as she'd thought it might be and if she were to think of marriage—but of course that was ridiculous. She had no wish to marry again, even to a gentleman as generous and good-natured as Lord Frant…and he'd given no indication that his affections had turned towards her, except now and then there was that look in his eyes. Jane did not wish to believe it. She was not ready to feel love again; it would be a betrayal of Harry. Besides, she did not think it true: it was merely Mama being a matchmaker again, of course.

'I do hope that Viscount Hargreaves will come this evening,' Melia said. 'He thought that he might be in Ireland, but perhaps…' She stopped, aware that Jane was staring at her. 'What have I said?'

'I wish you will not set your heart on that gentleman,' Jane said gently. 'I believe he has little fortune and though that would not necessarily prevent the marriage there are other considerations…'

Jane halted once more, because she knew she could not tell Melia what she feared. She must simply let the girl make up her own mind and hope that she came to her senses in time.

'If he'd been given what he was owed…' Melia blurted out but then stopped, her face turning red. 'No matter…' She turned away in some confusion. 'Yes, I dare say you are right, Jane.'

Jane would have pressed her to finish what she'd

been saying, but they were on the point of leaving for the duchess's ball and she did not want to spoil the evening for anyone. An argument with Melia would cast a shadow over what should have been a happy evening.

Smiling brightly, she walked to the door, which was opened promptly by her footman. Outside, the carriage was drawn up and another footman stood ready to assist the ladies into the carriage. The viscount came last, sauntering down the stairs as if there was all the time in the world.

'Will, dearest, do hurry,' Jane told him with a warm smile. 'Mama shall not be pleased if we are late.'

'Oh, I tremble in my boots at the thought of it,' Will said and laughed. Their mother was dearly loved by both but had never made the least attempt to keep either of them in check.

'No, do not be wicked, dearest,' Jane said and poked him in the ribs. 'Move up and do not squash my gown.'

'That would never do,' Will murmured mischievously. 'I should not wish to be in your black books, Jane.'

'How can anyone do anything with him?' Jane appealed to Sarah, who laughed but looked as if she had enjoyed the banter.

'I think the viscount but means to tease you,' Sarah said, her eyes resting warmly on the young man, who had moved over to the corner to give his sister room to spread her gown.

So they travelled to the duchess's grand home in the west of town, three of them chattering and laughing and only Melia silent in her corner. She was subdued and thoughtful and Jane was relieved that she had not scolded her, for the girl's spirits were already lower than they had been when she first came to town. It was a pity if she'd given her heart to a man who did not deserve her, Jane reflected, but then they were arriving and one of the duke's flunkeys was opening their carriage door so that the ladies could descend from it to the red carpet spread out to keep their dainty shoes clean, for even outside such a house as this the streets might be stained with dirt.

Then they were inside the magnificent and lofty entrance hall with its floor of shining marble and the magnificent wide staircase leading up to the first floor, where the duchess was standing to receive her visitors.

Jane led the way up the stairs and was graciously welcomed by her mother. Curtsying, Jane waited until the others had greeted the duchess and then remained with her for a few moments while her brother led the two young ladies along the landing to the first reception room.

'I am delighted to see you looking so well, my dear,' the duchess said warmly as Jane kissed her cheek.

'Thank you, dearest Mama.' Jane smiled at her. Seeing some of her mother's friends arriving, she inclined her head. 'I shall leave you to greet your guests and we shall talk later…'

The reception rooms were overflowing with happy, smiling people. Porky was circulating, as was the duty of the host, but when he saw Jane he nodded to his companion and left him, coming to meet her with hands outstretched.

'My very dear Jane,' he boomed at her and kissed both her hands in turn. 'How delightful you always look—charming and pretty, just like your mama.'

'I thank you, sir…' she said and dipped a slight curtsy.

'Now, none of that nonsense,' he chided and patted her cheek. 'I am your dear Porky and father, I hope?'

'You are a dearer one to me than I ever had,' Jane said and kissed his cheek, which made him blush with pleasure. 'I hope you know that, Porky?'

'You make me proud indeed,' he said. 'The duchess looks beautiful this evening, did you not think so?'

'Mama is always beautiful,' Jane said, 'but I think that rather lovely diamond tiara is new?'

'Ah, yes, a little bauble it pleased me to buy for her,' he said. 'Off with you to the ballroom, Jane. Do not waste your time talking to an old fellow like me—there are many fine young ones waiting to greet you, my dear.'

'But I enjoy talking to you,' Jane said, and accepted a glass of champagne from one of the footmen circulating, and then saw that Melia, Sarah and Will had been waylaid by friends and had not yet reached the ballroom either. Taking a few sips of her wine, her eyes searched the room but the tall figure of Lord Frant was nowhere to be seen and she was aware of disappointment briefly, before finding herself surrounded by several gentlemen clamouring for dances. She handed over her card, smiling particularly at two officers who had been Harry's friends.

'Major Harding, Lieutenant Brandt…' she said. 'How pleasant to see you again. Are you both on leave?'

'Yes, there is very little true soldiering to do at the moment,' Major Harding replied with a smile. 'We have been with Wellington in Vienna but now we are officially on leave. I intend to sell my commission shortly—and George here is wavering on the brink.'

'Trouble is, my father won't let me help with the estate,' the young man with melting brown eyes said and grinned at her. 'What is a fellow to do but spend his time in town, drinking and gambling—and that don't please his lordship either.'

'Find some employment, George,' Major Harding chivvied him. 'It is my intention to import wine—and to set up a breeding stable for thoroughbreds...'

'Oh, you should talk to Lord Frant,' Jane said impulsively. 'I believe he means to race horses...'

'Are you speaking of Captain Frant?' The major's eyes gleamed. 'We were great friends in the old days, but then he sold out and went to India.'

'I was not aware that Lord Frant had served as captain,' Jane said, liking the honest, open manner of the officer. 'Not when...when Harry and I were with you, I think?'

'No, a few years previously. He was my first commanding officer on the Peninsula...'

'Ah...' Jane nodded. 'He had intended to attend this evening, but I am not sure—he may have left for...' The words faded as her eyes were drawn across the room and she saw the very man entering. Yet something was wrong and she heard murmuring around her, not realising at once what it meant—and then she saw that he was wearing a sling on one arm and there was a dressing applied to his forehead. 'No...excuse me, please...'

Jane made her way through the room, unaware that people turned their heads to watch her or of the whispers and smiles, quickly hidden behind a hand or a kerchief. She reached the newcomer and stood staring up at him, searching his face and seeing that it bore small scratches as well as a binding on the forehead.

'Lord Frant, you have been hurt...' she croaked, her lips barely able to move for the shock of seeing him thus.

A rueful smile lit his eyes and he reached out with his right hand to touch hers. 'A mere accident, Lady March. I was advised to rest for a few days, but I could not forgo the pleasure of seeing...of the duchess's ball...'

Jane felt warmth flood through her as his smile seemed to caress and she knew what he had meant to say. It was the pleasure of seeing her this evening that had made him come, despite his injuries. Oh, no! How vain she was to think it.

'What happened, sir?'

'Oh, the merest incident,' he declared, dismissing his sling as if it were nothing. 'A toss from my horse, no more...'

Jane was certain there was more behind the accident as he described the fall, but it was clear he would say nothing, at least this evening.

'I am happy to see you,' Jane said. She suddenly realised that everything had become brighter, although until that moment she had not been aware of missing him. Now she realised that had he not come the evening would have seemed less for it. 'Though I do not think you will be able to dance this evening, sir.'

'No, perhaps not,' he said ruefully. 'I had looked forward to our dances, my lady, but they must wait for another time. Perhaps you will sit with me and take a glass of wine—or walk out on the balcony...'

'Yes, of course,' she said. 'I had reserved two dances for you...'

'I am glad you remembered that I asked for them,' he murmured throatily and Jane's heart jerked and then raced in a manner it had not done for some years. For a moment as she looked into his eyes it was as if her heart reached out to his and her breath came faster, making her aware of something she had not felt for a long time—a desire to be kissed by a man other than her late husband. Yet in an instant the desire was replaced by regret. She could never...must never let herself love again: that way lay too much pain and hurt. It was safer to remain where she was, in her own little bubble.

'Yet should you truly be here?' she asked as she re-alised she had been silent too long.

'If one always did what one ought it would be a dull life,' Paul said and laughed as her brows rose. 'I have often taken risks, as this gentleman may tell you...'

Jane saw that Major Harding had come up to them and was giving Paul a quizzical look. 'What mad esca-pade brought you to this, Captain Frant?'

'That is fine talk, coming from the wildest fellow I ever had under my command.' Paul laughed and of-fered his right hand, which was gripped and held. 'Jack Harding—how are you? A Major now, I hear?'

'Yes, but unlikely to go further now that Boney is safely tucked up out of harm,' Major Harding said, grinning. 'I am thinking of setting up a stable—and Lady March told me you have a similar idea. We must dine together one evening and talk of this…'

'Yes, indeed. I should enjoy that,' Paul told him. 'Perhaps tomorrow at my club—at eight?'

It was agreed and then Major Harding left them to claim a partner for the next dance.

'This was one of your dances,' Jane told Paul. 'Would you care for a turn on the balcony, sir?'

'Only if you stop calling me sir,' he said. 'Frant if you must, though I prefer Paul. I believed we were friends, Jane?'

'You know we are,' she said as he offered his arm and they made their way through the crowds to one of the long doors that stood open to admit fresh air and passage to the various small balconies. Her heart had opened to him earlier but now she had herself under control and was the polite society lady again. 'Now, tell me the truth—what happened to you?'

'My horse was spooked by a stray ball as I rode home from Newmarket yesterday.'

'You were shot at?' Jane felt severely distressed by the very idea and it must have shown in her face for Paul squeezed her arm against his side comfortingly.

'No, I fancy it was a poacher or some such thing— unless he was a poor shot. Unfortunately, my horse was not trained to the sound and reared up, sending me crashing to the ground—though I held on to the reins, luckily, and Adam was there to help me up…'

'Viscount Hargreaves was with you?'

'Yes, thankfully. He helped me to mount and got me to the nearest inn, where I was seen by the local doctor. A good man, who informed me that I had no broken bones and would live but must take it easy for a day or so.'

'Thank God someone was with you...' Jane was shocked to discover how much the idea that he could have lain hurt...particularly if the shot had wounded him.

'It was fortunate, but it is not the first time Adam has come to my aid,' Paul told her. 'I suffered from a fever on the ship returning from India and I believe I should have died had Adam not cared for my needs.'

'I did not realise that he had been such a good friend to you.'

'No, he does not speak of it, but he is a decent fellow,' Paul said and smiled as they took a turn on the small balcony and looked out at the pretty gardens, which were enhanced by fairy lights strung in the trees and bushes. 'It was a successful meeting for both of us and we leave for Ireland next week to buy land for our young horses—of which we now have six.'

'So it is definite that you will set up your stables in Ireland together?'

'Yes, I see no reason for it not to go ahead now,' Paul said softly, speaking almost to himself. 'I believe Adam intends to purchase a house there, where he will live for some part of the year, though he enjoys Society too much to bury himself there for ever.'

'Did he not come with you this evening? Melia thought it was his intention…'

'I believe he has another engagement, one more to his taste…' Paul frowned but shook his head, apparently wishing to leave the subject of his friend there. 'I was determined to keep my word and come—though I fear I present a sorry appearance. We must hope the sight of me does not distress the ladies…'

'There is nothing unpleasant in your appearance,' Jane assured him. 'I am glad to see you, Paul, though I am sorry if you are in pain.'

'Sweet Jane,' he said and gazed into her eyes for a moment before moving his hand to her cheek and caressing it lightly with the tips of his fingers. For a moment her breath caught and she almost swayed towards him as the need to feel his arm about her swept over her, but in an instant she had conquered the foolish desire. She must not let her longing for Harry confuse her; she did not know this man well enough to care for him—surely she could not be so inconstant. Only a few weeks ago she'd believed that she would never feel love or desire again. And now? Now she was not sure how she felt. 'You look beautiful, as always.'

'You flatter,' Jane said and laughed, but the look in his eyes was having a disturbing effect on her. She felt young and excited again, like a girl at her first ball. 'But it is most pleasant…and the evening would not have been the same if you had not come.' She felt her cheeks flush as he smiled down at her and for a moment it was as if they were the only two people in the world. For a moment then Jane thought that if he had held her and

kissed her she might have given herself to him…and
then another couple came out onto the balcony and the
lady called out to them, breaking the spell.

'Is it not warm this evening, Lord Frant? I swear I
thought I should melt if I did not catch the air…'

Paul moved back, turned and inclined his head towards her. 'You are very right, Lady Catherine. It is the
reason Lady March and I came out. Yet after a while it
seems cool…do you not think so, Lady March?'

'You are very right.' Jane took her cue. Besides, it
would be safer in the ballroom, for her emotions had almost betrayed her. 'Take care you do not stay too long,
Lady Catherine. We should go in, Lord Frant.'

'Oh, but I wanted to hear what happened to you,'
Lady Catherine said, placing a hand on Paul's arm to
delay him. 'Everyone is whispering different tales—is
it true that someone tried to kill you and that they might
have succeeded had Viscount Hargreaves not ridden up
with your groom?'

'Exaggeration,' Paul said and smiled at her eager-
ness. 'It was merely a little tumble from my horse. Excuse us, please, Lady March grows cool…'

Giving Jane his arm, he swept her back into the ballroom. Jane was aware of the pretty young lady staring
after them. The daughter of an earl, she was betrothed
to a marquis, but there were whispers that her father
was desperate to get her married to curb her wildness.
Some gentlemen spoke of her being no better than she
ought, but as yet the remarks had not come to the lady's
ears or those of her father or betrothed.

'I believe Lady Catherine came out in order to corner you, my lord,' Jane said with a teasing look. 'She enjoys excitement I understand…'

'That young woman is the bane of her father's life,' Paul replied with an amused smile. 'I knew her father years ago and his wife was a flighty one—unfaithful to him for years, though he believes that his first two sons are his own.'

'You think Lady Catherine takes after her mother?'

'I would not besmirch a young woman's reputation, though others are less circumspect,' Paul said. 'I have heard tales but, gossip being what it is, I am inclined to discount most of it.'

'I think she likes you,' Jane teased but he shook his head.

'No, I think her more interested in Adam. He has escorted her to some function or other on more than one occasion, for their families were friends…but I do not think the earl would countenance a union between them…'

'You think Viscount Hargreaves might wish for it?'

'As I believe I mentioned once before, he needs to marry money—but Lady Catherine's father wants more for her.'

'She is engaged to the Marquis of Barnchester.'

'A man old enough to be her father,' Paul said and frowned in disapproval.

'Yes, that is a sad thing,' Jane agreed. 'I do not agree with such marriages, for they can bring little joy to either partner, I think.'

'Barnchester needs an heir,' Paul murmured. 'After that, I dare say she will do much as she pleases…'

'Yes, perhaps,' Jane said but could not help feeling sorry for the lovely young woman who was so full of life. How must she feel about being married off to a man so many years older? Jane would never have agreed to such an arrangement. 'Does she have money of her own—or is she in need of a fortune?'

'Oh, her family is rich enough, but her father believes in keeping the coffers filled. The earl is full of juice, they say, but he wants a title and fortune for his daughter so if he has his way the match will go ahead.'

Jane nodded, and then turned her head to look up at him. 'My next partner comes to claim me, but I shall see you for the dance before supper.'

'How ridiculous these customs are,' Paul said. 'If I could dance I should want to keep you to myself and dance the whole night long...' He raised her hand to his lips and kissed it, and there was something in his eyes then that set her heart racing once more. 'Yet I am not too selfish to keep you from the pleasure of dancing, Jane. Go to Brandt and enjoy yourself. He waltzes well, as do all Wellington's aides...'

Jane moved from his side reluctantly, though she greeted her partner with a smile and went willingly with him to the dance floor. She enjoyed dancing and soon discovered that the man was an excellent dancer. Their dance was soon over, and though she looked for Paul she did not see him to speak to again as she went from one dance to the next with a succession of partners. When she caught the occasional glance it was to see him engaged in conversation with the Prince Regent and some political gentlemen.

However, Paul did not forget their second dance and came to claim her. The touch of his hand on her arm set her pulses racing and she wished that they might dance the beautiful waltz that was about to begin for she would have liked to be in his arms, swaying to the music.

Once again they went out to the balcony to take some air, before moving into the supper room. For some moments they strolled in the peace of the cool evening air, but others had the same idea and they were never alone. Jane looked at Paul and saw the slight frustration in his eyes, as if he too wanted some time alone with her, but then he asked if she was ready to go into supper and the moment passed. Here they were joined by various gentlemen, friends of Paul's, Melia, Sarah and Jane's brother.

'Have you enjoyed your first ball in town?' Jane asked of Sarah and was greeted with a bright smile.

'Oh, yes, it is lovely to dance—and your brother dances so well, Jane. He has danced with me twice and introduced me to his friends; I have sat out no more than three dances—and on two occasions I spoke with Lord Frant. He is such a pleasant gentleman, Jane. I know he likes you very much, for he spoke of you in the warmest terms.'

Jane refrained from asking what Paul had said about her, but she saw that his eyes were upon her and her heart began to race. Until this evening she had not truly understood how much she had come to like the quiet gentleman—and how much she enjoyed his company.

All too soon the last dance was over and people began to drift away as the sound of the music ended.

Paul remained until the last and came to her as she and her friends were preparing to leave.

'I hope you will call when I return from Ireland, to see how my house improves,' he said and held her hand for a moment longer than necessary. 'Bring Melia and your cousin—and your brother, if he cares to visit.'

'I cannot vouch for Will, because he always seems to have so many engagements,' Jane replied and looked up at him. 'Sarah and Melia will be delighted to accompany me, I know. Your ward must take an interest, for perhaps one day—when you have taken a wife—she may reside within the walls of your home.'

'Yes, perhaps she may,' he said and there was a hint of laughter in his eyes. 'I shall hope to see you—the day after tomorrow, perhaps?'

'Yes, in the morning,' Jane said. 'We shall look forward to it.'

'Goodnight, sweet Jane,' he said and his eyes spoke more.

'Goodnight, Frant,' she said and smiled up at him.

They went out to the carriage together. Will handed his sister, Sarah and Melia inside and then climbed in after. Jane caught a glimpse of Paul's face as he turned away. She thought he looked tired and sad and her heart caught. She wished that she did not have to leave him... For a short time on the balcony that evening she had almost believed that she was ready to love again.

Alone in the darkness, Jane wrestled with her thoughts. How could she even think of caring for another man when she had loved Harry so much? She knew very little of Paul Frant and, from the way Lady

Catherine had looked at him, Jane knew that he was a
man who drew women to him—how could she be certain that he wasn't simply flirting with her?

In truth, she knew nothing of him. His past was a
closed book to her and he might be an adventurer or a
rogue for all she knew—she had sensed that he was not
telling her the truth when he'd spoken of his injury, so
what was he hiding?

Paul's arm was aching as he entered the house, hand-
ing his cane, hat, gloves and cloak to his manservant
with a sigh of weariness. That country doctor had known
what he was talking about when he'd told him to rest for
a few days. He felt weary after standing for hours, talking, smiling, catching up with old friends—and all the
time his eyes followed Jane, his mind could not quite
shut out the ugly suspicions.

Whoever had shot at him from behind a tree had
meant to wound, for he had fired a second time before taking flight as Adam and the groom came riding up and Adam had instantly taken a pot-shot into
the darkness.

He must have an enemy, but he had no idea of who
it might be—or what he had done to bring on such hatred. Why would anyone wish to kill him?

He'd been puzzling over it since the incident the previous evening, just as dusk was falling. Had the villain
aimed only a little straighter, Paul might have been
badly wounded or even dead.

His first thought was that his half-brother wasn't old
enough to conceive such a plot—nor would the boy or

his mother know that he would be on the road from Newmarket to London that evening. Very few could know that, because he had not decided until the last moment…unless he was being followed by someone who was waiting for such an opportunity.

Yet who could hate him that much? Adam had suggested it might be his stepmother. Perhaps she believed that if he were dead her son would become Lord Frant. Yet the boy was already heir to everything of worth left in their father's possession at his death. Paul was the one who might have borne a grudge but did not. So why would the dowager Lady Frant want him dead?

It made no sense. Indeed, if anything, she'd seemed apologetic when Paul had paid her a fleeting visit out of courtesy. She'd made it plain that she made no claim on him and he'd told her that he bore her and the boy no malice. Whatever his father had done, he had done, and that ended with his death.

Having lived so many years abroad, Paul could not think that any of the friends he'd made in the Army— or since his return—would want to harm him.

Was it something to do with India? Paul thought he might have made enemies there. He'd risen fast and gained a fortune, much of it by hard work but some because of what he'd done to help the young Prince escape his captors. Could it be something to do with that— perhaps one of the soldiers Adam had commanded had resented that Paul should receive so much more in reward than he or anyone else? Perhaps there was some truth in that point of view, though they had merely done their job, while he had risked his life with no thought of reward.

Paul had broken down the door of that burning hut and rescued the Prince at some cost to his person—but the soldiers had fought the tribesmen and some had been wounded. They should have received a reward for it and Paul was not certain how much of the two thousand gold coins paid to their captain had gone to the soldiers...

He frowned as his manservant eased him out of the tight coat he'd worn to the duchess's ball. The bandage beneath showed a few spots of blood and the wound stung. Paul had lied when he said he was injured in the fall; he had taken the ball in his arm and the force had knocked him from the horse. Had the ball pierced his chest...but he would not dwell on such thoughts.

The assassin, for such he must have been, had not taken enough care with his aim and so Paul lived. Yet next time he might not be as lucky. He knew he must do something to protect himself—and he must employ an agent to discover the reason for the attack.

He felt the frustration of not being able to devote his mind to the woman who dominated his thoughts. Jane had looked so lovely and for a moment on the balcony he'd felt she'd invited his kiss—and then that woman, Lady Catherine, had intruded and the mood had been shattered. The spoiled beauty was a nuisance and had tried to pique his interest on more than one occasion but, like others of her ilk, she had failed—something that would displease her if she guessed it. Yet perhaps she'd done him an unwitting favour.

If Paul's life were truly at risk, it meant he could not ask Jane to be his wife. She had suffered a terrible loss once; Paul would not wish her to suffer another. He would continue to be friendly, but a proposal of marriage was not to be thought of until he had discovered his enemy and could take the precautions necessary.

He was about to retire when someone knocked at his door.

'It's Adam. May I speak to you?'

'Yes, of course. Come in,' Paul said and picked up the glass of whisky his valet had poured for him.

'I could not retire without enquiring how you were,' Adam said, standing in the doorway, his golden locks dishevelled and in his shirtsleeves. 'It was foolish to risk the wound opening again by dancing...'

'I did not try to dance, but I saw Jane—and met some good friends. I do not think you know Major Harding? He served with me many years ago...before we met in India.'

'I am glad you met friends,' Adam said and hesitated, then, 'but have a care, Paul. Someone meant to kill you last evening. You have an enemy, my friend— and it might be anyone...'

'Yes, I've realised that,' Paul said. He was about to confide his plans but thought better of it. 'I cannot imagine who...but I am sure that ball was meant to wound or kill me.'

'Had we not come along when we did...' Adam shuddered. 'We delayed to help a lady whose coachman had lost his way, and if we had been but a moment longer...I am certain he meant to finish you off as you lay there, but at the sight of us he made off into the trees.'

'Yes, that was fortunate,' Paul said and frowned. 'What have I done that someone should wish to kill me, Adam?'

'Men have many reasons to kill,' Adam muttered and something in his eyes at that moment made Paul wonder if he still harboured resentment against him because of Annamarie. 'Jealousy, anger…even resentment over a slighting word has been known to move a man to murder.'

'Yes, I suppose, but I do not think my half-brother or his mother hate me that much… If he were older, but…'

'An assassin works for a few coins in the hand,' Adam said. 'Do not look for reasons; accept that you are hated and watch your back, my friend.'

'Yes, I shall.' Paul grimaced and eased his shoulder. 'Was your evening a good one?'

Adam laughed ruefully. 'I think my luck resides in the turf rather than the tables. I lost five hundred guineas this evening, but I still have the funds we need for our venture. The day after tomorrow we leave for Ireland and I shall not gamble again before then so stand in no danger of losing what I have.'

'You have not yet received the money from your lawyer, I think?'

'No, but that will buy land and perhaps a house,' Adam said. 'I shall have that, whatever happens at the tables, Paul—for I shall not risk my land or the share in the future we plan together.'

'I am glad of that,' Paul replied with a lazy smile.

'I should not like to lose my partner. Now, if you will excuse me, I'm for my bed.'

Adam laughed softly and went out, leaving Paul to his thoughts, which were neither clear nor pleasant as he crawled into bed and closed his eyes.

Chapter Ten

Jane knew better than to visit her mama too early the next morning, but in the afternoon she drove to her house to take tea with her and found that several other ladies and gentlemen had formed the same intention. It was impossible to have a private word with Mama, but both Melia and Sarah found friends there and Melia seemed happier than she had the previous evening, when Captain Smythe and his sister Anne asked her to go walking with them in the park the following day.

Sarah also seemed lost in her thoughts as they drove home, though she answered when Jane spoke to her and discussed their plans for the evening, which were to dine quietly at home before joining a few friends for a trip to the theatre in the evening.

Jane enjoyed her evening, and when in the interval Major Harding entered their box she greeted him with a smile. His invitation to go riding the next day was accepted with pleasure and he spent the whole of the interval at her side.

Will had accompanied them that evening and he sat between Melia and Sarah, entertaining them both and providing ices and drinks in the various intervals for their pleasure. Melia was more talkative than she had been for a few days and Jane heard her agree to go riding with Will the next afternoon.

Jane watched her brother's face as he turned from Melia to Sarah and asked her if she would like to ride with them. Sarah hesitated, and then said she would very much like it if a horse could be found for her. Will promised that he would see her mounted properly and Sarah smiled, and then the lights dimmed for the last act. Just before the lights lowered, Jane noticed that someone was watching them from below in the pits through a small pair of opera glasses.

For a moment she wondered who the gentleman was and why he stared so intently, but then he seemed to become aware that she had noticed and inclined his head, turning his attention to the stage. Jane was soon drawn into the performance and forgot him, though later that evening, before she retired, she mentioned it to her brother.

'Did you notice that gentleman in the pits?' she asked. 'He seemed to be very interested in us...I suppose you did not notice him?'

'No, I cannot say I did,' Will said and smiled. 'You are a lovely young woman still, Jane. I am sure a great many gentlemen stare at you, dearest—and it might have been Sarah or Melia who was attracting his attention.'

'Yes, very likely,' Jane said, but she was still uneasy.

The man had been staring at her—and something in his manner had struck her as being odd. Yet perhaps Will was right and she was making too much of it.

Jane was soon asleep and no dreams came to disturb her rest. In the morning she decided she would visit one or two of the furniture makers' warehouses and see if she could find the missing items needed for Lord Frant's house. Both Melia and Sarah were engaged to friends so she would go alone...

As she left the second of the two cabinet makers' establishments feeling pleased with the purchase of several pieces, Jane stood for a moment in the side street and took stock. A cab had brought her here and she would need to find one to take her home. Had she realised the warehouse was as secluded as this, she would have brought her own carriage, but she'd expected it would be within easy reach of the showrooms. She believed that Lord Frant would be well pleased with the items she had purchased on his behalf, and there was no need for her to look further for the moment.

Ready to go home, she decided that she would return to the warehouse and ask if someone could summon a cab for her. As she turned, Jane was suddenly accosted by a man she'd never seen in her life. He was dressed in a brown coat and breeches with a dark hat pulled down low over his brow and the hand he placed on her arm was not quite clean about the fingernails.

'I reckon yer be the one I be lookin' for,' he grunted and thrust his face closer so that she could smell the sour odour of his breath. 'I've been told to warn yer that my mistress will have a reckoning if you continue your pursuit of her man. If you know what's good for yer, yer'll go home and forget him…'

'What are you taking about?' Jane suppressed the trickle of fear that ran through her. 'I have no idea who your mistress is—or her man…'

The brute pressed his face closer to Jane's. 'I reckon yer knows, all right. It ain't no use playin' the innocent with Pyke. I'm warnin' yer, and if yer ignore me warnin' yer'll be sorry.'

Jane wrested her arm from his grasp but he grabbed at her again and threatened her with his fist.

'Hey, you!' a man's voice cried. 'What do you think you're doing? Unhand that lady at once or I'll make you sorry you were born…'

Instantly, the man ran off down the street and she turned to find herself face to face with the gentleman she'd seen watching her from the pits at the theatre the previous evening.

'Sir,' Jane said, breathing deeply to steady her nerves, 'I must thank you for scaring off that brute.'

'Was he after money?' he asked and looked at her in a puzzled manner. 'You are Lady March, are you not? A friend pointed you out to me last evening at the theatre…'

'You were staring at me through your opera glasses,' Jane said after a moment. Her fright had subsided now and she was angry. 'Did you arrange this incident…to gain my favour?'

'You wrong me,' he said and smiled oddly. 'I was not privy to your intention to visit the warehouses of

Master Morrison. I came only to complete a purchase myself.' He tipped his hat. 'Excuse me; I shall not impose on you a moment longer...'

'No, please, stay,' Jane said, realising that she had been rude. 'I was shocked by that rogue's attack—and it seemed so odd that you should stare at me last evening...'

He laughed softly, his teeth gleaming against skin that had obviously been exposed to the sun often. 'Does it surprise you that beauty such as yours should attract attention? Yet you asked me to tarry—may I be of some assistance?'

'I came here by cab and need to summon another but I am not sure where to find one...'

'You will not find one here, my lady,' he said and inclined his head. 'Captain Richard Hershaw at your service. My carriage waits for me. I shall instruct my driver to take you home...'

'Oh, no, I could not impose on you,' Jane said at once. 'The warehouse manager will know where to hire a cab for me. I should have retained the last one but was not sure how long my business would take me.'

'I would have thought it safer for a lady of your standing to come accompanied by your servants in your own carriage,' Captain Hershaw said, a smile flickering in his eyes. 'Yet I know that some ladies are of an independent mind and I understand that sometimes you may wish to be alone. Please, take my carriage. I am well able to find my own way home.'

Jane hesitated for a moment and then thanked him. 'You are kind, sir—and I have not been polite...'

'Give me your address and I shall instruct my man,' he said and walked over to the carriage. Jane followed and was helped inside. Captain Hershaw doffed his hat to her and the carriage moved off.

She watched from the window and saw her rescuer walk into the warehouse. Leaning back against the squabs of the comfortable carriage, Jane closed her eyes for a moment. The small incident had alarmed her, but she would have been foolish to refuse the offer of a man who was obviously a gentleman.

For a few moments wild ideas that he might have been trying to kidnap her ran through her mind and she wondered if she had been a fool to step willingly into his carriage, but they vanished as swiftly as they came. Some half an hour later, when the carriage stopped outside her brother's house, Jane realised that she had indeed mistaken Captain Hershaw's intentions.

Of course he had not planned to rescue her from that brute or yet to kidnap her. It was, as he said, a coincidence that he had happened along at the right moment… and yet something lingered at the back of her mind, a suspicion that she was being duped in some way. She could not fathom the purpose if it had all been arranged, for had he wished to abduct her the opportunity had been his—so why did she feel it would be foolish to trust Captain Hershaw too much?

Caught up in the busy social whirl, Jane forgot the unpleasant incident at the warehouse over the next few days. She told no one that she'd been threatened, nor did she say anything of Captain Hershaw. When she found his calling card with the others in the hall, Jane made no mention of it. However, when her brother told her that he'd added the captain's name to the list of guests they had invited to a musical evening, she asked him who the gentleman was and how Will came to know him.

'Hershaw?' Will wrinkled his brow. 'He was introduced to me by a friend last evening at my club. I won five hundred guineas from him, Jane—so I thought the least I could do was invite him to dinner to make up for it.'

'I did not think you gambled for high stakes?'

'I do not often. It was a game of piquet. Although I seldom play for more than a few guineas, Hershaw suggested the stakes and I felt obliged to agree.'

'I should not make a habit of it,' Jane advised.

'Have you heard something against the man? I did not think you knew him.'

'We have met but once somewhere,' Jane said. 'I know nothing ill of him—but I would not trust him too far, Will.'

'I am not a gambler, my love,' Will said, 'but I must offer the man a chance to regain his losses—it is a matter of honour, dearest one.'

'Yes, I know…' Jane sighed for she knew her words would fall on deaf ears. She feared that Captain Hershaw meant them no good but could not put her fears into words, for there was no reason behind her distrust—and Will would laugh if she said it was her womanly instinct.

Jane wished that Lord Frant was in London. She could have asked him for his opinion and knew he would take her concerns seriously. How long did he intend to stay in Ireland? she wondered, and wished that she'd asked him, but their last meeting had been brief and she had not liked to press him. Jane had no claim on Lord Frant…but she would feel so much happier when he was home again.

Melia had taken to going out with Miss Anne Smythe and her brother Captain Smythe, the godson of Sir Henry Clarke. They called for her in the mornings to go riding or shopping, and in the afternoon she was invited to tea at their house. Jane, her brother, Sarah and Melia were invited to dine for cards and music, and during the evening Lady Clarke spoke to Jane about her ward.

'I believe you are dear Melia's chaperon. You know her guardian well I understand?'

'Yes, I know Lord Frant—and her aunt, Mrs Bellingham.'

'I was wondering if she had a dowry?' the lady said frankly. 'My husband's godson and heir is quite taken with her and I believe her to be of good family.'

'I know nothing ill of her family,' Jane said. 'I understand her guardian settled a sum of money on her, but I am not at liberty to disclose it…'

'No, of course not. I should not dream of asking. Of course my godson thinks it of no concern—but we like to do our best for our dear ones, do we not?'

'Yes, certainly,' Jane said. 'Has Melia shown a particular interest in your godson?'

'Has she said nothing of it to you?' The lady sounded surprised. 'They are forever in each other's company. I thought you would have remarked it.'

Jane shook her head. She'd seen Melia departing with her new friends but had given little thought to it, but if the girl had thoughts of marriage…surely she could not be so changeable? It was only a matter of weeks since she'd declared herself madly in love with Viscount Hargreaves. Had she given up all thought of him since he'd neglected to keep his promise and attend the duchess's ball?

Jane turned the conversation. She was not Melia's guardian, merely her chaperon for a short time—and she almost wished that she had never agreed to bring the girl to town. Will would be hurt if she turned her attentions to the young captain. He must be feeling that Melia preferred almost anyone rather than he, and that must be hard to bear.

Jane did not feel able to remonstrate with her guest. She did not wish to tell Melia where to bestow her affections. Indeed, if she were so shallow, it might be best if she married someone else. Will would be hurt but he would recover—if she married him and then turned her affections elsewhere it must be far worse. Better that his eyes should be opened to her failings now.

Although she said nothing to Melia, Jane spoke to her brother the next morning. She had come down to breakfast early, as she often did, and found him already in the parlour. From his dress, he had been riding and returned with a good appetite.

'Ah, I see you have been out already. I have agreed to go riding with Major Harding later—and I believe Sarah has promised Mama that she will call on her. I am not sure of Melia's intentions…'

'I understand she goes for a drive and then takes luncheon at the house of Sir Henry and Lady Clarke. Sir Henry is Captain Smythe's godfather...'

'We dined there last evening... It seems a little excessive to spend so much time in their company.'

'I dare say Melia has her reasons...'

'Will, dearest,' Jane said, looking at him in concern. 'His godmother asked me about her prospects last night...'

'Am I to wish her happy then?' A flicker of regret showed in his eyes. 'I suspected as much when I saw the way he looked at her—he is besotted with her and, since he has his own fortune, I doubt his godmother will sway him against her.'

'I am not sure she wished to—and it matters very little to me. It is you I am concerned for,' Jane said. 'I think Melia unkind to treat you so ill...'

'She is in love with Hargreaves,' Will said bleakly. 'I asked her and she confessed it was so—but he will not marry her because she does not have enough fortune...'

'Your fortune is surely large enough to satisfy her?'

'You are wrong, Melia,' Will said. 'She told me that she was sorry but she could not offer me her heart and so would not marry me...because she likes me too well. I think she intends to marry John Smythe because he adores her and will not question her. Yet if Hargreaves were to offer, she would abandon all others...'

'I am so sorry for your pain,' Jane said and went to him, touching his hand. 'I know you loved her.'

'Yes. Perhaps I still do in a way, but the blinkers have fallen from my eyes, Jane, and I see her for the heartless creature she truly is.' Will sighed. 'Better now than if we had married… John Smythe is welcome if he can get her. I shall not envy him.'

'Truly?'

'Truly,' he said and smiled at her. 'I shall recover, Jane—and next time I shall make sure that the woman I give my heart to is worthy of it and can love me in return.'

'You will feel easier in time…'

'Do not think I suffer as you did when you lost Harry,' Will said and kissed her cheek. He looked long into her eyes. 'You have not seemed as happy as you were, dearest—is it Frant's absence?'

'Perhaps…yes,' she admitted. 'I did not think I could care deeply again, Will, but I think…' She sighed and shook her head. 'Oh, I am not sure. Perhaps I am foolish to hope that I might find love again. We are friends but he has given no sign of more.'

'You think not? From what I have observed, I believe he truly cares for you,' Will said and frowned. 'Does he stay in Ireland much longer?'

'He did not tell me of his plans—but I thought it was his intention to return, leaving the viscount there to oversee the young horses.'

'He told me he will have his stables at his estate in Cambridgeshire. I think he hopes to race one of his horses at the autumn races.'

'Then surely he will return soon,' Jane said. 'Now, before I go out I must speak with your housekeeper, Will, and make the arrangements for this evening.'

'Yes, I would have everything as it ought to be, but

I know I can leave that to you,' Will said. 'I shall leave you now and go up to change. I have business this morning—and this afternoon I have promised to take Sarah for a drive in the park…'

Jane watched her brother leave the parlour and was thoughtful. Will had taken the news of Melia's desertion more calmly than she'd believed possible. Could Sarah's arrival in town have something to do with that—or was she being fanciful?

'I saw Frant this morning as I came to collect you,' Major Harding said when they had been for a brisk canter about the park. 'We acknowledged each other in passing but did not stop to speak. I shall call on him later and discover his plans—when he means to go down to the country.'

'I did not know he had returned,' Jane said and her heart skipped a beat. Paul was in town once more—and yet he had not sent word. Perhaps his smiles and soft words had been merely flirtation? Yes, she had been foolish to imagine more. They had such short acquaintance and love did not happen that way, did it? Jane had known Harry most of her life and loved him long before he asked her to marry him. 'Had I known, I would have sent an invitation for this evening…'

'I dare say he will call on you soon,' Major Harding said and smiled. 'I believe my old friend is much taken with you, Lady March. I have tried to steal a march on him while he was away, but I think I have not made much progress.'

Jane lifted her clear gaze to him. 'Your friendship gives me pleasure, sir.'

'But your heart belongs to another,' he replied and the look in his eyes was warm with affection. 'Paul is my friend and I would not come between you for the world—but, should he let you down, know that I would stand in his stead and it would make me happy to have you for my wife.'

'I think that is the nicest thing anyone has ever said to me,' Jane said. 'Know that I value your friendship and would have it continue.'

'I shall always wish to be of service—to you both…'

Jane could only thank him. She liked and respected the major, who was an honourable man, but she loved Paul Frant. His absence had revealed the truth to her and she could not wait to see him again.

However, he did not call on her that afternoon, and in the evening Major Harding told her that he had spoken briefly with Lord Frant, who had told him that he would be in town only for a few days before he left for the country to set things in order at his estate.

'Oh, I had thought he would be in town longer…' Jane could not keep the disappointment from her voice, though she schooled herself not to show it in her expression. She must have been mistaken in him. The doubts had set in now and she scolded herself for having been a fool.

'He will come.' Major Harding pressed her hand and then frowned as he glanced across the room at a newcomer. 'Hershaw here? I should not have expected to see that man at your house, Lady March.'

'My brother invited him because he won a substantial sum from him the other evening.'

'Then warn your brother to make sure he does not lose far more the next time they play...'

'You do not trust him?'

'I served with him in France for a time,' Major Harding said. 'He was accused of cheating at the tables by another officer and they were to fight a duel—but someone told the commander and Hershaw was sent off on a mission. I heard later that he had been sent to India...'

'To India?' Jane was suddenly alert. 'What became of him there?'

'I have no idea, but I believe he is still in the service, though why he has returned to England I do not know.'

'I am glad you warned me. I did not trust him but could not give a reason to my brother—now I shall warn him at the first opportunity, but not this evening. Captain Hershaw is our guest and must be shown respect, but I would rather he was not invited again.'

'Be careful of him, my lady.' Major Harding frowned. 'There was some scandal about one of the officers' wives...'

'Yes, I can believe it,' Jane said. 'He can be charming, I dare say, but he does not appeal to me.'

'I am glad to know it—and remember what I have said, Jane. If ever you need me, you have only to ask...'

Jane smiled and thanked him. She did not get another chance to speak with him in private that evening, but she was aware of Captain Hershaw's eyes following her wherever she was in the room and he kept her talking once or twice during the evening, asking her

if she would permit him to take her riding one morning that week.

Jane excused herself on the grounds that she was
busy and saw a gleam of annoyance in his eyes, but he
accepted her excuses and told her he would ask again.

She was not sorry when the evening was over, and
afterwards spoke to her brother alone.

'I should prefer it if you did not ask that man here
again, Will. Meet him at your club if you must but...I
cannot like him. The way he looks at me...'

'Yes, I noticed it,' Will told her. 'Be at peace, dearest.
I managed to lose six hundred guineas to him at cards
this evening and so the debt is paid. I doubt I shall have
much to do with the man in future.'

'I am so glad,' Jane said and kissed his cheek. 'Did
you not think Sarah splendid this evening? She kept
Lady Clarke and Mrs Holbein amused for ages after
dinner.'

'Sarah makes a good hostess and friend,' Will said
and looked more like his old self as he grinned. 'Cease
your matchmaking, sister. It is not necessary. I am perfectly able to make my own plans for the future.'

'Will...' she breathed and looked at him expectantly,
but he laughed and shook his head.

'Go to bed, Jane, and stop worrying. I have made up
my mind to nothing—and you shall know my thoughts
as soon as I know them myself...'

Jane was smiling as she went up the stairs. Lord
Frant was home, Will did not need his sister to watch
over him and there was nothing to worry her...

Chapter Eleven

Jane waited at home the following morning and her patience was rewarded when Lord Frant came to call on her just before luncheon. She was in her parlour at the back of the house and welcomed him with both hands outstretched. He took them and kissed her on both cheeks.

'I am so glad you are home. Is your injury recovered?'

'Perfectly,' Paul said and held her hands a moment longer. For one fleeting glorious moment he seemed to drink her in, as if his eyes could not have their fill of her. Jane longed for him to give her a sign that he felt as she did but there was nothing except that look of longing in his eyes. 'I have been impatient to see you, Lady March. I wanted to thank you for making my house into a home.'

'So you are happy with everything?'

'It is all quite perfect—but it leaves me with no excuse left to visit you.'

If he cared for her he would not need an excuse!

'You may always call on me as a friend—surely you know it?'

'I have hoped it,' Paul said. 'Indeed, I have hoped for more—but certain things prevent me from speaking of what lies in my heart.'

'What things?' Jane asked, puzzled, as she looked into his face and saw that his eyes were veiled, holding secrets. Why could he not speak openly if he cared for her? He spoke of his hopes and yet she sensed a withdrawal in him that had not been there at the start. 'Yet I should not ask—I have no right…'

'I would give you every right,' he said huskily. 'May I ask you to be patient with me for a time, Jane? I have business that will keep me from you—and there are some situations best dealt with before I can come to you with an honest heart.'

'Of course,' she said shyly, and her heart beat faster as she saw the look in his eyes. Surely his eyes did not lie when they spoke to her of love and need and wanting? She felt herself melting in the heat of that gaze and longed for him to take her in his arms and kiss her until there was no need for words—but it did not happen. 'Yet if I understand your words it would seem that I do have the right to ask what keeps you from speaking plainly.'

'Will you trust me, Jane? Will you believe me when I say it is as much for your sake that I do not speak now as anything else? I do not wish to involve you in…' He shook his head, an expression of frustration in his eyes. 'No, you must trust me because I cannot have you exposed to this…'

'I shall trust you if you ask it,' she said. 'Yet I do not understand why you may not be open with me.'

'For the moment I am not free to speak of what is in my heart concerning you, Jane.'

'Then I must wait until you are free...'

'I came to tell you that I leave for Cambridgeshire tomorrow,' Paul said. 'Major Harding is to accompany me. I asked him if he would bear me company for a few days while I set much needed work in train—and then I shall return to town. I hope to make up a party to dine one evening and a trip to Vauxhall gardens another...'

'Then I shall look forward to your return,' Jane said and restrained the urge to tell him that she did not want him to leave again so soon. How provoking his air of mystery was. She was not a tattle tongue and he might have told her whatever worried him in confidence. 'I had hoped you might come to the theatre with us this week, but your business is urgent, I dare say.'

'I fear it presses,' he said and looked regretful, because she had not been able to hide her feelings: he asked her to trust him and yet he did not trust her enough to speak of what was bothering him. How could he care for her if he could not tell her what was in his heart and mind? 'You do not know how much I wish that I might stay in town—but we have purchased horses to be trained and must make sure they have a roof over their heads.'

'Viscount Hargreaves remains in Ireland?'

'Yes, it is better for him. In town he becomes reckless. In Ireland he will attend to business, as he must.

Perhaps one day he will be rich enough to repair his family estates and then he may marry.'

'Yes, as you say, it is for the best,' Jane agreed. 'It will give Melia time to heal her broken heart, I think.'

'My ward has been in real distress?' Paul looked concerned.

'No, not truly,' Jane said. 'I believe she loved the viscount in her way but she finds amusement to heal her hurts.'

'Ah, I thought as much,' Paul said. 'If I believed it was a true match between them I should consider whether I could do more than I have so far.'

'I am sure you have been generous enough.'

'Perhaps—but I would not have either of them languish of a broken heart.'

'Well, Melia does not languish. She is out with her friends now.'

'Then I shall wait and see what happens,' he said and smiled. 'I had hoped there would be time for you to see my house—but when I am ready to entertain will be time enough, I dare say.'

'Yes, of course,' Jane agreed, though she'd hoped to see it privately long before he entertained others.

'Well, I must leave you,' he murmured reluctantly. 'Please forgive the briefness of this visit. I have business to attend before I leave and my lawyer awaits me now.'

'Of course…' Jane said and offered her hand. He took it, held it and smiled and then he went from the room, leaving her to stare after him in frustration and disappointment.

She had hoped for so much when he returned from

Ireland and now he had left her for the country and nothing had changed between them. For a fleeting moment his eyes had spoken to her heart of love, and his words had seemed to suggest he truly cared for her, but he had not spoken plainly of love or marriage and Jane could not be certain that what she hoped was true.

Hearing voices in the hall, Jane realised that Melia had returned and dashed a hand across her face lest any foolish tears should be upon it. As she went out into the hall, she realised that Melia was not alone and frowned as she saw that Captain Hershaw was with her.

'Richard brought me home,' Melia said with a dimple. 'I was caught in a rain shower when he saw me standing in the doorway and offered to bring me here.'

'I did not realise it had been raining,' Jane said truthfully.

'Oh, it was nothing much and stopped before we were home,' Melia said, blushing. 'However, it was so nice not to walk…'

'I thought you were shopping with Miss Smythe?'

'I was, but she wanted to go to the library and I did not so I thought I might as well take advantage of Richard's offer.' She darted a roguish look at the man, who smiled and bent to kiss her hand. 'He must stay and take nuncheon with us—please say he is welcome, Jane…'

Jane hesitated, reluctant to say the words that would give the impression she was happy for the man to come informally to her brother's house, and in that instant Captain Hershaw relieved her of the necessity.

'I have an appointment I must keep,' he said. 'It was delightful to have your company, Miss Melia—perhaps you and Lady March would honour me by being my guests at the theatre one evening…your cousin also, of course,' he added as Sarah entered the house.

'You are kind,' Jane said. 'We must consult our diaries. We have so many engagements it is hard to find a space for new ones…'

His eyes darted a look of anger at her, but in a moment it was gone and he was smiling. 'Of course, of course. I have no doubt we shall meet everywhere, Lady March. I am given entrance by most, you will find…'

In another moment he had gone, leaving Jane with the distinct impression that she had made an enemy of him. Yet a little voice at the back of her mind told her that he had always meant her harm…or perhaps to harm her brother through her. Did he hope to fleece Will? It was unlikely her brother would be drawn in again… but if not her brother's fortune, who else did he think he might get to through Jane?

It was not until after luncheon with her family that it occurred to Jane it might possibly be because she was known to have a close friendship with Lord Frant.

Remembering the night Paul had come to the ball with a binding round his head and his arm in a sling, Jane felt a cold shiver at her nape. Paul had said there were circumstances that kept him from opening his heart to her. She'd thought it matters of business…but had the shot that sent him crashing from his horse been meant to kill him? Was he afraid to tell her of his love because she was a widow and he thought he might also be killed violently?

The thought made Jane sick with fear. She tried to

tell herself that she was jumping to conclusions, to dismiss her foolish fears, and yet they had taken root and she wondered if he was in danger. Did Paul suspect that his life might be at risk—and was that why he'd asked Major Harding to accompany him to the country?

'When did you suspect that your life was in danger?' Major Harding asked.

They had stopped at an inn for the night and were talking over a meal and wine. Paul was silent for a moment, then, 'When my horse almost ran into a wire stretched between two trees in Ireland. The first time, when someone shot at me, was inconclusive. Adam rode upon us in time and the rogue made off. I could not know if it had been an accident or an attempt to murder me.'

'Hargreaves? I know of him, but have not met the gentleman—do you trust him?'

'A few weeks ago I would have said implicitly. He saved my life on the ship coming over—and I cannot think he has reason to want me dead…'

'You're not as sure of his loyalty now, are you?'

'I do not want to believe that he could be to blame,' Paul said reluctantly. 'Yet he was one of only a few that knew my route on both occasions…and he might resent that he received only two thousand gold coins while I received much more for saving the Prince's life.' Paul had no need to explain the circumstances of the rescue because Major Harding knew it all, though not from Paul's lips.

'So you do suspect he might be behind the attempts but do not wish to believe it.'

'I have to accept that it is possible,' Paul said reluctantly. 'It would be a bitter thing to me if I should discover that beneath his friendship lies only hatred.'

'Has he said or done anything to give you pause?'

'No, not truly—except that he told someone else he had been unfairly treated in the matter of the reward…'

'Yet, even so, it would be a spiteful fool who would hold such a thing against you to the extent where he would seek to take your life.'

'Yes…' Paul frowned. 'That is what I thought but I cannot think of anyone else who would wish me harm.'

'What of Hershaw?'

'Hershaw…?' Paul sought for the memory and frowned. 'That was so long ago…surely it could not be. Why now?'

'He was suspected of cheating and it was on your recommendation that he was sent away.'

'Yes, I remember now. Colonel Forster asked me for my opinion and I told him that I did not trust the man. I forget—where was he sent?'

'To India…you did not meet him when you worked for the Company?'

'No, never to my knowledge: India is a huge country and our troops are everywhere. I had little to do with the interior, being stationed in the mountain regions, as was Adam Hargreaves.'

'I saw him the other evening at Viscount Salisbury's house and warned Lady March to be a little wary of him. She told me that she did not care for him but must treat him as her brother's guest, but would warn him to be careful.'

'I dare say he goes everywhere in Society,' Paul said. 'He was not proven a cheat but only suspected and warned in private by the colonel. His reputation was not truly sullied by the charge, though if rumours persist...'

'I think he has not long been in London,' Major Harding said and frowned. 'He may have returned because an uncle left him a small estate. If he has come for business it might have occurred to him that he could settle an old score at the same time.'

Paul smiled oddly. 'It would relieve my mind if I could think of him as my enemy rather than Adam Hargreaves.'

'Of course there is always me,' his old friend said and grinned. 'I might have accompanied you for the chance of putting a ball through your head.'

'Had it been you I should already be dead,' Paul said and chuckled. 'You need only one shot, Jack.'

'Yes, there is that,' the major said and his eyes gleamed with amusement. 'Have you taken precautions to protect your back?'

'Some, but now that you have warned me there are others I need to set in motion,' Paul said with a grimace. 'Both attempts so far have failed. I am certain there will be a third. I only wish I understood what I have done to merit them...'

Had he known the identity of his enemy, Paul would have spoken of what was in his heart to Jane. He knew that she had been confused and hurt by his ambiguous words and felt he'd made a mess of things. Perhaps he should have spoken openly and told her that he loved her deeply but feared that his enemy might succeed in his aim of murdering him. Something in him had held back, because Jane had been robbed of happiness once and if she gave her heart to him it would be broken if he were killed. He'd been on the verge of telling her that night on the balcony before they were interrupted, but it was as well he had held back. Paul knew now that his enemy was determined to harm him; he just couldn't be sure why or who…

'Are you enjoying yourself, Lady March?' The voice made the back of Jane's neck prickle and she turned to look at the man who had come up to her unnoticed. It seemed that she could go nowhere these past days without meeting him, and she had a feeling that he was following her. He'd boasted that he was welcomed everywhere and it appeared that it was no idle remark. 'I know you love good music and I think we shall be royally entertained this evening.'

'Yes, I believe Madame Justine de Rigorini is much admired,' Jane replied. 'I would have thought you more inclined to cards, sir?'

'What makes you think I prefer cards to music and the company of a beautiful woman?' he asked, his voice smooth and even but a gleam of something in his eyes that made her stomach clench. 'I am a man of many interests and tastes.'

'Yes, of course. I meant no insult,' she said. 'My brother is here but I think he chooses the card room, but my cousin Sarah and Miss Bellingham will listen to the music with me.'

'I have invited some friends to an evening party of my own,' he continued as if she had not spoken. 'Perhaps you and your brother and your guests would be gracious enough to accept my invitation?'

'It is not usual for a single gentleman to host such a party?'

'Oh, my aunt, Mrs Sargent, is to host it for me. You may be acquainted with the lady. I believe she is an acquaintance of the duchess.'

'Yes, I do know Mrs Sargent,' Jane said and inclined her head. 'You must send me a card, sir, and we shall see if we have a free evening—and now you must excuse me…'

Jane walked away, not bothering to turn her head though she knew his gaze followed her. Mrs Sargent was indeed an acquaintance of her mother's but not a lady she liked. Mama did not much like her either; she was received everywhere and to snub her would be extremely rude, but she was never invited to one of the duchess's more intimate affairs.

'Did I see you speaking with Captain Hershaw?' Melia said as Jane went to sit down with the others, who were waiting for the music to begin. 'He is such a charming man, is he not? I believe he means to invite us to his party…'

'Yes, but I do not care to accept an invitation from that gentleman,' Jane said. 'I do not care for him and it might be best if you did not welcome his company too freely.'

Melia shot her a resentful look. 'It seems that you do not care for any gentlemen I like,' she muttered beneath her breath.

Jane frowned but did not chide her. She had no wish to fall out with her charge in public, nor was it her business to prevent Melia forming a friendship with the captain. If he made her a proposal of marriage it would be for Lord Frant to decide whether or not to accept it.

Jane had begun to think recently that it would have been better had she not asked the pretty young woman to accompany them to town. She had done so because her brother wished it, believing there was an understanding between them, but it seemed that Melia bestowed her affections easily on a handsome face. First it had been Viscount Hargreaves and now Captain Hershaw. Neither was suitable, in Jane's opinion, and had the girl been her sister or ward she thought she might have immediately removed her from town. In fact, the only suitor Melia had encouraged that Jane thought suitable was Captain Smythe.

It was, in any case, almost time that she began to think of going home. They had been in town several weeks and Jane had purchased all the new gowns she needed for a while. Will had mentioned leaving towards the end of the following week and Jane thought she would go with him, though had either Sarah or Melia been courted by suitable gentlemen she might have remained longer.

No, she would tell them in the morning that they must make any last purchases they needed and return books to the lending library. She herself intended to purchase a parcel of the latest books to take home to the country. It would seem quiet after so many balls and parties, though if she removed to Bath she and Sarah would have a good deal of company there. Will entertained his close friends at home, and Jane asked their neighbours to dine once or twice a month, but it was mostly just the two of them—three with Sarah, for Melia would return to her aunt's home, unless an engagement should be announced between her and Will. Jane did not think it likely now.

Would she see Lord Frant before she returned home? Jane hoped he would call on her before then, but if not…perhaps he might one day chance to call on them in the country…

Her heart ached when she realised she might not see him for months on end, if at all. He had hinted that he cared for her, and surely she'd seen it in his eyes—but if he truly cared for her would he not have spoken of his feelings and asked her to be his wife? The fact that he had not done so had raised doubts in her mind and she wondered if perhaps it was his habit to flirt with ladies who came his way. If that were the case Jane would be very disappointed… No, she would be hurt for unwisely she had begun to care for him rather too much for her own comfort.

Chapter Twelve

Jane sat opening her letters and cards when Will walked into the parlour. He was dressed for riding, the smell of the stables still on him. He smiled at the pile of letters before her.

'Even in town you have so much correspondence,' he said. 'I wanted to tell you that I intend to go home on Friday next, Jane—but if you wish to stay in town a few weeks longer one of my friends will be pleased to escort you home. George Brandt is coming to stay for the shooting in September. He likes you, Jane, and I know he would gladly put aside all other pursuits to be of service.'

'Lieutenant Brandt is a pleasant and attractive man,' Jane said. 'I enjoy his company and so does Sarah, I believe.'

'Oh…?' Will's brow darkened and Jane laughed, her suspicions confirmed. 'I had not realised she was interested in him.'

'I meant only what I said. Sarah finds him pleasant company, as I do—but neither of us has romantic inclinations towards him.'

Will's expression did not lighten. 'Is it that fellow Frant, Jane? I thought he cared for you, but he went off to Ireland and then to the country—I am sorry if the rogue has hurt you, sister.'

'Lord Frant is not a rogue,' Jane said and made herself smile at him, even though his words echoed thoughts that continued to haunt her despite her efforts to ignore them. 'Nor has he hurt me. I knew he had business in the country that would take some time. I hope he will return to town before we leave, but I intend to return with you, Will—no matter what…'

'I'm glad, for the house seems empty without you, love. You will not take yourself and Sarah off to Bath too soon?'

'Perhaps next spring,' Jane said and her eyes quizzed him. 'Will that be long enough for you to decide, dearest one?'

'Yes, I dare say it will,' he replied and shook his head at her. 'I had hoped you might marry…for I would not spoil your plans, Jane.'

'You must think of your happiness,' she told him. 'I can find a dozen companions if I choose…'

'But I want you to be happy. Have you met no one else you would wish to marry…or is your heart given to Frant?'

'I believe it may be,' Jane confessed. 'For a long time I did not think I could love again—not as I loved my dearest Harry. Now I think perhaps I have met someone I can respect and love. It may be in a different way, for it was a wild sweet joy I knew with Harry, but I think this time it would be just as sweet, but not the same.'

'What does Mama say?' her brother asked. 'She hinted to me weeks back that she thought you would make a match of it—but then Frant went off to Ireland and I know she is anxious for you again.'

'Mama would have me marry; any decent and wealthy man would do, as long as she thought he would make me happy. Was it her suggestion that you should invite Lieutenant Brandt to stay?'

'She might have mentioned it,' Will said, 'but George is a good fellow, Jane. I like him—and he likes you very much.'

'Major Harding likes me too,' Jane said. 'Shall you invite him to stay for the shooting?'

'If you wish it. I shall also ask Frant…if he can spare the time from his business…'

'Invite all three,' Jane said impulsively, because perhaps if he thought she had suitors Paul would make up his mind to speak plainly, 'and do not let your fears for my happiness stand in the way of your own, my dearest one. I shall consider each of the gentlemen and if I can find it in my heart to marry, you shall be the first to know.'

Will laughed and made a wry face, for she'd given him his own words back again. Jane laughed too, because they were so very close and she knew that her brother would wish her to be settled before he proposed to the lady he now hoped to make his wife.

Jane could not help but be pleased that he no longer wished to marry Melia Bellingham, for she had proved herself spoiled and flighty. Once they went home, she would return to her aunt's house—unless she accepted a proposal of marriage from someone before then.

* * *

'Go home next week?' Melia looked at her in sullen disappointment. 'I thought we should stay until the end of the season at least.'

'It is almost over,' Jane said. 'Most of the important balls have been held—apart from Lady Marshall's ball next week. We shall attend that on the Wednesday evening and then prepare ourselves to leave, by visiting friends to say our farewells and any last minute errands you may have—but you have several days before that…'

'We shall miss Captain Hershaw's affair…'

'As I told you, I did not mean to accept it,' Jane said and was glad to have a valid excuse for refusing it. 'Surely it is not so important to you? You have made so many friends and been invited everywhere. You must have known it could not go on for ever?'

'Yes, but…' Melia stared at her sulkily. 'I have not yet received an offer of marriage. I hoped…' She broke off and her cheeks heated.

'I do not think either your aunt or Lord Frant would agree to a marriage between you and that gentleman,' Jane said gently. 'I thought there was someone else… Miss Smythe's brother likes you very much. Perhaps if you smiled on him…'

Melia pouted. 'I do like John and his sister Anne, but there are others I like better. You've told me neither of them is suitable and I think that is unfair of you. What right have you to tell me who I may marry?'

'I have none, of course,' Jane said. 'You mistake me if you think I mean to forbid you, Melia. I hoped to advise you, because I would wish you to be happy and

I do not think you would be happy with Captain Hershaw. I think him a gambler and perhaps not a man to be trusted with the care of a young girl's heart.'

'And Adam?' she demanded. 'Is he also not to be trusted?'

'If he had asked you, I would have been happy for you,' Jane said softly. 'I think his reasons for not doing so were honourable—he cannot afford to give you the life you deserve. Yet it was unkind of him to raise your hopes in vain.'

'I should be happy living in a cottage with him,' Melia cried and promptly burst into tears, running from the room and slamming the door behind her.

Jane watched her leave sadly. She did not wish to cause the girl pain, even though she'd given Will some heartache when he'd first realised her promises were lightly given and not to be trusted. Yet she'd spoken only the truth. Viscount Hargreaves was a man who many young girls might break their hearts over, but he needed to marry a fortune and could not afford a young lady with only seven thousand pounds to her name.

Melia apologised later that day and a wary truce was called between them. Jane did her best to mend the breach, but could not think it was so easily done. Melia wanted to live in London and to continue the round of parties and dances that would go on all year, but that would mean accepting a man who wished for the same kind of life and Jane did not think that Adam Hargreaves or Captain Smythe was interested in living permanently in town. However, there was nothing more she could say and it was up to Melia to decide what she wanted from life now.

At the card party they attended that evening, Jane was happy to see that Melia joined her friends, Miss Smythe and her brother, and appeared to spend a noisy happy time with them. She seemed in better spirits than earlier and told Jane that Captain Smythe was taking her riding the next morning. Jane nodded and smiled and they parted on good terms.

Sarah had taken the news that they were leaving for the country in much better heart. She looked pleased and made a list of everything she'd seen that she wished to purchase and went shopping with Jane that morning. They bought material, books, sewing items for embroidery, sweet bon-bons, soaps and perfumes and many small luxuries that were not available in the country.

'We shall have so many trunks that we shall need another coach to carry them all,' Sarah said and laughed. 'Oh, I have enjoyed my stay, Jane. I cannot thank you enough for all you have done and given me.'

'It gave me so much pleasure,' Jane said and then her heart caught as she saw the gentleman walking along the street towards them. It was clear that he had seen her and immediately came up with them, a smile on his face. 'Lord Frant, I am glad to see you return. I was afraid we should miss you, for we go home next week.'

'Ah, that is unfortunate,' Paul said and looked regretful. 'Business has kept me from your side too long— but perhaps I may call on you in the near future? I hope that things will be settled soon enough.'

'You are very mysterious,' Jane said and gave him

her hand. He held it to his lips briefly and her heart fluttered as she saw the fire burning deep in his eyes. He did care for her—he must! If not, he was a heartless flirt to look at her so. 'You have been sorely missed, sir.'

'As have you,' he said. He smiled as he saw all their packages. 'I see you have been busy. May I walk with you and assist in the carrying of all these trifles?'

'This is only a part of the whole,' Sarah told him. 'Many of our purchases are to be delivered. We were just about to seek an ice or some coffee, were we not, Lady March?'

'Then allow me to treat you both to an ice at Gunter's.' Paul smiled at them both, though his gaze lingered longer on Jane's face. 'Perhaps we may go to the theatre together, all of us, before you leave town?'

'We are free this evening,' Sarah told him, a hint of mischief in her voice.

'Then I shall arrange it,' Paul murmured. 'Thank you, Miss Sarah, you are very good to aid me so—theatre and supper later it shall be.'

Jane had planned to spend the evening at home because it was a rare thing in London to have no engagements, but she accepted the invitation with pleasure and her heart lifted at the thought.

Perhaps there would be a moment or two for them to speak alone...

Jane was surprised to find that Melia had brought guests to take luncheon with them for she had not mentioned her intention earlier. However, she smiled and welcomed Miss Smythe and then her brother.

'I feared we might impose on you,' Captain Smythe said, 'but Melia insisted that you should be the first to hear her news—she has done me the very great honour to say that she will become my wife...'

Jane was stunned for she could never have expected it. Surely Melia had given no indication of her intention to accept the young man's proposal? However, she recovered quickly and congratulated them both and then called the butler, sending him for champagne to celebrate.

'I know I must speak with Lord Frant,' the young man said, looking very happy and a little bemused, as if he had not quite expected this himself. 'I hope that he will think me worthy...'

Since Captain Smythe was of good family, not fabulously wealthy but rich enough to not care about his wife's dowry, Jane could not think that her guardian would have any objections. He would, no doubt, be grateful to see her well settled and happy.

'I am happy for you both,' Jane said and kissed Melia's cheek. 'I think it a good match for Melia—and I am certain her family will think the same. Lord Frant is in town, I know, for we spoke no more than twenty minutes since.'

'Then I shall take my leave and call on him,' Captain Smythe said and inclined his head.

'Will you not stay to luncheon?' Melia begged, dimpling at him.

'No, for I would have this settled. I shall return later, if I may, Lady March—and we shall settle details of our visit to my parents and your aunt. Come, sister. We

must leave these good people to their luncheon and return later…'

After they had gone, Jane looked at Melia. 'It is a
good match for you, Melia—but are you happy with it?'

'Yes, of course I am,' the girl replied but her eyes
did not meet Jane's.

Jane said no more on the subject, but told her and
then her brother when he came in a few minutes later
of their arrangements for the evening.

'I shall not accompany you,' Will said, 'but you have
no need of me if you are with Frant.' His eyes dwelled
for a moment on Melia's flushed face. 'I must wish you
happy, Melia. I am sure you will be… Captain Smythe
is a decent man.'

'Will, I…' She hung her head and could not continue,
but Will took her hand and smiled.

'We are still friends, Melia. You never promised to
wed me, merely to consider the idea. You have broken
no promise to me—and I hold no grudge against you.'

Melia laughed in relief and said, 'We should not suit,
Will. I like the town too much and you prefer the country—Captain Smythe is an officer and I shall enjoy
living in married quarters, for there are parties and
regimental balls. For now, he is based in town, but his
regiment may soon remove to Bath for some months.'

'You will enjoy a military life,' Will agreed and
turned away.

After that the conversation was general. After lunch
Will left them to keep an appointment with some friends
and the ladies went up to their rooms to rest or write letters. Jane had changed into an afternoon gown of coral

silk when Captain Smythe and his sister returned. It was clear that the news was good and they had made plans to visit their parents in the country almost immediately.

'We shall leave before the last ball of the season,' he informed them. 'I cannot wait to introduce Melia to my family, and my sister will accompany us—and we shall invite Mrs Bellingham to stay if she so wishes...'

'I am very glad everything has worked out well for you both,' Jane said. Melia's sulks had disappeared completely and she seemed perfectly happy to leave town, knowing that after her wedding she would return as the captain's wife.

'Lord Frant invited us to accompany you to the theatre this evening,' Captain Smythe went on, his enthusiasm carrying all before him. 'However, I want to take Melia to meet my grandmother and so we shall go to her house this evening...'

Jane could only smile and agree and feel relieved when sister and brother had taken their leave so that she could prepare for the evening. Her own thoughts were only for the pleasure that lay ahead and the hope she would have a little time alone with Paul Frant...

'You look beautiful this evening,' Paul said when he greeted her, presenting her with a small nosegay of red roses. 'I have missed seeing you, Jane. I hope that one day soon I shall see much more of you.'

She smiled and murmured her thanks, holding the roses delicately to her nose to smell their scent, but could not say what was in her heart and, despite his compliments and his attentions to her that evening, he did not say the words that would make it possible for her to open her heart to him.

The play was a comedy by Sheridan and well received by the audience, and the music and dancing that followed was pleasant. It was only as they were leaving the theatre after the performance that Jane's gaze was drawn to a lady and gentleman she knew: Lady Catherine and, with her as her escort, Captain Hershaw. She had no other chaperon and that seemed odd since she was engaged to be married to another gentleman.

Captain Hershaw seemed unaware of her but Lady Catherine saw her and her eyes narrowed, a look of something that could only be dislike or anger in her eyes. Jane inclined her head slightly and was given a frosty nod in return, but then Paul spoke and Jane turned to him. When she turned back the pair had gone, mingling with the crowd as the theatre emptied.

The four of them ate supper together in a discreet restaurant and enjoyed each other's company, Sarah and Will seeming to find a great deal to talk and laugh about. On being told that Melia and Captain Smythe were not to be of the party, Jane's brother had decided to accompany them after all.

'Your cousin is a pleasant girl,' Paul said softly when the other two were laughing at some jest of their own. 'Your brother seems happier than he was a few weeks ago.'

'How observant of you,' Jane replied in the same hushed tone. 'I think they like each other but it is early days yet, of course.'

'Of course.' Paul looked into her eyes with such long-

ing that her heart caught. 'Would that I was free to follow my heart, Jane. I long to speak but I may not for
the moment. Indeed, it would have been wiser had I not
come at all this evening, but I could not forgo the pleasure of being with you...forgive me if I seem reluctant
to be plain, but I may not speak openly yet.'

'You do seem to speak in riddles,' Jane said and
frowned, for she did not care for this mystery. 'If something troubles you, I would be happy to listen.'

'You are everything that is lovely and precious to
me,' Paul told her. 'Yet I have good reason to keep my
silence—but know that I care for you deeply. If I could
I would ask you to be my wife.'

What impediment could there be to his asking her to
be his wife if he really wished for it? Jane was puzzled
but, even though her honest nature would have preferred
things to be plain, she sensed that his secret was something he felt unable to share with her.

She touched his hand. 'I see that you are sorely troubled, my friend. I must tell you that I value your friendship and perhaps more, but if there is some barrier...'
She was puzzled for he seemed so strange.

'One that I hope may soon be overcome,' Paul replied and pressed her fingers. 'Now, may I order more
champagne?'

'No more for me. I think perhaps we should be leaving.' She looked across the table, catching her brother's
eyes. 'Are we ready to leave, Sarah—Will?'

'Yes, quite ready,' Sarah said. 'It has been an exciting day and I grow a little tired.'

It was agreed that they should leave and Lord Frant

called for his account and asked that the carriage should be brought round. Sarah and Will seemed content and did not say much as they were driven home but, after they had gone in, Jane asked if Paul would care for a nightcap before he left.

'Just for a moment in private,' he said and followed her into a small parlour, but, as she would have rung for brandy, he stayed her hand. 'Now that Melia will no longer be with you, I must visit her aunt and make arrangements for the contract for her marriage—and then perhaps I may visit you at home?'

'Yes, certainly you may, Lord Frant. I have already asked Will to invite you for the shooting in September, but if you wish you may call at any time.'

'I would hope to be with you before the month is out,' Paul told her. 'I can only pray that circumstances are more favourable by then...'

'Yet you will not tell me why you are troubled?'

'Jane, my love...' He reached out and drew her against him, looking down into her face for a long moment before he kissed her, softly at first and then with increasing passion. She felt a little shudder run through him as though he controlled his passions. 'I love you beyond reason, have done so since we first met—but I dare not ask you to be my wife until this business is finished...'

Jane felt herself melting into him as he held her close, her lips still warm and tingling from the passion of his kiss. 'I believe that I have come to love you, Paul,' she whispered. 'I did not think it could happen again but, though it is different this time, I know that I care deeply for you.'

'Oh, Jane, my love, I adore you,' Paul said and now she could not doubt it for she saw his love for her blazing in his eyes. 'I vowed to keep my distance to hold you safe, but how can I not speak now when my heart cries out for it? I want you for my wife, Jane—will you be mine, sweet love?'

'Yes, I will marry you—if it is what you truly wish.'

'I wish for it with all my heart, yet I must ask you that our love remains secret for a time—will you do that for me? Will you trust me, Jane? I think it better for your peace of mind that you do not know all my reasons, but hope that you will believe in my sincerity and wait until I can come to you freely.'

'Yes, if you wish it,' she said, for how could she refuse? She was swept away on a tide of happiness. 'I know there must be a good reason for what you do...'

'Believe me when I say I ask for your discretion only because I love you and seek to protect you from those who might seek to harm me through you. I have an enemy, Jane, and, though I am almost certain of his identity, I cannot name him yet.'

'Then I shall tell no one; even my brother and Sarah shall remain in ignorance.'

'Thank you, dearest Jane.' He kissed her softly. 'I shall treasure your promise and will return tomorrow after luncheon to bring you a token of my love...and now I must leave you.'

Jane smiled and kissed his lips and then allowed him to leave her. She was lost in a sweet dream as she walked up the stairs to her own bedchamber. Paul loved her and she knew that she loved in return. The future looked bright, for surely this time she would not be robbed of her happiness…

Leaving her, Paul felt a flickering of unease. He had meant not to speak openly yet of his feelings for Jane. Indeed, it would have been better for her sake if he had not taken her to the theatre—but he had needed to see her and then when she'd smiled his feelings had overcome him. He could only pray that his weakness in speaking would not endanger her safety. Yet surely what had passed between them was unlikely to reach the ears of his enemy…

Jane went shopping in the morning for some items she had remembered she would need when they got home. Paul was not coming until the afternoon and so she seized the last chance she might have to visit various establishments.

On her return she glanced through the visiting cards on the silver salver in the hall, a little surprised to find one from Lady Catherine. Flipping it over, she saw an urgent message.

I must see you privately. Please come to tea at my house this afternoon. I have something I must tell you.
Catherine Radcliffe

Jane stared at the message, frowning over it, for she could not understand why the lady should need to see her urgently. They knew one another but could never have been called friends and Jane had thought the other woman disliked her... But stay, perhaps she feared that Jane would speak of what she'd seen on leaving the theatre the previous evening. The young woman had clung to Captain Hershaw's arm, fluttering her lashes at him and flirting with him—at least until she became aware of Jane's gaze.

Paul meant to call that afternoon and Jane had no intention of perhaps missing him by answering Lady Catherine's summons. She did not wish for private conversation with someone she did not particularly care for. Instead, she would write and tell her that she was too busy to call that day but would be at home the next morning if Lady Catherine wished to see her.

She sent her letter off and spent the time during luncheon talking to Melia of her plans to leave London the next day with Miss Smythe and her brother, and discussing with Sarah any errands that needed doing before they too left London.

Will had promised to take Sarah driving and they left the house soon after the meal was finished. Melia went upstairs to write a letter to her aunt in her room and Jane retired to her parlour to wait for Paul's arrival.

He came at three, looking distinguished in a blue coat, long riding boots and pale breeches, his hat of beaver and bearing a silver buckle at the front. His gloves were of finest leather, his linen pristine and he looked every inch the wealthy gentleman about town.

Jane rose to receive him, holding out her hands. Paul took them and kissed them, and then handed her a flat red leather box. When she opened it she saw a beautiful diamond necklace.

'This is lovely, Paul,' she said. 'But we are not formally engaged; I ought not to accept it.'

'I have ordered a ring to be made, and perhaps tomorrow you could visit the jeweller and have your finger sized,' he said. 'The necklace was my mother's, given her by her father when she married and passed to me when she died. I know she would like you to have it, dearest Jane.'

'Thank you, I shall treasure it,' Jane said and closed the box. She looked up at him. 'I wish I understood why we cannot speak of our engagement to the world.'

'Forgive me—I want to shout it to the rooftops. I ought not to have spoken until these matters were settled, but I have waited too long already and feared to lose your regard. Please try to understand, Jane—it is difficult...'

'Hush, you do not need to tell me,' Jane said, making up her mind that she must trust him. 'You have your reasons and I accept that we must wait...'

'You fill my heart with joy every time I look at you,' he said and moved to take her in his arms and kiss her once more. 'I love you, Jane, and I want to marry you—as soon as it is...possible.'

She sensed that he had almost spoken a different word and wondered at it, but to question every word would show a lack of faith and she let the moment pass. Paul had told her that he loved her and she must accept and believe.

'Then I shall wait patiently for you to come to me,' she said and smiled up into his eyes.

'Tomorrow I have business I must see to,' Paul said, 'and the day after I leave for the country to visit Melia's aunt. I must see the date for the wedding set and talk contracts with her aunt and her husband-to-be—and by then you will be in the country. I may be able to call on you again tomorrow for a few minutes, but cannot be certain, so do not wait in for me.'

'Come if you can,' Jane said. 'You will stay to take tea with me now? Melia will be down shortly, though Sarah and Will have gone for a drive and will not be back until later.'

'Yes, I shall stay. I wish I had no engagements for this evening, but there are people I must see and I am engaged to dine with Major Harding…'

'Ah, yes, I believe he stayed in the country with you when you were last there?'

'Yes—and I was very glad to have him. If he had not…' Paul shook his head. 'I may have been wrong to ask you to tell no one of our understanding, Jane. You should feel free to tell your cousin and Will…perhaps your mama, if you wish? Yet it would be better if it went no further than your immediate family.'

'My brother and Sarah,' Jane said and smiled. 'I do not think Mama needs to know at this time because she would swear to keep it private and then tell everyone— and nor does Melia. She is a friend but no more and… she might not keep our secret.'

'No, she might not,' Paul agreed. 'I shall speak to your brother when I visit you at your home.'

'Yes, he will expect it,' Jane said. 'I am of an age to please myself in the matter of marriage, but my brother would think it a courtesy, I know.'

'I shall have your ring when I come down,' Paul said, 'but…' He broke off as Jane shook her head and realised that they were no longer alone. Turning, he saw Melia standing just inside the door.

'Forgive me,' Melia said. 'I did not wish to intrude, Jane, but I thought you might be waiting tea for me.'

'And so we were,' Jane said, smiling at her. 'Please come and sit down, my dear, and I shall ring for tea. Lord Frant wanted to speak to you, I believe. He intends to follow you down to the country in order to speak to your aunt about the wedding preparations…'

'Yes, I am sure my aunt will wish to discuss them with you, sir,' Melia said, but she did not look at him and Jane thought there was a sulky look about her mouth again, almost as if she had begun to regret her promise to wed Captain Smythe.

Chapter Thirteen

Jane was writing letters in her private parlour the next morning when the door was suddenly thrust open and Lady Catherine walked in, followed by a harassed maid, who apologised to Jane.

'Milady insisted, ma'am,' she said. 'I asked her to wait but…'

'It's all right, Tilly,' Jane said calmly. 'You may go. I was expecting Lady Catherine…' She stood up and greeted her guest with a smile and extended hand. 'I am pleased to see you, Lady Catherine.'

'Are you?' the other woman said rudely. 'I quite expected to be refused entry after your note.'

'Forgive me, I expected guests and could not come to meet you, as you asked.'

'You might be sorry that you did not. I've been told your guest was Lord Frant—and when you hear what I have to tell you, you may wish you had not been at home to receive him.'

Jane was puzzled. 'I'm sorry. I have no idea what you mean.'

'Have you not heard the latest gossip concerning Lord Frant?' Lady Catherine's eyes gleamed with spite. 'I know you two have been close so perhaps that is why you have not been told…'

'Told what?' Jane asked, her gaze narrowed. She had coldness at her nape and knew that she would not care for whatever it was that this woman had come to tell her.

'You may think Frant intends marriage,' the lady said and a cruel smile played over her mouth as she taunted, 'but you shall be sadly disappointed if you hope to be his wife. No decent woman could consent to marry him now…'

Jane's fists clenched at her sides, but she refused to be drawn. Lady Catherine had come here hotfoot to tell her this news but Jane would not press her.

'Don't you want to know?' The other woman laughed. 'Oh, you think yourself so secure—but I had this from Lady Moira, and she has been in his confidence…as well as from other lips…'

'Lady Moira was to have been Miss Bellingham's chaperon but Melia chose to stay with me. I do not see what you think so amusing in this…'

'Lady Moira told me herself. She was shocked when she heard it and confronted him, for she would never have agreed to chaperon the girl in the first place if she'd known…'

'Melia is a perfectly respectable young lady,' Jane said, feeling angry; although the girl had hurt Will she would not allow her character to be besmirched.

'It is not the girl but Lord Frant himself…' Lady Catherine's eyes gleamed with malice as she chose her words with deliberate spite. 'Lady Moira has been told by someone who knows the facts that he was married to a girl…a half caste Indian whore…'

'Ridiculous!' Jane said. 'Paul would never…' Her words stuck in her throat because Paul had spoken of circumstances that prevented his announcing their engagement or marrying her. 'He couldn't be married to a girl of that class…'

'Oh, she isn't of the lower class,' Lady Catherine said with great satisfaction. 'Her mother was the daughter of an earl but she became an Indian prince's concubine and her daughter is a whore—she gave birth to Lord Frant's child soon after he left India. It seems she claims he wed her in secret and she named him as her child's father…'

'No, I do not believe you,' Jane said. She refused to believe the other woman's spiteful words; they must be spoken out of malice, for there was no other reason to come here and speak so to her. 'Paul does not have a wife or…a child…'

She looked proudly at Lady Catherine. 'I do not know what you hoped to gain by coming here this morning, but you have failed if you believed I would listen to your lies. I do not know the truth of the matter, but I am certain Lord Frant would not have left his wife in India, nor would he have kept her existence a secret.'

'Men are all deceivers,' Lady Catherine said coldly. 'You may believe what you wish, Lady March—but I have been your friend in this by coming here. People are whispering about the way he is received here. You have no chaperon and you have been to his house with just his ward. Some say you are his mistress—a single gentleman and you still too young to be a true chaperon to any girl…'

'I hope I know Lord Frant well enough to be certain that it is perfectly proper for his ward and her chaperon to visit during the morning hours.' Jane raised her head proudly. 'We were hardly alone, for there were servants present. You will please leave my house, Lady Catherine. I have no wish to continue this conversation.'

'You will learn soon enough,' the other woman said. 'Be careful that you do not lose your reputation in the meantime. Believe me when I say that several ladies believe you to be his mistress. If you continue this way you may find you are not welcome everywhere, as you have been in the past.'

Jane took a step towards her. She was seething with anger and wanted to slap Lady Catherine's sneering face but held her temper in check, her hands clenched at her sides.

'Leave now or I shall ring for a footman to escort you from the house.'

'I'm leaving…' The other woman laughed scornfully. 'At least I know what I'm getting when I marry. I shall give the marquis an heir and take as many lovers as I choose—but I shall not be fool enough to lose either my heart or my reputation…'

Jane stood frozen to the spot as Lady Catherine swept from the room. Tears were burning her eyes but she refused to let them fall, despite her humiliation. She stood motionless for some minutes and then sank down to her chair. It couldn't be true—Paul could not have a wife in India and a child…

He would not have spoken to her of love if that were the case. She could not believe him so false and yet…he had begged her to keep their attachment secret for the moment. He had seemed so strange but she'd thought he was telling her his own life might be at risk when he'd spoken of an enemy.

Slowly, the tears began to trickle down her cheeks. For a while she left them unchecked, but then she dashed them away. She would not let Lady Catherine's spite hurt her because she believed it arose from jealousy. The night they'd all met on the balcony at the duchess's ball, Jane had seen something in the other woman's eyes. Lady Catherine had tried to make Paul notice her that night but he hadn't; his eyes had been only for Jane, and that would have aroused the other woman's ire. She was used to attention and to getting what she wanted—but was that enough to make her come to Jane with a vicious rumour?

That was all it could be—just a rumour. Paul loved her, Jane, and he would never do anything to hurt her… and yet he had told her that he was not yet free to wed her…

Might it be that he needed to free himself of a wife he no longer cared for? No, no, that was dishonourable and cruel and Jane could not love a man who would treat a woman who loved him thus.

Getting to her feet, Jane went slowly from the room. The housekeeper called to her as she began her ascent of the stairs but she did not answer. She needed a little time alone in the privacy of her bedroom.

'Thank God I caught you before you left,' Major Harding said. Paul was dressed for visiting and on the point of leaving to keep his promise to Jane. He'd had little time for anything these past few days, but intended to spend the afternoon with her, even if it meant he left some work undone.

'Something wrong?' Paul asked with a lift of his brows. 'I was just on my way to visit Lady March. You could walk with me if you chose.'

'I think you need to hear this,' his friend said, 'and in private—it's being whispered of all over town. A scurrilous lie, I am sure, but you should hear it, if only to be prepared…'

Paul sat down and invited the major to sit, but he continued to stand, looking uncomfortable.

'They say you have a wife…and she a royal bastard of mixed blood…in India. Apparently she had a child soon after you left and named you as the father. She claims to have married you in secret…'

'That is a lie,' Paul said but felt as if a jug of cold water had been thrown over him. 'Annamarie is not my wife—and I have never lain with her. The invitation was there but never taken up.'

'I have no doubt you speak the truth, but you know what the gossips will make of such a tale as this…' Jack Harding hesitated. 'Unfortunately, it is not the worst of what they are saying…'

'Go on,' Paul said grimly. 'Get it out, man.'

'They are linking Lady March's name with yours and whispering that she has been too free, visiting your house without a proper chaperon and allowing you access to hers... They begin to hint that she is your mistress...'

'Damn their wicked tongues to hell!' Paul said furiously and jumped to his feet. 'I care little for what they say of my having a wife in India. It is not true and I can prove it—though if Annamarie had a child it would be harder to prove I was not the father...' He struck one fist into the other. 'I should like to strangle whoever started the rumours...'

'Lady Moira told me what people were saying. She pretended not to believe it, but there was something about her manner...'

'I thought her a friend, but when I told her that I no longer needed her services for Melia she was angry—but I cannot think she made up the tale. How would she know of Annamarie? No, someone who knew me in India has done this...'

'We knew you had an enemy. He has tried to kill or injure you three times now. Once on the way home from Newmarket, in Ireland—and again in the country, when your saddle was tampered with...'

'Fortunately, you suspected something and discovered it before we went riding that day...' Paul was thoughtful. 'Yes, we knew I had an enemy who wanted me dead—but this is different. It is spiteful and meant to hurt another as much as I...'

'Yes, I detect a woman's hand in this,' his friend said. 'Which lady have you so mortally offended?'

'I have no idea,' Paul said. 'I knew Lady Moira was not pleased to be told she was not needed as Melia's chaperon—but there is no one else…' He paused, his gaze narrowed and thoughtful.

'You have thought of someone?'

'Lady Catherine…' Paul said. 'I thought it of no importance, but she did make the attempt to engage my interest on more than one occasion. I greeted her politely but could not give her the attentions she craved.'

'Lady Catherine is a flirt and proud, too spoiled for her own good. Yet how would she know of this girl in India?'

'I do not see how she could—unless…' Paul stared at him. 'I saw her the other evening at the theatre with Hershaw.… He followed me from India by the next ship, I think…'

'Then I think we have our answer.' Jack smiled grimly. 'Adam is in Ireland and could not have tampered with your saddle—and he certainly has not been seen in town with Lady Catherine.'

'Yes, I begin to think I wronged Adam even to consider that he meant me harm,' Paul said. 'It was something Melia said to me… I thought he had told her lies and that made me believe he might have had a hand in the bungled shooting…'

'Your ward? She has no cause to hate you or spread malicious rumours?'

'No sensible cause, though she thinks I did not give her a large enough dowry—or she did, but now she is to marry someone else and has forgot she ever wanted Hargreaves…'

'Then I think we should concentrate our efforts on Hershaw,' Jack said and Paul nodded.

'He is the most likely to be behind this latest attempt to bring me harm. Three attempts to kill me have failed, and now he thinks to ruin me by casting filth on my reputation. I shall find a way of letting it be known that I am not married and the child is not mine.'

'I doubt you will be believed, as far as the parentage of the child is concerned,' Jack warned him. 'The men will not blame you for that—but the women may not wish to welcome you as warmly as they did.'

'It is Lady March I think of,' Paul said. 'If it were not for the whispers concerning her, I should ignore them and let them do their worst.'

'Yes, it is her reputation that I care for too,' Jack said grimly. 'I shall do my best to scotch the rumours, believe me.'

'Thank you, my friend. I care not for the wagging tongues of spiteful women—but I would not have Jane hurt for all the world and, as for the other business, I think we must lay a trap for my enemy...'

Jane washed her face and changed into a walking gown of dark green, which she wore with a velvet bonnet tied with ribbons to match her gown. A silk shawl was draped over her shoulders. She had refused luncheon, telling her housekeeper that she had a headache and asking to be left alone, but now she needed to go out in the fresh air. Sarah would accompany her if she wished it, but Jane needed to be alone.

Sitting on her bed had not served. She was in too

much agitation to settle or sleep, and now her head really had started to ache. One thing she was certain of: she could not receive Paul that afternoon if he called—so she must make her escape and give herself time to think before she spoke with him again.

He would no doubt wonder why she had gone out rather than receiving him as she had expected to do, but Jane did not feel like asking the questions that raced through her mind. Paul had spoken of love and trust and she wanted to trust him, but it was difficult to forget the gleam in Lady Catherine's eyes. Clearly, she had enjoyed passing on the shameful gossip—for if Paul had deserted his Indian wife when she was carrying his child, he had behaved badly.

Yet would he have spoken to her of marriage if the stories were true? Jane could not believe it, but her treacherous mind would not let it go. She loved him and she ought to trust him, because with love came trust—and if it did not could it be true love?

Leaving the house, Jane told her footman that she would be back in time for tea. She did not want her family to worry if they discovered her room empty, but she wanted neither company nor sympathy and she was afraid that her emotions would show too easily. She felt as if her heart would break because she was tortured by her doubts.

What had Paul meant when he said he was not free to marry her yet? He wanted her, loved her, but he had asked her to keep their understanding secret—what honourable man would do that?

The thoughts kept going round and round in her head

and she could find no answers to her questions. She wanted to believe that his reasons were honest and that he was not the man Lady Catherine had implied. *Her* motive was easy to read, Jane thought. She'd wanted Paul for herself. Although promised to a man much older and with a respected title, she would have jilted him, had the opportunity arisen for her to marry a man as wealthy as Paul. He might not have the marquis's title but he had youth and strength and his fortune was vast, so it was said… Yes, Jane could think of reasons why both Lady Moira and Lady Catherine might want to spread poisonous lies…but why had Paul wanted to keep their engagement a secret?

If it were not for that, Jane would have dismissed the whole story as nonsense, for she could not believe Paul would seek to keep such a scandal from Society. It was almost certain to leak out if there was any truth in it. Only a fool would believe they could keep such a secret and Paul was not a fool. Indeed, she found him intelligent, amusing and honest…and she was the fool to let Lady Catherine distress her.

Jane found that she was heading for the park. It was a pleasant afternoon and she felt that a good brisk walk would help to clear her head, both of the headache and her doubts. All she knew of Paul was telling her that she should trust him and yet it was hard not to let the doubts creep in… If only she could be certain that he truly cared for her…

If she was sure that Paul loved her Jane would care little for the gossip. Some of the more spiteful ladies might watch her to see if she quickened with child but her friends would dismiss the tales of her being Paul's mistress as nonsense. Yes, perhaps she had been a little careless, calling at his house with just Melia—but the girl was his ward, and Jane had been married previously. She was not a vulnerable young girl. Surely only those with nasty minds would make anything of such meetings. There had been nothing clandestine in them, for Paul's servants had been in the house and Viscount Hargreaves and Melia…

Entering the park, Jane saw an acquaintance and nodded to her, but the woman looked through her. She sighed because the dowager Lady Benbow was a stickler and just the sort who would cut Jane if she believed the rumours. Oh, well, there was nothing to be done. She would simply have to ride out the storm and hope at the end she would still be accepted into the homes of her friends.

It was very hot. Jane felt beads of sweat on her brow and more trickled down her back. She headed for the trees because it would be cooler there and she was not yet ready to walk home. In her haste to leave the house she'd forgotten her reticule and had no money with her, so that meant she must walk all the way home again. Had she thought, she might have taken a cab when she was ready to return…though she could ask the cab to wait and ask her footman to pay for her. Yes, perhaps she would do that when she was ready, but for the moment she would simply walk in the shade.

She had been strolling, lost in thought, for almost half an hour when she heard a sound behind her. Turning, she gazed into the face of a man she knew and a shiver ran down her spine as she saw the look in his eyes. It was a look of malice and intent to harm.

'What do you want?' she asked, looking about her as she took a step back. 'Have you been following me?'

'Yes, of course, for weeks, but I never expected you to make it so easy for me. Lady Catherine must have done her work better than she knew...'

'That was you?' Jane gasped and moved back. 'Why did you send her—what did you hope to gain?'

'Exactly what I have,' he replied and grinned. 'You alone and vulnerable. There is nothing like sowing doubt in a woman's mind to make her do something foolish—but I thought you would be harder to deceive...'

'Get out of my way,' Jane cried defiantly. 'It was all lies. I know Paul doesn't have a wife...' But her words ended abruptly as a cloth was placed over her nose and mouth from behind and she felt herself losing her senses. She was falling...falling, though she did not know it, into the arms of the man who had followed her.

'Forgive me, my lord,' the viscount's footman said when he admitted Paul to the parlour. 'I believe Lady March went out earlier. If you would care to wait I shall make enquiries as to whether she has returned. Perhaps some refreshment while you wait?'

'Nothing, I thank you. I thought Lady March was expecting me. Did she say when she was to return?'

'I will enquire for you, sir.'

Paul stood looking out at the rear gardens, frowning because he had expected Jane to be here. Surely she knew he meant to call and spend some time with her before he left town? Why would she have gone out when she knew she would have company—unless Lady Catherine had been here before him? No, that would not make her leave the house. Jane must know it was a wicked lie—surely she did?

He turned as someone came into the room and he recognised a footman he'd seen before on his visits to the house.

'Lady March went out two hours ago, my lord. She said that she would be back in time for tea…'

'Ah, I see…' Paul looked at his watch. Perhaps Jane had an errand and did not expect him until then. 'I shall leave and return later…'

He was frowning as he walked from the house. He would call into his club and make the situation clear to one or two trusted friends who could be relied upon to refute the scurrilous lies that were circulating. Just as he reached it, however, he saw someone coming out and looked at him in surprise.

'Adam, you here?' he said. 'I thought you settled in Ireland?'

'Yes, I am, but there was a small matter of business that my lawyers wanted me to settle. I intend to return this evening. Our horses are being well cared for, Paul. There is nothing to concern yourself with…'

'I was just surprised to see you,' Paul said and placed a hand on his arm. 'You were in the club—did you hear a rumour concerning me?'

'If you mean that nonsense concerning Annamarie, I told the man who uttered it that I would knock it down his lying throat if he said such a thing again. I know you did not marry her—nor is the child yours…'

'Then she has a child?' Paul wrinkled his brow. 'I can scarce believe it.'

'If there is a child I have heard nothing of it—though there could be one,' Adam said. His expression changed to one of anguish. 'I cannot tell you here; it is too public. I never intended anyone to know, but now I must tell you. Where can we go to talk in private?'

'Come home with me, Adam, and I will listen to your story.'

'I should have told you sooner, but she begged me not to…'

'Come, my friend, walk with me and we shall speak in private…'

'I fear you will think the less of me once you know the truth.'

'We are friends,' Paul said. 'You saved my life on board ship when I lay ill of a fever—and I might have died that night as we returned from Newmarket. I believe you are not my enemy, though there were moments when I wondered.'

'And I gave you cause,' Adam said. 'I was bitter and resentful when I learned the true extent of my father's debts—but there were other reasons, as you will soon learn…'

'I wish you had told me this sooner,' Paul said when Adam had finished his story. 'I always sensed that you cared for Annamarie—but you told me she would not look at you…'

'For a long time that was true,' Adam said and grimaced. 'She wanted you, but one night after she learned
that you had booked your ship for England, she came to
me and...' He faltered, his voice caught with emotion.
'She declared that it was always I that she had loved
and she gave herself to me. Yet afterwards she cried
bitter tears and I knew that it was you she truly loved.'

'I could never love her, though I felt sympathy for
her, caught between two worlds and never belonging
to either.'

'When she learned that I had become the viscount
she begged me to wed her and told me that she was
with child—my child...though I wasn't sure whether
she lied...' Adam hesitated. 'She believed that I would
be rich and would send for her to come to me here...
and I promised she would be received in society as my
wife...'

'So when you learned you had nothing you resented
what I had...' Paul looked at him hard. 'Knowing that
Annamarie was your wife, why did you let my ward
think you cared for her?'

Adam had the grace to look ashamed. 'I suppose I
wanted to punish you a little for having everything that
I wanted and I knew that you were concerned for her...'

'Not the action of a gentleman,' Paul said severely.
'You might have broken her heart.'

'I doubt she has one to break,' Adam said. 'She is
a flighty little madam, Paul—yet I should not have let
her think I cared. There is only one woman I have ever
loved—but when she learns that I have only a small
house in Ireland and a share in your racing stables...'

'If she loves you, it will be enough for her, Adam.'

'No. Annamarie loved you. I was second best and she took me only because she'd given herself to me in a fit of pique and feared the consequences. She will not want me when I tell her I have nothing to give her...'

Paul turned from him and took a few paces about the room, his thoughts working furiously. 'There is a way you might appease her,' he said. 'It is not what she hoped for or what you might wish...but it is a way for you to do what is right, Adam.'

'If you can tell me what I need to do then I shall do it,' Adam said. 'I have racked my brain, but I can find no solution—my wife would never consent to live in Ireland.'

'Yet she might be content to remain in India in her own palace—the palace I was given as a reward for saving the Prince's life...'

Adam stared at him in disbelief. 'You would do that for me? I could not ask it of you, Paul. I do not deserve such generosity...'

'No? You saved my life.' Paul smiled oddly. 'I have no need of pink palaces, my friend. My future is here in England—but if it can be of use to you...and it seems I owe a debt to Annamarie, though it was not of my making. Yet if my rejection of her made her come to you as she did then I share the responsibility...'

'She will never love me as she loved you but I have a title and if we live in a palace I think she will accept her fate.'

'All my lands there will be under your care and you will be my agent. I shall trust you, Adam, and in caring for my business affairs in India you will find both respect and wealth for yourself.'

'I can never thank you enough.' Adam squared his shoulders. 'As for the money you let me think was mine to invest in the land in Ireland—the stables are yours, Paul. As soon as you find another partner to take my place I shall return to India.'

'First there is something you may do for me,' Paul said and smiled. 'You may come with me and tell Lady March the truth of your marriage to Annamarie...'

'Yes, of course. When would you have me visit her?'

'Come with me now,' Paul invited. 'She should be at home now—and do not look so chastened, Adam. I've always suspected that you loved Annamarie. I am sure she will be happy when she has your child and you beside her. As for any coolness between us, it is forgotten now that you have told me the truth.' Paul smiled wryly. 'I do understand the power of love, my friend, and I think at times it makes a man lose all reason.'

'Indeed, you are right.' Adam looked rueful. 'Yes, I shall tell Lady March, and I must also see Miss Bellingham and beg her pardon if I led her on...'

'There is no *if* about it,' Paul said severely. 'Yet it hardly matters now, for she is to marry Captain Smythe and I truly hope she will be happy...though, as you said, she is flighty and it would not surprise me if she leads him a merry dance, but that will not be my concern...'

Chapter Fourteen

'Did Jane say nothing to you of her reasons for going out?' Will asked of Sarah as she came back to the parlour and told him that Jane was not in her room. 'It is unlike her to go off on her own like this without telling anyone.'

'She told John that she would be back for tea and it is now half past four,' Sarah replied. 'I have not seen her since she said she had a headache…'

'I know that my sister likes to walk when she has a headache, but it is so rare that she does—and she ought to have been home by now…'

'My lord—Viscount Hargreaves and Lord Frant are here.'

Will frowned at his butler, and then inclined his head. 'Pray show them in, if you please. Perhaps they may have some news of Jane…'

'Salisbury,' Paul said and held out his hand, 'I was hoping to see Lady March—she has returned from her walk?'

'No, she has not and I grow anxious,' Will replied. 'It is so unlike her to go off alone and not tell anyone where she is going…'

'I fear you have good cause to worry,' Paul said and handed him a piece of crumpled paper. 'I was about to leave my house when this was delivered—by an urchin who immediately ran off, I'm told.'

Will scanned the paper and then stared at him in bewilderment. 'Why was this sent to you, sir? If my sister has been kidnapped, the demand for her ransom should surely have been addressed to me?'

'We had not yet got round to announcing our intentions to the world,' Paul replied. 'I see I must be plain with you—I asked Jane to be my wife and she accepted me, but I begged her to keep it secret for a while.'

Will was puzzled. 'I do not see why you need to keep it a secret—unless you meant until you had told the family?'

'No, sir. It was more serious than that…though I had not told Jane. Would that I had warned her to be careful of him, but I did not imagine that he would do such a vile and desperate thing as to kidnap her.'

'Your enemy?'

'Yes. You may have heard some scurrilous rumours?' Will shook his head. 'No? There is talk of my deserting an Indian wife, who has since had my child. It is a lie, as Adam can confirm, for she is his wife and the child his—but before this there were three attempts on my life. I did not wish to worry Jane so I did not tell her everything, but it was my reason for keeping our understanding a secret—to protect her.'

'Someone knew of it,' Will said, his gaze narrowed. 'Someone must have passed the news on to whoever has used it against you.'

'I have told no one,' Paul asserted. 'If it was learned of, it must have come from Jane or someone here.'

'If my sister said she would keep a secret she would not speak of it, even to me,' Will said and frowned. He glanced at Sarah. 'You did not know?'

'Jane said nothing, but I suspected it,' Sarah said. 'I would never have spoken of it…' She hesitated, then, 'I think Melia might have heard something… She might not have been so circumspect. I believe she could be… spiteful and she was a little jealous of Jane.'

'Yes,' Will admitted. 'I had not realised it until recently, but she was spiteful about Jane and you, Sarah, on occasion. Yet would she have deliberately set out to harm Jane?'

'I doubt she meant to harm her,' Paul said. 'She is thoughtless and probably did not think telling someone could cause harm…'

'But who did she tell—and why should that cause harm to my sister?'

'If she told the man who hates me he would feel it cause to strike against her in order to harm me—this note is proof of that, if proof were needed.'

'You know who this man is?'

'I believe so,' Paul said. 'Years ago I spoke out against him because I believed he was a cheat at the card tables. He was sent away from the regiment on active service and I did not see him for many years—until he returned from India some weeks ago. Yet I would not have believed he could hate me so much—unless he has other cause...'

'Hershaw!' Adam spoke. 'He was not of our regiment, but he came to the region some months before you left...he asked me about you and I told him you had grown rich and powerful because of what you did the night you rescued the Prince from the flames.'

'While you and the others held the tribesmen at bay,' Paul said. 'I have not forgotten your part in the affair, Adam.'

'I but did my job,' Adam admitted. 'You broke down the door of that burning hut; you dashed in and brought out the Prince at some cost to yourself. You deserved the praise and the rewards.'

'But what does this have to do with Jane?' Will demanded. 'Why has she been kidnapped?'

'Because my enemy knows that it is my vulnerable spot. If anything happens to Jane... I do not think, I could bear it.'

'It would kill Mama,' Will said. 'In God's name, why didn't you tell us, Frant? I could have had her watched wherever she went...'

'That was my duty and I believed she was being watched over,' Paul said. 'I came straight here in the hope of finding it a hoax and Jane safe with her family, but I shall seek out those I had paid to watch for her and demand an explanation for this...'

'We must find her,' Will said. 'Jane is my sister. I care for her—as does Sarah and my family. We must get her back unharmed.' He frowned, then, 'You will pay the ransom?'

'I would pay three times over what he demands,' Paul said, 'but I fear he would take the money and laugh in my face—perhaps send her back more dead than alive. No, I must find her and bring her home...'

'How do you expect to do that?' Adam asked, looking grim. 'I shall help you, Paul. Whatever you ask, I am happy to do...but where do we start?'

'I must consult the men I employed to watch her back and mine. One of them should have followed her. It surprises me that he did not report this abduction himself before the rogues could do so themselves...'

'Tell me what I can do to help,' Will said. 'If you need more agents, more men to help you find her, you know I shall do all I can to aid you.'

'Yes, of course,' Paul said. 'For the moment there is nothing you can do but keep your cousin safe. You will hear from me again as soon as I have news. Come, Adam, we have work to do...'

Jane came to her senses slowly. Her head hurt and she was conscious of feeling sick, a dull aching sensation all over her body. As the light in the room strengthened, she could feel soreness at the back of her head and her wrists hurt. She touched one wrist and winced because she could feel where the ropes had chafed against the softness of her skin.

She had been drugged and dragged off to a waiting carriage. Her memory of what happened then was cloudy, but she seemed to recall that she had tried to fight off her captors and almost got away—until one of them had hit her on the back of the head. After that they must have tied her hands, though she had at some time since been released from her bonds.

How long was it since she'd been captured? Jane had no idea, but she thought it must be morning now. There was a faint light coming from the windows, which had thick drapes over them but were not quite drawn together. She rolled over and tried to put her feet to the floor but the feeling of sickness swept over her and she vomited, the foul-smelling bile spilling out of her to the floor. Her mouth tasted as bitter as gall and she thought they had forced her to drink a few sips of something, probably to drug her, as the cloth soaked in some foul mixture, which they'd put over her nose in the first place, had not put her right out. She'd recovered enough to kick the shins of her captor and run, but of course they'd caught her because she'd been disorientated and frightened. Jane had seen real hatred in the eyes of the man who had captured her and she did not think that he intended to let her go. She had not been taken for a ransom.

If she could get to the window and discover where she was… Had they brought her to a house in town or were they in the country somewhere? She listened hard, but could not hear anything that would help her to identify her whereabouts.

She stood up, immediately felt dizzy and fell back onto the bed. It was no use; she felt too ill to even think about making an attempt at escape, even if there was a chance of it.

Jane lay back against the pillows and closed her eyes.

Her head was throbbing. She could not remember feeling this ill before, even when she'd had the influenza.

Hearing a key in the lock of her door, she kept her eyes shut as heavy footsteps came towards her, sensing that there were two men in the room even though she could not see them.

'She's still out. I reckon 'e 'it 'er too 'ard. If she dies it'll be us that swings fer it. Mind me words, Herb, he'll be off scot-free and us'll be for the 'igh toby.'

'He's a rotten swine, the captain,' Herb said. 'I 'ates 'im, but I daresn't do other than wot 'e says. If'n I'd known it was a woman I'd never 'ave gone along of it. But I dare say the devil would 'ave shot me if'n I'd refused 'im.'

'I reckon you'm be right,' the other man said. 'Put the tray down there, Herb. If'n she wakes, she might want a drop of water and a bit of this 'ere cheese. As I says it meself, it's a rare bit o' cheese, that—tasty and fresh.'

'Seems a waste ter leave it if she's gonna croak…'

'He's payin fer it, and there's a pot of soup downstairs. Reckon we'll leave this in case she wakes and have our soup and bread in the kitchen with Sophie.'

'Sophie'll 'ave me guts fer garters if'n this one croaks. She created somethin' awful when she see it were a lady… She says we'll all be 'ung fer this night's work…'

Jane heard the men leaving and locking the door behind them. She opened her eyes cautiously, but she was alone again. Sitting up carefully, she managed to pick up the small jug and pour some liquid into the thick earthenware cup provided. It tasted good, cool and fresh, like spring water. Jane seldom drank water in town that had not been boiled first because it was often contaminated—this water was good and she thought they must be in the country. As if to confirm her thoughts, she heard a cock crowing the hour. Yes, that was a country sound—but they could surely not be too far from town, unless she had been unconscious for more than one night.

Suddenly becoming aware of a need to relieve herself, Jane struggled to first sit up and then to put her feet to the floor. She was still a little unsteady but she managed to walk to the window and pull back the curtains enough to let in some light. Glancing round, she saw the room was furnished with heavy ill-fashioned pieces made by a carpenter rather than a cabinet maker, but there was a rather crude commode chair, and she sighed with relief as she made use of it.

She saw a washstand in one corner, and on examination found water for cleansing herself, a lump of coarse soap and a rough cloth to dry on. It was all of the poorest quality, but the cloth was clean and she was glad of the chance to wash her face and hands. Returning to the bed, she looked at the tray and saw that the cheese and bread were fresh, though the bread was not white but thick dark bread that looked home baked with coarse-grained flour. However, the tiny piece she broke and ate with a morsel of cheese tasted good and she ate half the bread and all the small slice of cheese.

At least she wasn't to be starved, Jane thought. The men who had checked on her sounded reasonable enough, though clearly the kind of rogues who sold their services to a man they feared. She imagined that they would not baulk at murder if she were a man, but the thought of killing a gentlewoman had given them cause for concern—and Sophie sounded as if she might have some influence with at least one of them. It was Sophie she had to thank for the soap and towel, and the bread and cheese. If she had any chance of getting out of here alive, it must be through Sophie—and she would hope that next time food was brought it would be the woman herself.

Jane sat on the bed and hunched her knees to her chest. She knew the name of her captor and she'd seen hatred in his eyes. Right from the time of their first meeting, Jane had been wary of Captain Hershaw but she could not imagine why he wanted to harm her. What had she done that had so offended him?

Yes, she had perhaps made it clear that she did not wish him to make himself free of her brother's house, but was that cause enough for him to abduct her? It seemed so strange that he should look at her in that way—as if he wanted to inflict pain on her...or some-one else.

Was it possible that the person he truly hated was Paul Frant? Jane came to the conclusion in a flash, be-cause it fitted with the rest. Lady Catherine had been at the theatre with Hershaw and she knew they'd been noticed—was it because of that Jane had been told of Paul's wife in India? Had they hoped her distress would lead her to do something foolish? If so, they must be pleased with themselves for she'd walked neatly into their trap.

Her brother would be frantic with worry—and Paul, would he be anxious too? Yes, of course he would. He'd sworn he loved her and she ought to have trusted him and ignored Lady Catherine's lies, for she was now certain that they had been concocted especially for her sake, to make her act foolishly—and that was her own fault. Paul had told her that he wished to keep their attachment secret in case his enemy sought to use her against him—which was exactly what he had done, but it was Jane's own foolish behaviour that had put her into danger. Will often told her that she ought to take a maid when she walked out in town, but she'd laughed and told him she was perfectly safe. While that was probably so in the grounds of their country home, it was clearly not the case in London—but she had not realised she had enemies.

Hearing a sound outside the door, Jane sat on the edge of the bed. She'd eaten food and made use of the water for washing so there was no point in pretending to be asleep.

The door opened and a woman entered. She looked at Jane and nodded, smiling as if she were pleased to see her sitting up and relatively unharmed.

'My man said as he thought you was awake, milady,' she said. 'I came up to see for myself and see to things… he said as you'd been sick earlier.'

'He spoke of Sophie—are you she?'

'Yes, milady, and I must tell you that I was angry with Herb and my brother for bringing you here in that state. It was a wicked thing to do—but you mustn't think too hardly of them, for it was that wicked man as made them do it. He's a rare cruel devil that one and they be fools for havin' to do with such a one as he.'

'Tell me,' Jane said, 'were you once in service to a lady, Sophie?'

'Aye, my lady, I was—and a sweeter, gentler lady was never to be found. I loved her and stayed with her until she died of a fever and they turned me off; 'twas then I married Herb and came here—and there's times I curse myself for a fool. He's not a bad man, milady, but easily led—and my brother was never to be trusted, though as a boy none had a sweeter nature.'

'Do you know what Captain Hershaw intends to do with me?'

'Ah, you know him then,' Sophie said and looked concerned. 'It would be better had you not seen his face for he will not let you go now—for a crime such as he plans the penalty is death at the end of a rope.'

'Do you know why he hates me?'

'I doubt it's you he hates, milady—but the man you care for. My man heard him in his cups one night, vowing to be even with his enemy. He thinks he can deal him a blow through you from which he will never recover.'

'Did your man hear the reason for his hatred?'

'None that he told me, but it seems it was something that happened long ago…'

'Yes, I see,' Jane said and bit her lip. 'I think he means to hold me here to lure Lord Frant to his doom—and then he must kill me too…'

'Aye, 'tis what I suspected from the start, milady.

I've told Herb that if he stands by and does nothing I shall leave him…'

'If you help me to escape I would see you all rewarded for your trouble.'

'I dare say you would, milady, but money won't help my Herb if the captain suspects us.' Sophie gave her a measuring look. 'I would help you but you must play your part—are you brave enough to fight for your life?'

'Yes, I believe so,' Jane said. 'I have never had cause before—but what would you have me do?'

'He has gone somewhere for the moment,' Sophie told her. 'When he returns for his meal he will probably call for drink. I could make sure that he became drunk more quickly than he thinks and when he comes to gloat over his prisoner, as he surely will…you must be ready.' Sophie brought out a heavy iron bar with a hook on the end, used for hanging meat in the kitchen. 'Hide behind the door when he comes and then hit him as hard as you can, but do not drop the weapon for I would not have him know I gave it to you…'

'I shall do as you suggest,' Jane promised and took the weapon from Sophie.

She was aware that even in his drunken state Hershaw would not be easy to knock down and if she attacked him he would most certainly retaliate—and yet she knew it was her only chance, for he could not let her live.

'I wish I could simply let you go now while he's out,' Sophie told her. 'Yet he is an evil man and I fear that he would kill us all.'

'Have you considered that he may do so anyway

when this is over?' Jane said. 'Once you have served your purpose it would be an unnecessary risk to let you live.'

'Yes, I've considered it, but my man thinks he's too useful to the captain,' Sophie said and shook her head. 'I think this mad venture will be the end of us all, milady—but I've done what I can for you and there's an end to it.'

'You know where they've taken her?' Paul stared at Jack Harding with a mixture of disbelief and wonder. 'How—please explain?'

'I happened to see Lady March enter the park yesterday afternoon,' Jack said. 'She looked to be in distress and I wondered if I should go to her and ask what was wrong, but, knowing that you worried for her safety, instead I followed at a distance. For a moment I lost her as she sought the shade of some trees. Forgive me, Paul, it all happened so quickly and they had her before I could do anything. I was unarmed and there were four of them. I thought it best to follow and watch—and that is what I did.'

'Is she in town? A prisoner in some low house?'

'They had a carriage waiting and took her out of town. I had no horse, but I commandeered one from a friend who rode by in the park and followed. The house in which she is a prisoner is some two hours ride beyond the town, a deserted place tucked well away near some sheltering woods. I remained there all night and then I saw two young lads and asked if they would keep watch over the place. If anyone took a woman away they were to follow and discover the new hiding place and one must return to tell me when I came back…'

'Do you think they will do as you ask?'

'Yes, for I gave them half a guinea and promised the other half on my return—and one asked if I needed a groom and I said yes, I would take him if he did as I asked.'

Paul gripped his shoulder. 'We must return at once. I shall send word to Jane's brother and gather my men. I pray God that he has not harmed her.'

'You know who took her then?' Paul nodded grimly. 'It was no surprise to me that Hershaw should be a villain. I have thought it but there was never any proof. He will not be admitted to any house in England again when I have finished with him.'

'If I get my hands on him, he will not live,' Paul muttered. 'If he has harmed her I will see him dead before nightfall.'

'Better to leave him to the law,' Jack cautioned. 'We have enough evidence to hang him now—and I would see justice done.'

A nerve flicked in Paul's cheek and for a moment his hands clenched and then he smiled oddly. 'It is as well you are here, my friend, for I have been in agony all night. I knew not where to search. I feared her already dead and my anger has been building. Yes, the law shall have him—but if they do not take his life I will…'

'We must waste no more time in talking,' Jack said. 'Gather what you need and let us go. The longer she remains in that devil's power, the more likely that he may harm her.'

* * *

It had been a long day for Jane, cooped up in the stuffy bedchamber with nothing to read and only water to drink. Sophie had brought her some soup and bread at midday, but since then no one had been near her. She thought someone had arrived an hour or so earlier, for she heard shouting downstairs, but since then nothing.

How long must she sit here and feel the anxiety gnawing at her stomach? She'd told Sophie that she would use force to protect herself but she knew she would find it difficult to strike hard enough to fell Hershaw, for he was a big man—and she could never bring herself to kill him, even though he might deserve it. She would beat him about the shoulders and body if she could and then make her escape.

As she heard sounds outside her room, her body tensed and she gripped the iron bar tightly, her heart racing with fear. Standing so that she would be behind the door when it opened, Jane took a deep breath. She would only have one chance to escape, for if she attacked and did not succeed she was sure he would kill her.

The door swung slowly back. A man entered and moved towards the bed, looking at the shape Jane had formed beneath the covers.

'Still asleep, bitch?' Hershaw demanded, his voice slightly slurred. Sophie had done her work well, plying him with strong drink and perhaps more.

Jane rushed at him and struck a blow against his back. He gave a yell of pain and rage and turned on her, his eyes blazing. Jane struck out again and caught him

on the shoulder, but it was her last blow for he caught
the bar and held it, wrenching it from her by force of
his superior strength.

'You damned bitch!' Hershaw cried. 'Murder me,
would you? I'll see you in the ground afore the night
is done, but first I'll have a taste of what you give to
him…'

'No!' Jane struggled as he grabbed her by the arms.
'Don't you dare touch me, you filthy brute.' She pushed
him back and then heard sounds in the house. Shouting and screaming and one shot and then Sophie's voice
yelling in anger. Hershaw grinned and looked towards
the door. 'He comes at last—the one I hate…and he
shall see you die before his eyes.'

To Jane's horror, she saw him pull a pistol from inside his jerkin and point it at her. His hand was not quite
steady but his finger was on the trigger. Did he mean
to kill her or Paul first?

She heard voices outside the door. It was flung back
and Paul charged in, armed with two pistols, Jack Harding close behind.

'Stay where you are,' Hershaw warned. 'I shall kill
her before you can get to her, Frant. You may kill me
but come one step closer and she dies first.'

'Don't be a fool,' Paul said and Jane thought that she
had never seen him look so grim. 'I have this place surrounded. You cannot get away. If I don't kill you, one
of my men will…'

'Do you think I care what happens to me once I have
my revenge? You took all from me when you made
those charges against me…and she swore to me that

you had ruined her life. Her child is yours and you plan to marry another…and now I have been told she lies ill on her bed in India because of what you did, her child lost and her mind wandering…'

'If you speak of Annamarie, I am sorry to hear of her tragedy but she was never my wife and I have never laid a finger on her,' Paul said calmly. 'If she lied, it was because she hoped you might do something foolish— but I have only your word that she named me when she knew it was a lie…'

'Damn you, Frant, I loved her and I'll have your life for her pain if I die for it…' Hershaw took a firmer aim, holding his right arm with his left in an effort to keep it steady. His finger was on the trigger when Jane bent to retrieve the iron bar and struck. She brought it down on his arm with all the force she possessed. He screamed in pain and his finger squeezed before the pistol dropped to the floor and the ball embedded itself in the wall. 'You bitch…' He lunged at Jane but before he touched her Paul's pistol spoke and the ball struck his leg. He fell, writhing in pain and cursing them both. 'I should have killed her first…' he muttered and promptly passed out.

'Jane, are you hurt?' Paul asked as he covered the ground between them and drew her into his embrace. 'Forgive me, I should have instructed my men to keep a closer watch, but I did not expect him to abduct you. Oh, my love, I have been so afraid. I knew he hated me, but not the extent of his hatred or the true reason for it.'

'Annamarie—is she the Indian Princess that Lady Catherine said was your wife?'

'Yes. She is very beautiful in her way,' Paul said gravely. 'I think she expects homage and if she does not get it, it makes her angry. I angered her because she made it clear she wished to be my wife and live in my palace but I ignored her—indeed, I am guilty of treating her as though she was a spoiled child. I did not think her capable of such lies…and I pity Hershaw, for she would never have had him. Yet I pity Adam more, for she is his wife…and I must tell him what Hershaw revealed and I know it will cause him pain.'

'And the child is his?'

'Yes, so he claims, but I wonder…'

'Poor Adam,' Jane said softly, for she understood what he meant. This woman who would lie to set one man against another was not to be trusted and her child might already have been conceived before she married him, but it was not for either of them to speculate. 'No wonder he was adamant that he could not marry Melia—and yet it was not kind in him to lead her on…'

'No, and I have told him. I think he regrets it now… as he regrets other things, but he will return to India and live in the palace that I have given him. He will be my agent there, for I shall never return to India. My home is here now, Jane, with you…'

'Oh, Paul, forgive me for causing you so much trouble. I was distressed and did not think what I was doing…'

'Do not think of it,' he said and kissed her softly. 'Come, I shall take you to the carriage and you will return to town with your brother. I must remain here until the magistrates have been and have this rogue under lock and key.'

'Is Will here?'

'Downstairs, seeing to the woman and her husband, I imagine. He knew I should not be satisfied unless I dealt with the rogue myself, though he would have come had I not told him his part was keeping an eye on the others.'

'Be careful, Paul. He would still kill you if he could and he is only unconscious…'

'His men have dispersed,' Paul said. 'Only one of them put up a fight and once Jack fired over his head, he surrendered and begged pardon. He claims he was forced to help Hershaw and I believe him.'

'Yes, I am sure it was so,' Jane said and sighed. 'Must you truly stay?'

'Yes, for my word will be needed; otherwise Hershaw will lay false charges. I must see this thing through, my love—but when all is done I shall come to you and we shall begin to plan our wedding…'

'Was he the reason you wanted to keep our understanding secret?'

'He had already made three attempts on my life— and then he heard from someone that we were promised to each other and changed his plans to include you…'

'Three attempts to kill you…' Jane stared as the horror of it finally hit her and she realised how close they had both come to death. 'You did not tell me.'

'I did not want you to worry for my sake, but I did not suspect that he intended to harm me through you until I was told of the rumours. I made arrangements for someone to watch over you, but for some reason my man did not see you leave your house. But I hardly thought Hershaw would kidnap you and hold you hostage in order to torture me before he killed us both.'

'Paul…he must be evil or mad…'

'Perhaps a mixture of both,' Paul said. 'I believe he had a run of bad luck on the horses recently. He tried to make up for his ill luck at the tables and was caught placing a card he had secreted from his sleeve into his hand. He managed to hush it up, but once the story got round he would have been ostracised and I think he lived by what he managed to win cheating some young fool at the tables.'

'And so he decided to take his anger out on you— is that it?'

'Yes, it seems that way.'

'Who told you all this?'

'Adam told me when he learned of your abduction. One night when Hershaw was in his cups he'd spoken of his misfortunes and blamed you, though his reasons were incoherent…'

'Why did Adam not tell you before?'

'He had his reasons,' Paul said. 'Perhaps he too felt some jealousy, Jane—but it is over now and we are friends again. He will return to India to his wife and I shall stay here and run my stables…and marry you, if you will have me.'

'You know I shall,' she said and kissed his cheek. 'But if Adam is to return to India, how will you manage your stables?'

'Perhaps he will have me for his partner,' Jack said, coming to the doorway to look at them. 'We have them all under control, my friend. The magistrate is on his way—and perhaps Lady March should be if you wish to protect her good name...'

'Yes, of course,' Paul said and gripped Jack's arm. 'Take her down to the carriage, my friend, while I see that he is taken care of...' A moan from the man lying on the floor gave warning that he was coming to his senses. 'I'll bind his wrists and bring him down—and then we'll talk...'

Chapter Fifteen

'Oh, Jane, I am so glad to see you back,' Sarah said and rushed to embrace her. 'I wanted to come to find you, but Will said I must stay here in safety. He would not hear of my coming but I have been so anxious for you all…'

'There was no need,' Will said. 'Between us we had more than a dozen men, all armed and ready to do whatever was required of them, but no blood was spilled—except that of the rogue who began this. He was wounded in the leg and will be lame for what little time remains to him. If my evidence has anything to do with it, he will pay the ultimate price for his perfidy.'

'I am surprised he still lives,' Sarah said. 'I thought one of you would kill him, for you were all so angry—as you should be. He treated you shamefully, Jane.'

'It was through my own foolish fault,' Jane said and laughed as Sarah looked outraged. 'If I had stayed safe inside the house instead of rushing out like a fool he could not have taken me so easily.'

'Yet he would have found a way,' her brother told her gravely. 'If he meant to harm you both he would have waited—and you could not live your life under the shadow of fear, Jane. Had Paul begged you to be careful it would have irked you.'

'Yet he would have done so had he thought it necessary,' she said and smiled. 'No one could have guessed what would happen. I wonder that a man should bear a grudge so many years.'

'Yet perhaps it was because of his run of ill luck of late,' Will said. 'He had nursed various grudges against Paul for a long time yet did nothing. Only when his fortunes fell so low did he think of such wickedness. I am not sure what he hoped to gain from it, but perhaps he thought, as Paul's ward, Melia might inherit his fortune when he died. I believe she would have wed Hershaw had he asked…and with a fortune to call his own he could have done anything. In time he might have seen her dead and returned to India in the hope of securing Annamarie's affections…'

'She must be very beautiful,' Jane said, 'to play on the hearts and minds of so many men—Adam Hargreaves and Hershaw, and who knows what others lie victim to her charms?'

It was in her mind that the beautiful girl had wanted the only man who had resisted her. Yet was Paul completely blind to her charms? For a moment jealousy raised its ugly head, but she squashed it before it could take root. She could not doubt that Paul loved her and she would not let herself wonder any more. Instead, she would think about the future with the man she loved…

* * *

'I suppose you think you have won.' The injured man threw Paul a look of hatred as he was pulled roughly to his feet. The magistrate had taken his evidence and a secure coach was waiting to take the prisoner into custody, yet still he was defiant. 'She promised to reward me if I made you suffer—she wants your life, Frant, and I doubt I'll be the last to be swayed by her.'

'She is another's wife, not mine—and her child was his,' Paul replied. 'Do not blame her for your decisions, Hershaw. She knew of your bitterness and played on it. All that has happened to you has been your own fault, because you resented me and thought to gain great riches from the woman you wanted. I doubt she would have kept her word, for her story was built on lies.'

'Damn you!' Hershaw said and tried to lunge at Paul even though his wrists were bound, but was restrained by the magistrate's men. 'You were always my enemy.'

'No, you were your own enemy,' Paul said and turned away as Hershaw was taken off, cursing and spitting defiance, his injured leg dragging on the ground.

'He will trouble us no more,' Jack said with satisfaction. 'You and your lady may walk in safety now, my friend.'

'Yes. I thank God for it—and you, Jack. Had it not been for your quick wits, I might have been searching for weeks and still not found her.'

'Oh, he would have let you know eventually, for your death was his intention, but she might have suffered in the meantime. I do not like to think what he had in mind this evening.'

'She had found a weapon from somewhere and was defending herself, but I think he must have overcome her resistance in the end.'

'Then it was a mercy we arrived when we did,' Jack said and jerked his head at the woman and her husband, who had been silently watching the proceedings awaiting their fate. 'What do you want to do with this pair? The other rogue ran off when we arrived.'

'That was my brother, sir.' Sophie spoke up. 'It was I gave milady the weapon to defend herself. She came to no harm in this house. We but did what that devil commanded, my lord—he would have killed us all if he'd known.'

'Yes, I imagine so,' Paul said. 'Jane told me that you had helped her and I shall not move against you this time—but the magistrate warned you of your fate if you break the law again.'

'If my man attempts such a thing I'll take my hand to him,' Sophie said and gave her husband such a look that he jerked back as if he believed her.

Paul hid his smile. 'Very well, woman. Keep your man on a leash, because if he ever comes near my lady again I shall kill him.' He turned back to Jack. 'Gather the men. I would return to London and speak with Jane…'

Jane was sitting in her parlour at her writing desk when Paul was announced later that evening. She turned, gave a cry of pleasure and ran to him. His arms opened to receive her, holding her close to him for a moment before he spoke.

'You are safe now, my love. Hershaw is safely locked away and will harm neither of us again. He was a bitter, twisted man and a dangerous enemy, but I did not expect he would use you so ill, Jane.'

'That was my own fault. If I had not allowed Lady Catherine to distress me I should not have laid myself vulnerable to his schemes.'

'She has a vicious tongue and meant to hurt you, but I doubt she knew what lay in his heart, or what he was capable of.'

'No, I am sure she did not. Lady Catherine spoke out of spite and jealousy. I think you must have slighted her, Paul…or I have done something to arouse her hatred.'

'She was at the theatre with Hershaw. Perhaps she thought we might speak of it to her betrothed and spoil her marriage plans, for he was merely an amusement to her. She would not have married him, because she requires a prestigious title and a fortune.'

'I should never have dreamed of such a thing,' Jane said. 'Let us forget her and the other one…though I think her the more dangerous of the two. If Annamarie would move a man to murder because of some imagined slight…'

'It was the reason I could never like her,' Paul said. 'She is proud and beautiful in her way, but I thought her cold of heart. She offered herself to me and I refused her… I knew it angered her but did not imagine she would inspire a man to murder because of it.'

'Yet if he had not already hated you, she could not have done it. Adam loves her and has every reason to feel jealousy, but he does not hate you…'

'No, I must admit that for a while I thought he might be my enemy but, despite knowing that the woman he loves preferred me, he did not turn completely from me. I can only pray that his love for her will overcome her nature—for otherwise I think he will know only unhappiness...'

'What kind of a woman could be so vengeful?' Jane marvelled at it for she could never understand such wickedness. 'I could never urge a man to kill another, even if he had slighted me.'

Paul smiled softly at her. 'I know and it is that precious difference between you that makes me adore you, my sweet Jane. I loved you from the moment we met and if you had not found it in your heart to love me, I should never have married.'

'Oh, Paul,' Jane said, her throat catching. 'You know that I loved Harry. I never thought to love again, but I do—and as deeply. Harry was the mad, sweet love of first youth and you are the man I love now and will love all my life.'

'I thank God for it,' he murmured and bent his head to kiss her lips. 'How soon will you marry me, Jane?'

'We go down to the country soon and you must visit Melia and her aunt or she will think you have deserted her. As soon as you come to me, we shall set the banns and then we can begin our new life together...'

'Yes, you are right,' he said and sighed. 'The responsibilities of a guardian weigh heavily upon me, Jane. I would that I might stay by your side, but I must do my duty.'

'Do what you must and come to me,' she said and

lifted her head so that he could kiss her again. 'I shall look for you every day so do not tarry longer than you need, my dearest one.'

'You have my promise on that,' Paul said. 'We shall spend tomorrow together and then I really must leave for the country—when next we meet it shall be at your home...'

'I will accompany you to Miss Bellingham's home,' Adam said the following evening. 'I must make my peace with her—and then I shall sail for India. I cannot thank you enough for all you have done for me, Paul. You have stood as a good friend to me and there were times that I did not deserve it.'

'You loved a woman you knew had feelings for me and it caused you grief,' Paul said. 'Yet be comforted by the knowledge that I never once laid hands upon her. She is your wife and she must care for you or she would not have come to you that night, nor would she have wed you.'

'She wed me because she was carrying a child.' Adam frowned. 'I think she came to me out of temper and a wish to hit back at you through me—perhaps she thought I would be turned against you, but she never asked me to take your life.'

'You were not Hershaw and would not have done it,' Paul said. 'You had opportunity to see me dead by another's hand, but you did not take it.'

'No, for I am no murderer,' Adam said ruefully. 'I know Annamarie's faults, Paul. She can be both spiteful and cruel, but she has been taught harshly by her father's people when they turned her from the palace after her father's death. Now that she will have a palace of her own and my title, I can provide her with the life she wishes, I believe she will be content. Besides, she is my wife and, if Hershaw speaks the truth, she is desperately ill. If she still lives when I return, I shall do my best to make her happy. I can only hope that illness will have driven the bitterness from her heart.'

Paul kept his silence. He was not sure that Adam would ever find happiness married to the beautiful but vicious woman he so obviously adored, but love was blind. Words would not change Adam's heart nor would he wish to try. Love was a strange but glorious thing, which brought both great happiness and terrible grief. Adam loved his wife despite all and he could only send him on his way in friendship.

'Very well, if you wish to say goodbye to Melia you shall come with me,' Paul said. 'We shall ride together, Adam—and then I shall take my leave of you, because I stay only one day before I join Jane at her home…'

The man looked down at the battered body of the fool he had so easily duped into bringing him the only weapon he needed—a bottle of wine. It had been a pity to waste good claret on the oaf but, broken over the head of the obliging turnkey, it had proved sufficient to gain his freedom.

He took the keys to the outer door. His prison had proved no stronghold and he'd known immediately that money would sway the fool they had given charge of him. All he had to do was steal a horse and he would be away. Then he needed clean clothes and money, which he had hidden safely in case he had need of them.

The horses were in the stables behind the magistrate's house. No guards patrolled the grounds and there was only one unsuspecting groom in charge of the stables that night. It was a matter of a swift blow to the neck with the broken bottle and the fool fell to the ground, blood seeping from the wound as he tried to call out but could not speak.

Once upon his chosen mount, the man sped away from house and stable to open countryside. His first plan had failed and that bitch Frant planned to marry would be on her guard, but there was one other who would not be so wary. He might yet find a way to ruin her and bring Frant to his knees.

Annamarie's promise was in his mind as he sped through the darkness.

'Kill him for me and I will share everything I have with you...' she'd whispered as they lay together in the darkness. 'I will take you for my husband and you will live in a palace...'

He had been mad for her from the first time he saw her, when he was sent with a diplomatic mission to her mother. At first the girl had not seemed to notice him, but then one night she had waylaid him as he returned home from dinner at the Governor's house. Her smile had sent his wits spinning and when she offered herself to him in return for a favour, he had not stopped to think. He would have killed anyone for her at that moment—but when she spoke the name of the man she hated, he'd laughed with pure delight. Frant deserved all that was coming to him.

He had taken his time planning the downfall of his enemy, but somehow luck had been on Frant's side— but this time he would no doubt be planning his wedding to that bitch and would know nothing of his ward's elopement until it was too late.

Melia was a flighty little thing and he did not doubt that he would have her eating out of his hand within a few minutes of speaking to her. She would run off with him…and then he would make Frant pay, both in money and with his life. A ransom first and then a ball in his heart…

Melia was annoyed. She had expected that Lord Frant would be here sooner. The plans for the wedding could not go ahead until he came and the marriage contract was signed. Her aunt was strict about keeping the proprieties and she said it would be discourteous to speak to the vicar or plan anything until Lord Frant arrived—and her betrothed agreed.

'Your aunt is correct, dearest,' he'd told her. 'Besides, what does it matter? We have a lifetime ahead of us— and it is but a few days' delay.'

Melia did not know why she felt so frustrated. Until they came down to the country she hadn't truly known either her betrothed or his sister very well. Spending each day in their company, she was beginning to be bored. Anne was forever with her nose in a book, and her brother spent most of his time riding or speaking to the grooms. He did walk with Melia in the afternoons and was attentive in the evenings, but that was almost worse than when he left her alone to go riding or played cards with her aunt's guests.

The truth was that she had provoked Captain Smythe into speaking by saying that she was to return to her aunt's house and did not know if she would ever return to town. Managing to shed a tear, she'd had him gallantly trying to comfort her and when he'd suddenly proposed she had accepted him—and now she wished she hadn't.

Oh, what a bother it was! She had been so sure that Viscount Hargreaves was in love with her, but when she'd tried to push him towards a declaration he'd told her he couldn't afford to marry her. Melia had blamed her guardian, because Adam had told her of the rewards her guardian had received while he had only a few guineas. She'd resented that, because she was sure that Adam would have wed her if she'd had more fortune.

Then, after it was made clear to her that she would never persuade the viscount to wed her, she had met Captain Hershaw. He'd set out to captivate her from the start and, though she did not think him as handsome as Adam Hargreaves, he'd seemed to like her—but he had not spoken and so she'd seized her chance when Captain Smythe proposed. Now she wished that she had waited, for it seemed that only a lifetime of boredom lay ahead.

So it was with a mixture of anticipation and surprise that she heard Viscount Hargreaves announced as she sat alone in the parlour that morning. He entered and her heart raced at the sight of him. How handsome he was and she loved him. Yes, now that she saw him again, she knew that it was Adam Hargreaves she had always wanted.

'Miss Bellingham, forgive me this intrusion,' Adam said and looked awkward. 'Your guardian has allowed me a short time to speak with you alone…'

'You wanted to speak to me alone?' Melia asked and her heart raced. There could be only one reason for him to come all this way to speak to her! Her engagement had made him realise that he cared for her and he had come to beg her to break it off and marry him. The excitement was so intense that at first his words did not penetrate her mind.

'It was very wrong of me to let you think I was free,' Adam said and at last the words reached her. 'I found you attractive and I was disturbed by other things. I should not have been so free in my manner towards you, because I have a wife and child in India…'

'You have a wife…?' Melia stared at him in dismay. 'You let me think and you knew…you always knew that you were married…'

'Forgive me. I have regretted what I did and perhaps, had I been free…'

'How dare you come here?' Melia demanded. 'Why should I care what you have to say?'

She threw him a look of malice and ran from the room before she could shame herself and weep before him. Adam called her name but she did not look back. Her disappointment was such that she could scarcely bear it and she ran from the house, through the back gardens to the orchards beyond.

Leaning with her back against a tree, Melia let her tears fall. How could he come here just to tell her that he had a wife? Oh, how she hated him, and her guardian. Lord Frant must have known of the wife—why had he not told her at once? Why had he allowed her to humiliate herself by running after that hateful man—and why had he brought him here to hurt her in this way?

She hated them both. She wanted to strike out and hurt someone—to punish those who had wronged her.

'Miss Bellingham, I do not like to see you in distress…'

The voice broke into her fevered thoughts, bringing Melia's head up. She gasped as she saw him and dashed her hand over her cheeks.

'Captain Hershaw,' she said. 'I did not expect to see you here.'

'I could not stop thinking of you,' he said softly and smoothed his fingers over her cheek to wipe away the tears. 'I should have spoken sooner, my dearest Melia, but I dare not because your guardian hates me.'

'And I hate him,' Melia said, firing up immediately. 'He does not care for me—no one truly cares for me…'

'Then come away with me now,' he urged. 'Let me take you to France, where we can live and be happy. I shall find a way to…'

Before he could say more, a voice called out to him. 'Stand away from her, you dog! Melia, move away from him. He is a coward and a murderer…'

Melia saw her guardian striding towards her and, a little distance behind him, Adam. She lifted her head defiantly.

'You have never wanted me to be happy,' she said. 'I am going with Captain Hershaw now and you cannot stop me.'

'Think about what you're doing,' Paul warned. 'He is wanted for a hanging offence and means only to lure you away to get at me...'

'And I nearly had her,' Hershaw snarled, reaching out to grab Melia around the throat with one arm. He levelled a pistol at her head. 'I am taking her with me and I shall dishonour her and you, Frant. When I've done with her I shall kill her—and if you come near me I'll kill you too.'

Melia gasped. Her throat hurt where his arm pressed against it, but the pain of humiliation was far worse. She had come here to weep in private and he had offered her comfort, but it was just a trick. Filled with rage and hatred against the whole world, Melia bit his hand as hard as she could and heard him scream and jerk his hand away. In that moment of freedom, she wrestled with him and tried to take the pistol he'd held to her head. In her thoughts was only one desire—to see him dead at her feet.

He knocked her back so that she was felled to the ground and then fired at her guardian. Hearing the muffled oath, Melia thought he must have hit him and she rolled over, flinging herself at his leg and pulling at it so that he stumbled. He kicked out at her, his boot landing hard against her mouth so that she tasted blood and then he fired again.

Getting to her feet, Melia glanced round and saw that Adam lay bleeding on the ground. She ran to him, screaming, as she flung herself down on her knees and looked into his face. He was dead, Hershaw's ball having found its target too well. A pistol lay beside Adam. Melia's hand reached for it. She took it, turned slowly and aimed. Her shot caught Hershaw in the groin and he screamed in agony but levelled his pistol at her, and in that moment another shot rang out and Hershaw pitched to the ground.

Melia fell back, faint and sick of heart. She wished that it had been her ball that had killed him, but knew it was her guardian who had fired. She was aware of being lifted gently and carried indoors. People were around her. She heard their voices but did not know what they said, nor did she wish to know. Adam was dead. He had loved another, but still she loved him and she grieved that his life was lost. She turned her face to the wall and let the blackness take her.

'It is so shocking,' Mrs Bellingham said as she came from her niece's bedchamber after the doctor had been. 'To think that he might have made off with her, had you and the viscount not been there and seen what he was about.' She mopped at her cheeks with a lace kerchief. 'My poor niece—and it was all to be arranged for her wedding this very day.'

'Yes, well, that may have to be postponed,' Paul said, looking grave. 'Adam was badly wounded. I am sure she thought him dead, which is why she fired. I had been wounded and it took me a moment to steady my aim and he might have killed any of us if Melia had not acted as she did—she is a brave girl, madam.'

'Yes, indeed, but I think it has shocked her fiancé and his sister. They do not know quite what to make of her actions—and I must say it was not what I would have expected of my niece, or of any gentle girl.'

'I had not expected so much of her,' Paul said. 'I hope that she will soon feel better and I shall delay my departure until I am sure she improves. I must speak with her and see what can be done to sort out this mess.'

'He...that awful man is dead now?'

'Yes. I should have made sure of it before this, but I thought to bring him to justice. If Melia or Adam had died I should not lightly have forgiven myself.'

'Well, I cannot like what has happened, Lord Frant. I do not think my brother would have approved of the company she has kept since you became her guardian.'

'I would willingly have given her care to you, madam,' Paul said. 'But now I owe her something and I shall make sure she is happy with her chosen course before I abandon her to you or her fiancé.'

Paul walked down the stairs to write a letter to Jane to explain why he could not join her as planned. His arm was painful, but he was fortunate to have escaped further injury. Adam's wound was far worse and had barely missed his heart; another inch to the left and he would indeed be dead. As it was, he would be ill for some time and the doctor had stressed that he must not be moved for the moment.

It would be awkward for all concerned. Melia had not taken his apology well and Paul believed that she had been on the verge of running off with Hershaw, perhaps to spite them all. She, like Jane, was safe from

Hershaw now, but she would be bitter and it would be painful for her to know Adam was lying in his sickbed in her aunt's house. Paul was not sure what he could do to help her, but he blamed himself for what had happened. Adam was his friend and, in paying court to her, he had not been fair to Melia. Perhaps worse still, Hershaw's actions had been meant against Paul and Melia had unfortunately been caught up in the sorry mess. It was a miracle that she was not badly wounded or dead. Her bruises were superficial and Paul suspected that it was her broken heart that had caused her to turn her face to the wall.

Had he been careless in his duty towards her? Paul knew that he had been caught up in his own affairs, labelling the girl as a flighty miss. Yet now he felt that he might have been remiss and if there was a way to help her, he must find it. For the moment his own affairs must wait, even though he was impatient to be with Jane once more.

Chapter Sixteen

Paul's letter did not reach Jane for four days and she had begun to wonder why he did not come as he'd promised. Wild thoughts went through her mind and she pictured him lying dead or injured, so the truth was not so very shocking. He had a flesh wound, but Adam's was so much worse he feared for his friend's life—and Melia had taken to her bed and refused to leave it.

> *I wish I might be with you, planning our wedding. Yet I know you will understand why I cannot leave this house for the moment. I must make arrangements for Adam to be properly cared for when he is well enough to be moved—and I feel in part responsible for Melia's despair.*
>
> *It seems I wronged her in believing that she would soon recover from her infatuation. I now believe she truly loved Adam, and his confession that he was married to Annamarie deeply wounded her.*

*Had I not followed she might have gone with
Hershaw and, in his hatred for me, he would have
used her ill.*

*I would not ask it of you, Jane, but I believe
she needs a friend she can speak to of what is in
her heart. Her aunt is a good woman in her way
but she fusses foolishly. Come if you can, and perhaps together we can heal her wounded heart.*

Jane took her letter to Will and showed him. She
found him with Sarah in the parlour. They had been
talking earnestly, but Will saw at once that Jane was in
distress and read the letter she handed him. He agreed
that she must go to Melia and Sarah offered to go with
her.

'The viscount will need nursing and I have some
skill in that,' Sarah said, and looked at Will shyly. 'We
have something to tell you, Jane...' She faltered and he
smiled and nodded.

'Yes, my dearest sister. I am sure you have long
guessed it was my intention—but I must tell you that
I have asked Sarah to be my wife. We shall announce
our engagement but the wedding will wait until after
your own has taken place.'

'I had hoped that might be quite soon,' Jane said,
'but, should it be long delayed, you must not delay your
plans to suit me—I can quite easily stay with Mama
until my affairs are settled.'

'I knew you would say that,' her brother said and
gave her a quick hug. 'Sarah insisted we must wait,
but we shall call the banns for one month hence and

hope that Lord Frant's friend will have recovered before that…'

'He is severely wounded, but wounds of the heart may heal sooner than a broken heart,' Jane said. 'I think Paul is more concerned for Melia than he has written. I shall go to him this very day, Sarah. Are you sure you wish to accompany me?'

'Yes.' She looked at Will and he nodded. 'We must all help each other and I shall come with you, Jane.'

Jane accepted her offer and went at once to set plans in motion for their journey. She could not know how long they would have to stay with Mrs Bellingham and would take clothes for a few weeks, as well as all the medicines and clean linen bindings she thought necessary.

Will had decided to accompany them. 'I shall not stay to be a burden to Mrs Bellingham,' he said, 'but I have friends nearby who will welcome me and shall ride over each day to see how you go on.'

'I am glad of it,' Jane said, because she did not wish to be the cause of their parting at a time when they should be planning their wedding.

The journey took several hours and it was past six when they arrived at Mrs Bellingham's house. She had been expecting them and her relief was obvious for she welcomed Jane with open arms, sniffing into her lace kerchief.

'I am at my wits' end,' she declared to Jane as she ordered tea and cakes to sustain them until supper. 'Melia will not even speak to me…'

'Is Paul here?' Jane asked, looking about her, for she had expected he would meet her.

'He is with the doctor attending the viscount,' Mrs Bellingham said and gave a little sob. 'That such a thing should happen here! I have never been so shocked. We have had the magistrate here and doctors... Lord Frant was not satisfied with our local man and sent for a man from town. I am sure I do not know what things are coming to...a man shot dead, another dying and my niece refusing to eat or drink...'

'I shall go up to her,' Jane said. 'You may send a tray of tea with two cups and a little bread and butter and some chicken to the bedchamber, if you please, and I shall do what I can to encourage her to drink.'

'I will show you to her room,' Mrs Bellingham said. 'If your brother and cousin will take some tea...' She seemed torn between being polite to her guests and Jane's request.

'Your footman may show me up,' Jane said and pressed her hand. 'Pray do not worry so, ma'am. I am sure that Melia will be better soon.'

'Oh...well, if you think so...'

Jane left her with Sarah and Will and enquired direction from the footman who had admitted them. He took her up the stairs and she thanked him as he directed her to Melia's room. She knocked and entered, though Melia did not invite her to do so. The room was in darkness and Melia was lying hunched up on the bed, still dressed in what she had been wearing for days judging by its state. She had her face turned to the wall and did not look round as Jane spoke to her.

'Why are you in such distress?' she asked. 'Your aunt is distraught because you will not speak to her—and with Adam so ill…'

She saw Melia stiffen and then she rolled over on to her back and pushed herself up against the pillows, staring at Jane in disbelief.

'I saw him die…he was so pale and still…that devil killed him and it was my fault…'

'How could it be your fault?' Jane asked. 'I must tell you that Adam is badly wounded, but he is yet alive. I had it from your aunt but a moment ago. A new doctor has been summoned and Lord Frant is with him now.'

'He is truly alive?' Melia looked at her and for a moment there was light in her dull eyes. 'He was not killed?'

'No, he lives. I cannot promise he will not die, but he lives at this moment.'

'I am glad…' Melia gave a little sob. 'I hated him for a time that morning. He told me that he has a wife—and I loved him. Why did no one tell me that he was married? Had I known…'

'The viscount told no one of his marriage. It remained a secret until Hershaw spread a whisper that Lord Frant was secretly married to the Indian Princess and had deserted her. I was told in such a way that I became distressed and left the house alone—which led to my capture and imprisonment.'

She saw the shock in Melia's face. 'Yes, I was imprisoned by Hershaw's men, and he meant to kill me when he had finished his evil work against Paul—as he would have killed you, my love.'

'Oh, Jane, I did not know what was in his mind,' Melia said and tears rolled down her cheek. 'It is all my fault…I brought him to your house and encouraged him. I told him all the things he wanted to know about you and my guardian…I told him you had an understanding…'

'Yes, I thought it must have been you,' Jane said and saw the girl flinch. 'No, do not blame yourself for what happened, Melia. He would have found a way even if you had not told him anything…'

'I am to blame,' Melia insisted. 'I was selfish and thoughtless—and if Adam dies it will be my fault.'

'If you regret what you have done, give up this selfish remorse that is so distressing for your aunt…' There was a knock at the door and then a maid came in with a tray and Jane asked her to set it down.

After she had gone, Jane poured two cups of tea, giving one to Melia and taking one herself. 'There is a little bread and butter and some cold chicken, my love. Please try and eat a little and drink your tea. I have been travelling and truly need mine.'

'You are so kind to me and I do not deserve it,' Melia said and sipped her tea. She discovered that she was thirsty and drank it all. Jane poured them both another and Melia ate a few mouthfuls of the bread and butter and Jane tried one of the delicious cakes.

'Your aunt has a good cook, Melia.'

'Yes, she does,' Melia said and put down her empty cup. 'What am I to do, Jane? I am not in love with Captain Smythe—but I have promised to wed him…'

'You know that even if the viscount lives he will return to India—to his wife and child?'

'Yes…' Melia's complexion was pale but her expression was set. 'He never loved me. I was foolish to fall for a pretty face and charming manners. I see now that when he made excuses he was only being kind…'

'I fear there was a little more to it,' Jane said. 'He felt some resentment towards Paul and perhaps he flirted with you in a mood of mischief. It was not kind in him, Melia—but I think he relented when he realised the damage he had done. Paul has forgiven him and perhaps in time you will be able to do the same.'

'I do not know if I can forgive,' Melia said, 'but I pray that he will live and…be happy with his family.'

Tears were running down her face. Jane wiped them away with her kerchief. 'In time the pain of a love lost will lessen,' she said. 'I think you must decide whether you wish to marry Captain Smythe or not and tell him. He left to take his sister home, but said he would return in a few days. You should tell him at once that you cannot marry him if that is your wish.'

'I shall be an outcast from Society,' Melia said. 'When word gets out there will be a terrible scandal.'

'No, I do not think it need be so. Some people may be cool towards you and think you a jilt, but others will be kinder—as for the other business, it will be hushed up and your name kept from it, I am sure. Lord Frant will do all he can to protect you.'

'I shall never marry…' Melia said and looked so miserable that Jane leaned forward to kiss her.

'Do not despair, Melia. For a time you will grieve

but in time your heart will mend. One day in the future, Paul and I will take you travelling—perhaps to France and Italy. You may find happiness again. Besides, in a year or two your brief engagement will be forgotten.'

'Yes…' Melia sighed. 'I suppose it will…'

A knock came at the door then and Paul asked if he might enter. Melia said that he might and he came in looking apprehensive, but smiled as he saw her sitting up and the teacups.

'You are feeling a little better,' he said. 'I am glad, Melia—and I beg you to forgive me for all that has happened to you.'

Melia smiled, perhaps the first natural smile she'd given him. 'You were never anything but generous to me, sir. I was foolish and greedy, and I beg your pardon for the hurt I have caused.'

'I came to tell you that Adam is conscious. He asked after you, Melia, and said that he would like to see you when you felt able…'

'I will go and see him,' she said and then looked down at her crumpled gown, as if she had not realised the state she was in. 'Perhaps I should change first… this has his blood on it.'

'I shall help you,' Jane said and looked at Paul. 'We will talk later, my dearest.'

'Yes—and thank you for coming to our aid…'

He left the room and Melia stood while Jane unfastened her gown and helped her to change into a clean one. Melia chose a plain blue dress that had none of the fashionable style she had adopted in London, her hair caught up in a simple knot at the back. Jane thought she looked prettier than she ever had before.

'I shall leave you,' she said. 'Perhaps you will come down to supper later?'

Walking down the stairs, Jane went to the parlour where the others had been taking tea earlier. Paul was alone, drinking a glass of brandy. He turned as she entered and held out his hands to her. She went to him and he took her hands, drawing her into his arms and holding her.

'You spoke of a wound?'

'It was a mere scratch to my arm,' he said. 'I should not have mentioned it, but I had to explain… I needed you here, my darling. I could not reach Melia, no one could…she would not listen to us.'

'She thought Adam dead,' Jane told him. 'She blamed herself for his death. I think she both hates and loves him. He hurt her badly—and yet she could not bear to think her foolishness had led to his death.'

'Even if he had been dead it could not have been her fault,' Paul said. 'The blame is mine. I should have been more careful. I thought it right to leave Hershaw to the law, but I should have known that he would never rest until one of us was dead.'

'Why should he hate you so?' Jane touched his cheek.

'It was many things…mostly envy and greed, I think,' Paul sighed. 'Truly, I hardly understand such hatred myself. I once warned our superior officer that he cheated at the card tables and he was sent away in some disgrace, but that was many years ago. I can only think that he fell prey to the charms of a jealous woman…or perhaps it was his losses at the card tables…'

'We shall never know for certain,' Jane said. 'I am relieved that he is dead, Paul, though a man's death is never cause for celebration, I know.'

'No, it cannot be,' he agreed. 'Yet, unless the law dealt with him harshly, I think a shadow would have hung over us. He tried to kill Adam and he would have killed Melia had I not fired first.'

'Then it ended the only way it could,' she agreed. 'I hope that we shall never have to speak of him again, Paul.'

'I see no reason why we should,' he said. 'All has been settled with the magistrates and, though an inquiry may be held, there is naught to fear. We must wait until Adam is on his feet again—and then perhaps we can be married…' He smiled at her. 'You must decide where we go on our wedding trip, my love.'

'I think we should live a week or so alone somewhere—and then perhaps we could take Melia on a trip to France or Italy…'

He gazed into her eyes. 'I know of no other woman who would be willing to share such a precious time with her but I am grateful to you for the offer. I feel the need to make some recompense for her hurt.'

'Yes, I know, and I have promised that she shall go travelling at some point,' Jane said. 'Her heart weeps now for her grief but she is young and I believe she will recover well, given the opportunity.'

'Has she decided against marriage to Captain Smythe?'

'Yes—how did you guess it?'

'I knew from the way she wept over Adam that she still loved him. I wasn't sure whether she would marry for position and wealth.'

'I think she believed she could go through with it— but perhaps she was too young to know herself, Paul. I think she knows now that it will not do for her. I think this has made her wiser and perhaps better—and we must hope that she finds love in the future.'

'Yes, I shall pray for that,' he said and then bent his head to kiss her. 'Perhaps we need not wait too long to be wed, now that Adam is out of danger?'

'My brother and Sarah wish to wed soon. Mama will come down for the wedding—and we may have ours soon after. In six weeks, perhaps? It should give your friend time to recover and…'

Jane could say no more for Paul's lips were touching hers, caressing them with a tender sweetness that filled her with love and pleasure. She melted into his arms, murmuring his name as his kiss deepened.

'Jane, my love,' he whispered huskily. 'If I had lost you I do not know what I should have done…'

They were married in the church at Jane's home some seven weeks later. Although Adam had turned the corner and was now conscious, it had taken him some time to recover. Melia had helped Sarah with the nursing after the first few days and, as Adam no longer needed constant watching, Will and Sarah had married two weeks before Jane. They had gone away for a few days, but returned in order that Jane's brother could give her away, and Sarah stand with Melia as her maids of honour.

Will's wedding to Sarah had been lavish, but Jane had chosen to celebrate hers with just a few good friends. Major Harding was Paul's best man, and Adam was able to attend the wedding, even though he did not stay long at the reception, but retired to the room provided for him after the toasts were drunk. He had booked his passage to India in one month and everyone wished him a fair journey and happiness at the other end.

Melia had broken off her engagement from Captain Smythe and it was with a little smile on her lips that she told Jane he had seemed mightily relieved.

'It was all I could do not to laugh when he assured me he would always be my friend and did not hold my decision against me.'

'You will choose more carefully in future, I think,' Jane said and Melia nodded.

'I am not sure I can love again, but I shall certainly be more careful in future.'

On the morning of her wedding, Melia and Sarah helped Jane to prepare. She looked lovely in a gown of pale ivory silk shot through with rose and silver threads. Her bonnet was fashioned of pink velvet and tied with silver ribbons, her boots of soft cream leather and her gloves a pink lace to match the bonnet.

'You are beautiful,' Sarah said, her face glowing with happiness as she handed a posy of pink roses tied up with lace to Jane. 'Lord Frant is very lucky to have you as his bride, Jane.'

'I think I am lucky to have found him,' she said and

smiled at her dear cousin. 'I know you are happy with my dearest Will—and he looks as if he has the world in his pocket. If we are as happy I shall be more than content.'

'I am sure you will be,' Melia said. 'Lord Frant is both generous and caring—and I was a spoiled silly girl to ever say anything else.'

Jane knew that Melia had been thoroughly chastened, but she had recovered well enough to face the world with a proper dignity and was looking forward to the trip to Italy that had been promised her when Jane and Paul returned from the first part of their wedding trip.

In private she'd told Jane that she had forgiven Adam for hurting her and they had made their peace. She was able now to wish him happiness with his wife and Jane prayed that he would indeed find it—though, from what she'd heard from Paul, she doubted it. Annamarie was beautiful but cold, and it was more than likely that hers had been the voice that urged Hershaw to murder Paul.

India was a world away and Jane believed that all the bitterness and pain that Paul's enemy had caused was over and she had nothing now to think of but her life with the man she loved. She hoped that Adam too might find happiness; perhaps illness and loss would have softened the Indian girl's heart and she would learn to be happy with the man who loved her.

For her the future held only happiness and the pleasure that would come from being Paul's wife. Walking down the aisle towards him, she saw a shaft of sunlight pierce the stained glass windows and light up the altar with gold. It seemed a blessing on their marriage and, as she looked up into her husband's face, she felt her heart overflow with happiness.

They were wed and all Jane wanted now was to live in peace and happiness with Paul.

He came to put his arms about her as she stood near the window, looking out at the view across the park to a lake in the distance. In the dying embers of a summer sun, its waters looked almost pink as the huge ball of fire seemed to sink below the horizon.

'Your home is lovely, Paul,' she said and her cheek was close to his as his lips touched the arch of her white neck.

'This belonged to a friend,' he told her. 'He knew my mother well and loved her all his life and so when he died he left it to me. I had thought I might sell but when I saw the view from this window I knew it was the perfect place for us.'

'Yes, it is perfect,' Jane said. 'The gardens are lovely but in places unfinished and the work will be a pleasure to oversee.'

'You must order everything as you wish,' he murmured against her throat. 'You made my house in London a home and I pray you will do the same here.'

'I think there are improvements to be made, but it is already a home,' Jane said. 'I felt it when you brought me to it this afternoon. I believe it is a happy place, Paul.'

'It was and will be again,' he said and turned her in

his arms to kiss her. 'I love you…want you so much, my darling…'

'And I you,' Jane said and gave herself up to his kiss.

Paul swept her up in his arms and carried her to their bed. The fresh linen sheets smelled of lavender and felt cool to the touch as they lay together, wrapped in each other's arms, touching and kissing, becoming one in a sweet embrace that lifted them to the heights of pleasure. Their bodies fitted as one in a sweet bliss that neither had known before. Jane had been married and was able to give herself freely to the man she loved, his touch different from that of her first husband but just as sweet, and perhaps because the years had taught her the meaning of loss and sorrow she was able to experience an even sweeter joy in finding love once more.

They loved and slept and loved again, entwined as one, for ever in perfect harmony, the need of one perfectly matched to the other. And in the morning when Jane woke, she discovered that he was still deep in slumber beside her. All the worries and cares of the past months had melted away and he looked almost boyish as he slept, and then she bent and kissed him and his strong arms surrounded her, pulling her down to him so that her silky flesh surrounded him and his desire leapt once more to white-hot passion.

'You have made me the happiest man alive,' Paul whispered as they lay quiet once more. 'I shall always love you, my darling—and I thank God that I have found you.'

'Oh, Paul,' she whispered. 'I thought I should never

know true happiness again. Life is good and I know that, whatever the future brings, we shall be together.'

'Until the years pass and we are old and grey,' he teased, touching her nose with his fingertip. 'I dare say you will grow fat and I shall grow bent and grouchy…'

'Me? Fat? You wretch! Never!' she said, and threw herself on him, pummelling him with her fists until he began to kiss her and she could only smile into his eyes and give herself once more to his loving embrace…

* * * * *

If you enjoyed this story, you won't want to miss these other great reads from Anne Herries…Explore her
REGENCY BRIDES OF CONVENIENCE
trilogy now!

*RESCUED BY THE VISCOUNT
CHOSEN BY THE LIEUTENANT
REUNITED WITH THE MAJOR*